Serenity Lake Marina

SARASOTA GREEN

E-book ISBN 9798985882131

Print ISBN 9798985882148

Green Sea Publishing LLC

A Note from the Author

Dear Lovely Readers,

I'm so glad you found this book in the world. I put my whole heart into this story. It's perfectly *imperfect*.

These characters made me laugh, made me cry, surprised me, and I wanted them all to get what they wanted in the end. I truly hope you are inspired by Alex and JT's story.

Wishing you safe journeys, serenity, and sweet dreams.

Sincerely,

Sara

July 15, 2025

Dedication

for my father and my brother
traveling through the constellations
in dreams of music
your legacy
alive

Chapter One

July 4, 2017

Alex used to love the Fourth of July. Not now, not anymore. Today was going to be the hardest day. It had been hanging over her like a black hole in her solar plexus. Something intangible and terrifying. What could she do today? Who could she call? What could she do to run away from her feelings?

One year today.

She didn't want to think about it. She wanted to think about anything else.

There was nowhere to run anymore.

She'd run away already, and every time she ended up back at home. It always felt like surrendering, like giving up. Like she'd gone out into the world to make something of herself, and then ended up back here, tail between her legs, white flag in the air.

Home again having *not* made anything of herself.

She hit the snooze button and fell back into a dream. Since she had started teaching, she'd dream of her students. Since she'd started teaching in prison, dreaming of her students made her feel like she never had any time off. It had been less than a year since she'd begun, so maybe she would get used to it. Hanging out with convicted felons during the day and dreaming about them at night.

This morning there was a vague sense of the shy student in a fight, and Alex couldn't help him. Not a relaxing dream. There was something about a Jeep and a Jet Ski. There was something about a bookstore. The dream didn't make much sense.

The dream, however, was a respite from this reality.

A knock at her door woke her back to the present. The shades were drawn so far, the room was almost pitch black. She had no idea what time it was, only the day.

She had been dreading this day.

"Alex, it's eleven o'clock. I made us some breakfast." Alex wanted to stay cuddled right here under the blankets, but she shook them off and glanced at her cell phone on the nightstand. A message from her on-again, off-again saying, "Good night." There was some reassurance in their regular messages, but who knew when they'd be off again?

The date glowed at her. *July 4th*.

"Honey?" Diane opened the door. Cinnamon wafted into the bedroom. Her mom must have baked a pie, which meant there were those tiny little pinwheels made of pie dough, sugar, and butter somewhere out there, next to the bacon and eggs.

"Morning, Mom," Alex said. Diane entered the room, lifted the blinds so the sun came in, and sat next to her on the bed. The *dream room*, Aunt Skylar called it, all blues and butterflies and music boxes. A painting hung on the wall beside the mirror, a turquoise and black acrylic called *The Beach After Sunset*. Aunt Skylar had painted the stars to glow in the dark.

The familiar smell of corn lotion cradled Alex, as her mom wrapped her arm around her shoulders. Diane's light blue eyes sat wide and round under strawberry tendrils. Pink circles of blush highlighted her freckles, the rest of her unruly curls tied back in a knot. There was something her mom was keeping from her, but Alex had given up asking.

She didn't know if she wanted to know, anyway.

"It's going to be hard for all of us," Diane said. "We'll get through it together."

Alex put her head on her mom's shoulder. At thirty-five years old, Alex felt too old to be needing her mother's comfort like this. She was going to need everything today, though. It just wasn't all going to be here.

Chapter Two

"We could go to the festival," Diane said. "Come, eat some breakfast first. You're getting so thin."

Though Alex had been dreading this day, and knowing she needed to do something to keep her mind busy, she hadn't been able to make any plans. The on-again off-again boyfriend was working the holiday, playing music back in Florida.

She hadn't reached out to her old friends yet, though some of them she hadn't spoken to in years had reached out as early as yesterday. Over social media and over the phone. How did they even get her number?

Thinking of you.

I can't pretend to know what you're going through, but we're praying for you.

She knew these messages were well-intentioned, but they somehow cut deep into her heart. She'd never been good at other people's sympathy. Each message reminded her of the things she did not do or say.

There *was* this one that she treasured. One of her dad's friends, who at least seemed to get it.

I am holding you and your family this week with my whole heart.

This had made Alex cry the hardest.

Were they even still her friends? Some of them had been her friends way back when they were going to school together. She'd shared so much with so many of them, but when she left for college, they'd slowly lost touch. She had gone in an entirely different direction than all of them. When it was time to leave, she'd high tailed it out of there without looking back.

She felt the worst about her oldest friend from childhood.

JT had showed up the day her car was packed for Florida, and he almost cried right there in the driveway. He was so sad, why wasn't Alex sad? They had been inseparable for years, but when her car was full of books and gas, she was ready—like that Dixie Chicks' song—to run. Alex was excited to embark on a new adventure in her life. An adventure of the unknown. A chance to see the world.

Thinking of JT standing forlorn in the driveway overflowing with emotions made her feel bad she didn't . . . feel bad. Sure, she was going to miss him. But she wasn't going to miss high school, and she definitely wasn't going to miss home. The memory was like an emotional question mark she couldn't wrap her mind around. All these years later, she still felt ashamed for not comforting her friend. Maybe she would add that to her amends list.

Amends. Apologies for being such a jerk when she was drinking so much. A thing she also didn't want to think about. She couldn't carry the weight of it all. She wasn't strong enough.

God grant me the serenity . . . she let the rest of the prayer roll through her mind.

She wandered into the bathroom and looked at herself in the mirror. Shiny black hair hung haggardly around her blue-green eyes. Despite having her father's features, she was beginning to look more and more like her mom. She broke eye contact with herself; she couldn't get too deep today.

She could call her sponsor, though Kara didn't really under-stand, did she? She'd helped Alex learn how to get sober and stay sober, but when it came to this weight of living this life, now without her dad, there were no words enough, no comparable experiences.

She splashed some water on her face.

Her brother was struggling as much as she was, and there was nothing either one of them could do except: remember to eat. Try and sleep. Try to carry it or navigate it or move through the pain. Focus on things which needed to be done. Try and come up with words. Try and talk about it sometimes, try *not* to talk about it other times.

Sometimes answer messages. Sometimes not.

Today she felt like . . . not.

Sometimes she felt like it had happened yesterday, and sometimes she felt like it happened to someone else entirely. The truth is it could have happened to anyone. Could it have? Tragedy happens to people for no reason.

The text messages played on repeat in her brain.

Thinking of you.

Praying for you today.

I'm always here if you want to talk.

This past year they could come out of nowhere and startle her. Every time a message came through, a tiny piece of her heart tore off and dropped into her stomach, and that feeling could burst into an avalanche of tears. She had not even spoken to some of these people for years. Except for at the funeral. The confusing haze of the funeral.

What could she do that was constructive?

Alex left her phone on the nightstand and followed the smells of her mom's cooking to the kitchen.

"You should really go out to the festival."

Diane placed a glass of orange juice in front of Alex. A simple wooden thing, this dining room table, like most things in this house, was new.

Unfamiliar.

"I don't know if I feel like it, Mom," Alex said. She studied the tidy plate of eggs and bacon and gluten-free toast. Diane always went out of her way to cater to her family's newest dietary needs.

"Might be good to get out and *see* people." Her voice was soft and her face gentle.

"What if somebody asks me what happened?" Alex whispered. Her biggest fear. This was a small town. When someone asked what happened, they had already heard three different stories from three different people, most of which were exaggerated or false.

Living in a small town could be much like the old telephone game. Which is one of the reasons why Alex had left. She thought she had gone for good, the last time, but here she was again. Home in Ohio.

In the city, nobody asked you what happened. In the city, if somebody noticed you were crying at the grocery store, they just walked on by. In the city, nobody said, "You don't look very good today, are you all right?" In the city you had some privacy. Which was how Alex had started drinking so much and stayed drinking so much for so many years.

Well, and everybody drank in Florida. It was like a year-round vacation.

Alex didn't know exactly what happened, which is why she hated this question. And then there were the reporters calling and the police report and the detectives and the confusion, and the complete and utter shock. And who would want to revisit it? And why did everybody think they had the right to know, especially when Alex didn't even know? It wasn't any of their business, and even if it were, why did everybody think she wanted to talk about it?

She had made a fool of herself at the funeral. She almost fainted walking down the aisle of the church, and then when she got to the front, she could hardly stand. She had wanted to speak, she had written an entire eulogy and had it folded up on a note-card in her pocket, but when it came down to the exact time to get up and deliver it, Alex just faded into some kind of black. There was video of her uttering some words that didn't make much sense. She couldn't even remember the service, only the faces who passed by her, and their strange expressions of sympathy.

Faces she hadn't seen for almost twenty years but had seen daily in the twenty years before. Faces from her childhood, but not faces she knew anymore. Except for her coaches, and a handful of kind smiles, the whole thing was like being in a dark maze of mirrors, words repeating and swirling through the church like smoke and fog, and Alex, outside of her body somehow, wandering through it all like a zombie.

If she'd had some sort of appetite, then maybe she would have eaten, and would have been able to stand, and to talk. But all she remembered from the funeral was feeling like her body was made of steel, with no capability for emotion.

The feelings of others, which she usually made a point to tune into, simply bounced off her body and stayed out of her mind, keeping her in the blank, dark haze.

Where was he?

California.

What was he doing?

I don't know.

What happened?

He passed in his sleep.

How?

Something about his heart.

All of it felt so intrusive. It was too heavy, too hard; too much for an only daughter. The waves of grief could literally knock her to her knees if she didn't keep her guard up.

She turned a switch in her brain and focused on changing her thoughts.

"One day at a time," her friends in recovery said. "Where are your feet?"

What are five things you can see, five things you can smell, five things you are grateful for?

She focused hard on her plate. Her mom did make the best eggs. A sprinkle of water in the scramble made them light and airy. She had gotten used to eating by now, even when she didn't have an appetite. It kept her from fainting.

She was grateful she had woken up today, even if it were today.

"Get dressed," Diane said. "Let's go out to the festival and be social." She knew her mom needed to do something, anything, as much as she did. But her mom was better at people than Alex, especially when she was sad.

Alex finished her breakfast in silence and sipped her coffee. She was grateful for this day off. She'd been working so hard figuring out this new job, that her mind was constantly problem-solving, even in her sleep. Even in her dreams she was teaching, or something to do with teaching.

The job wasn't her first choice. She only applied to the community college because her feet and knees were getting so tired waiting tables, she thought it was finally time to turn in her apron and do something else. When she was young, it was fun. It was still fun, though not a highly-enough respected occupation. Waiting tables was challenging, like an intense workout. There was music, and laughter, and always something happening. It was also taxing on the body. A young person's game. Alex was not getting any younger.

That's where she'd been when she got the call. It was a busy night, Thursday Night All-You-Can-Eat Crab Legs, and she was on the floor by herself with twenty tables. It's why she hadn't answered the phone.

She'd seen her mom's text, "Call me when you get a minute?" And her mind had started racing.

For some reason, she had thought about her dad in California, and about the police. But she was juggling drinks for fifty people, trips to the bar, trips to the kitchen. She was moving. She wasn't a huge phone person. She'd told herself she would call her mom after her shift. The California thoughts drifted in and out, and like usual, she had dismissed them as her overactive mind.

She didn't know the difference between her fear and her intuition. Something the drinking had dulled. She was trying to rectify it, but for her dad it was too late.

Where are your feet?

She stood up from her breakfast and went into the bathroom again. She stared at her hollow cheeks in the mirror and the new wrinkles under her neck. She *did* look skinny. But she had spent the year simply trying to survive.

Some days she cried for hours and wondered if the grief could kill her. She brushed her teeth and turned on the shower. Maybe she should go with her mom. It would give her brain something else to focus on. Not just the day. Not just the text messages. Maybe she would even leave her phone at home.

When the water warmed, she stepped in and found the Dove soap.

She didn't want to go to the festival, but she didn't want to stay at her mom's house, either. What was she going to do all day? Wallow? Try not to have memories? The could-have, should-have, would-haves would eat her alive today, especially if she was here, home alone. She smoothed some vanilla shampoo and conditioner through her hair. Her *hair* was even thinner.

She wished her Nana Kate were still here. Alex and her grandmother had a special bond. They shared the same birthday, but also an understanding. Nana Kate could always see right through her and know what she was thinking, how she was feeling, and knew just how to comfort her. But she'd been gone for over a year now, too. Her dad's passing was like throwing kerosene on old embers of grief. Both of them gone now, empty places in her heart.

"Honey," Diane cracked open the bathroom door, and the steam rolled out. Alex was still in her towel. "JT's here."

JT?

Oh, my goodness, JT.

She'd been home for less than twenty-four hours . . . how did he know she was home?

Chapter Three

Alex had flown in from Florida for this week, she'd told herself, for her mom. The truth is, she felt lost again. What was she doing with her life? What had she accomplished? She'd wanted her dad to live long enough to see her succeed. To see her accomplish something *great*. She'd wanted him to be proud of her. Instead, she was a waitress with a huge student loan balance. She rented a studio apartment in Florida, and she barely had enough money to live over the poverty level.

She put the flight on her credit card and took a week off. Because it seemed smarter to be together as a family, even though her family could be difficult. In this year of reflection, she'd told herself that she had to be more accepting, kinder, more empathetic to everyone.

Less judgmental. More patient.

The last conversation with her father had not been a kind one, and she would never get to apologize.

"Tell him I'll be down in a minute?"

She dressed quickly, a sundress for the damp Ohio heat. No, a tennis dress showing absolutely no cleavage for the conservative Ohio women's judgment. Some sunscreen for her shoulders. The scent of coconut and banana calmed her. It reminded her of vacation, of the ocean, of freedom. She'd remember to put the nontoxic bug spray in her bag for the festival. Guess she was going.

Lately it seemed like life was happening to her, instead of her happening to life. That was a consequence of grief, she guessed. Roll with the waves.

Life on life's terms, her sober friends said. *When we cease fighting anything and everything . . .*

The slogans were always popping into her mind at random times, which was, maybe healthy. Healthier than the old obsession to drink, anyway. Always something about *finding a higher power* and *surrendering.*

Some of it made sense, and some of it didn't.

She walked down the stairs in her high-necked blue tennis dress, white zipper down the front. Shorts underneath, always. Her favorite turquoise flip-flops with the silver star on them. At least she'd be comfortable under examining eyes. The soccer moms might gossip and stare; she didn't want to give the guys anything to admire.

At least her legs were kind of tan from working.

The by-product of growing up overweight and being best friends with the guys instead of their girlfriends had created a new dynamic when she'd lost all the weight in college. She'd gone from the chubby girl who was good at sports to the girl with average dimensions: five-foot-six, 135 pounds. Maybe less now from the weight of the year.

Inside, she still felt like the chubby, geeky girl from Alvin and the Chipmunks. More like a Cabbage Patch Kid than a Barbie doll.

Now, sometimes, she would catch random guys looking at her like a Barbie. She'd never really gotten used to it. She wasn't sure if she ever would.

JT was standing at the bottom of the stairs in camouflage khaki pants, a black shirt, and a gray ball cap that said *Serenity Lake Marina* on it in cursive.

JT. Her best friend from childhood turned best guy friend in high school. The last time she'd seen him was at her dad's funeral. Before that, only a handful of times at her dad's shows, and at his wedding. Each one of those times, she'd been drunk.

Kind and familiar Jason Torrez.

"Hey," he said. "I hope I'm not intruding." His voice sounded like a high string on a bass guitar.

Alex wanted to ask how he knew she was home, but she was caught up with JT's eyes.

Kind, honest, sincere.

Golden hazel with spurts of yellow flecks you could only see when you were close. Long, curly eyelashes that looked like they'd been curled with an eyelash curler. Eyes that changed color depending on what he was wearing or what mood he was in. Eyes you could stare into and study and never get bored, that somehow concealed his true depth, unless he really trusted you.

If you were barely eighteen, drinking cheap strawberry wine and reminiscing by the pond in that moment between the past and your destiny. If you were staring into them the night after graduation on a hammock, and trying to decide if it were a good idea to date your best friend and ruin all the best friendship dynamics you'd ever had, or if you should just stare up at the sky and be grateful you even had a best friend.

Even if you wanted to kiss him. Even if it were the summer before you were going off to college.

Alex had stared up at the sky and pointed out Orion's belt.

It was the last time they'd been alone together, other than him seeing her off. They'd kept in touch with silly letters and the occasional phone call, though back then it cost money to call long distance, and she couldn't afford to rack up her phone bill.

They had drifted apart, like everyone else, and would only see each other at her dad's shows. By then Emily was there, turning heads of all the men in the room. Though it was subtle, and maybe Alex was the only one who noticed, Emily had always looked at Alex's dad some type of way. It was the only thing Alex didn't like about her.

JT and Curtis had gotten close over the years, and she knew JT had been as thrown off as she was at the news of his passing. She hadn't been able to talk to him at the funeral, or anyone else for that matter. Also, his wife had been there, standing between them. It had been sixteen years now since they were inseparable. Almost seventeen.

"You look good," he said. These memories surfaced as she descended the stairs, aware of her mom cleaning up the kitchen from breakfast. Aware her mom was pretending not to pay attention but paying attention to every word and move from her periphery.

Alex gripped the white railing of the stairs and felt the soft, cream carpet on her toes. It still smelled new in this house.

I do not look good.

"Thanks. Same to you." Her mom clinked dishes in the sink. She had a dishwasher but washed everything by hand.

"JT," Diane said, "I made some cinnamon pinwheels. Have one." She carried the paper plate over to him. He took one and smiled.

"I haven't had one of these since high school," he said. "The Diane special." Diane blushed and went back to the kitchen sink. Alex squinted to focus. She'd been crying so much she didn't know if she was losing her eyesight or her sanity.

He looked good. A stubbly beard and goatee over his copper skin had made him look older, finally. A smatter of freckles across his perfect nose. He always looked younger than the rest of their friends. "My good, Latino genes," he would say when the other guys teased him about his boy-face. "Wait until we're older."

Now, he looked like a man.

She had aged fifteen years in the last one. The bags under her eyes wouldn't go away. Her neck was skinny and wiry.

Some days she had to write "eat" on her to-do list.

"How are you?" he asked. This was the next question she

dreaded. She couldn't even begin. It was like asking someone who'd fallen into a cave and spent a year clawing themselves out—with no tools—how they did it. She didn't know how she had gotten through any day in the last year. Other than recovery.

Other than putting one foot in front of the other.

Other than trying herself to stay alive.

The question, her friend Layla said, was *unanswerable.*

"I'm here. Home again." She tried to manage a half-smile, but it was something else she couldn't control anymore.

Feigning happiness.

"Yeah." He did his familiar nervous tick, where he scrunched his shoulders and scratched his forearm, as if it were something that needed to be done instead of something that filled the space of awkward silence.

Alex's defenses lowered. She reached the last stair, bounced a couple of steps, and hugged him as tight as she could.

He smelled like dryer sheets and spearmints. His familiar arms, his familiar height. Just a few inches taller, he cradled her in his strength. His tee shirt was soft, like it was long-worn.

A wave of grief welled up in her horizon. She felt like crying, but she stopped.

There was a certain art to it.

The thing about grief was that when one of the waves came, you could let it knock you over if you completely surrendered to it, or you could try and swim with it, take a small little leap, and let it pass for the next time. Like body surfing, you pick the wave and ride it, try to swim over the top, or you dive under it, so it doesn't pull you under and crush you against the sand.

Today, she didn't want to cry. She wanted to dive through it or swim over it.

Today, she just wanted to get through *today.*

Chapter Four

She pulled back, embarrassed at her familiarity. She thought of his wife, and she thought of her boyfriend, and she didn't want to make anything awkward.

Alex grabbed hold of both of his forearms before letting him go.

"Thanks for coming. I needed that. How are you?"

"I'm okay, I guess," he said. "Thought you might want to ride over to the festival."

Alex did believe in this higher power thing sometimes, so when the Universe continued to suggest something, she did her best to pay attention.

This year she'd read every book about spirituality, God, and grief. *The Four Agreements* by Don Miguel Ruíz. *Life After Death* by Deepak Chopra. Her friend Layla had gifted her a copy of *Journey of Souls* by Michael Newton. She'd read every page and then ordered every book he'd ever written.

The books had given her some comfort, but only when she remembered to keep the wisdom in the forefront of her mind. So easily, she forgot. She hung on to every bit about *the soul cannot be created or destroyed.*

That we are love, and we are immortal.

She wanted to believe that. She really wanted to believe that.

But did she want to ride over to the festival today? What about JT's wife? Wouldn't everybody in town love to talk about them showing up together?

"Uh," Alex stuttered. The consonants just wouldn't come out. "How's Emily?" she managed.

Emily was everything Alex wasn't. She was tall and blonde, thin and sleek, with straight hair down to her waistline. She had the kind of legs that looked like they were born for high heels. Everybody liked her.

"I don't know," he said. "And I don't care." He tilted his head and looked at her from one eye hiding beneath his ball cap.

Oh my.

The third and final byproduct of grief, if she were counting, was that she still couldn't remember: life also goes on for other people. She wasn't the only human on earth dealing with something heavy.

It was hard to remember when you were only trying every day to survive, to do the basics. Self-care distilled into small, barely-there instincts: *Need to eat. Need to work. Need to sleep.*

What do I need in this moment?

Where are your feet?

Jason Torrez had never been one to be private with his life to Alex, but there was something holding under the surface he seemed reluctant to share.

It almost came out of her mouth. The innocent question. *What happened?*

She did not dare say it out loud. She would not kick him while he was down.

A loud bang exploded from outside.

Alex ducked. JT touched the bill of his hat and looked toward the front door.

"Fireworks!" Diane said from the kitchen.

Fireworks.

Of course. Alex straightened. The Fourth of July. The neighbors were setting off fireworks during the day. Small country towns.

"The neighbors are probably doing a test run," Diane said. Alex's eyes fell to the wooden placard by the front door, a gift all those years ago from Nana Kate: *May the road always rise to your feet; may the wind always be at your back.*

Alex looked back at JT and took an intentional breath in.

One day at a time.

JT said, "Emily took my son last week while I was at work. Left a note. Said she went back to Virginia Beach." His voice trembled. "She wants a divorce."

"Oh, gosh," Alex said. "I'm *so sorry.*"

Everybody her age had kids. Alex hugged him again. Something about his body was so comforting. She didn't have kids.

Diane wiped her hands on a towel and came into the living room.

"That's so awful," Diane said. "You've been working so hard to support them." Alex's mom was good at keeping in touch with people. So of course, she knew what he'd been up to.

"I wish I could call your dad," JT said. "Curtis would know exactly what to say."

How many times had she thought that over the last year? She wished she could call her dad.

"You two go and I'll meet you there. I've got some things to do around the house here before your brother gets in tonight. Also," Diane said, as she popped a cinnamon pinwheel into her mouth, "your aunt Skylar is coming over." She hugged Alex and JT, and put her hands on Alex's shoulders. Diane physically turned Alex's body, and nudged her toward the front door.

Alex would love to see her aunt Skylar. She was probably the only other person in the world who understood her. Or at least, didn't judge her.

"Let me get my bag," Alex said. She ran back upstairs, picked up her purse that doubled as a cooler, and made sure she had her things: bug spray, sunscreen, sarong—you never knew when you were going to need a towel to sit on or wipe your hands on, she had learned from her Florida friends.

And you never left the house without your bathing suit, so she threw it into the side pocket along with her favorite hat, grabbed her sunglasses, and went back downstairs.

Chapter Five

The noon sun warmed the pavement of the suburbs and tiny heat waves, almost imperceptible, rose into the air between the green manicured lawns. At 95 degrees, it felt like walking into a hot tub. Summer heat was different in Ohio; the lack of beach breeze made the air sluggish.

The lady across the street was bent over in her flowerbed, tending to some peonies, a white hat on her head. Alex followed JT around the tiny sidewalk of her mom's house, past the small apple tree, and out to a black Jeep that sat on the street next to the mailbox.

"Great car," Alex said.

"She wanted me to get rid of it, but I couldn't. Glad I didn't."

He opened the passenger side door and pointed to a lever at the top of the windshield. "Pull that handle." He then went to the driver's side and pulled a handle so the top unlatched. "Now lift up a little, and we'll fold it back." They lifted the top away from the front of the vehicle, and guided it back over the trunk latch, tucking it down just before the spare tire. His baseball bag sat there perfectly, a bat sticking out on one end.

"I always wanted a Jeep," Alex said. Her friend Layla in Florida had one, and they would tool around the beach with the top down, barhopping and catching the local live music acts. She always thought she'd have one by now. She thought she'd have something, anything, to show for her life by now.

JT cranked the engine and tinkered with the radio. He turned on the air conditioning. Van Halen's "Jump" came on. The sun beamed down on them, and she was glad she had worn her hat.

"Once you get one," he said, pulling the gear shift, "you won't want to drive anything else." He pushed on the gas.

Driving with Jason Torrez through Greenview Falls, Ohio, home of the Tigers. Population 4000. Her hometown.

Maybe this was okay.

"You want to stop at the restaurant?" He turned right out of the suburb section of town. "We could get a drink on the way. Take the edge off."

Carnita's, the local cantina, owned and operated by JT's parents. Her dad had played there off and on for years.

He downshifted, stopped, and then waited. He looked at her twice before she answered. She hadn't remembered his chin being chiseled like this; a clear line drawn from behind his ear. The stubble covered it, but it was there.

"Oh, no. Thanks. Unless you do." Her voice caught up with her thoughts. "I quit drinking last year." There was so much more she should say here, so much more to this story.

She'd been practicing and rehearsing for moments like these, where she'd tell her friends about her rock bottom, how awful the argument was, how she'd sat at her writing desk the next morning with a liter of vodka, all alone, telling herself that she didn't need anyone, nobody cared about her, and all she needed was vodka.

"Okay," he said. "Then we'll go straight to the festival." JT was not one to pry into anyone else's privacy. He turned left as the Van Halen synthesizer sang out of the stereo like a high-pitched trumpet.

JT drove through four-way stop signs and past houses of their old friends. Alex was overwhelmed at passing Coach's, then Gracie's. She knew everyone in town fifteen years ago, and where almost everyone lived. Now, she didn't know who was still here and who had moved away. They drove past the park where they met when they were kids, the playground where they used to swing.

She hadn't meant to go so far away, and stay away, but when it was time to go to college, she was ready for the next thing. And then she just kept going.

When they stopped at the crossroads in front of Gracie's, she said, "Is Gracie still around?"

"I think so. Her dad passed away, too, and she moved into his house over on Front Street."

Oh, man. Another thing Alex had missed.

"I have absolutely no idea what is going on in everyone's lives anymore," Alex said. "I feel kind of crappy about it."

JT smiled a half smile out of the corner of his mouth as he shifted. "Don't you keep up with them on social media?"

"I don't. I quit logging in." She wanted to say, *after my dad passed away*, but she didn't. There were too many people reaching out to her, too many strangers, too many memories with too many emotions. She didn't know how to grieve in public.

She couldn't count how many times some female acquaintance of her father's had messaged her: *"Your dad was my best friend . . . what happened?"*

Her dad had a *lot* of *best friends*. Of the female sort.

And they all wanted to know.

"Same," he said. "The internet is too weird."

Manicured lawns surrounded the humble brick houses, and before she processed the memories of her and JT riding bikes from one end of the city limits to the other, they were at the festival.

The old elementary school parking lot was roped off with orange cones and red, white, and blue ropes. Officer Sandborn was directing cars into the gravel lane that led back behind the football field.

"We're here," JT said. "Welcome home."

"JT," Sandborn said. "Alex, hey." He stared at her over his glasses with unspoken sympathy in his face. She hated that. But it was better than questions. "Park anywhere you like by the bushes."

Alex waved.

JT pulled ahead, turning the Jeep toward a line of bushes separating the houses and the school. Alex lowered the bill of her hat onto her eyebrows. She wanted to be invisible.

Chapter Six

What was she doing here, and what was she doing here with Jason Torrez on the first anniversary of her father's death? What was she doing at the hometown festival showing up with a married man, although, maybe separated, but her best friend from high school?

Since she quit drinking her mind could really race, and though she was working more at only observing, her thoughts sometimes made sense and sometimes sounded crazy. She didn't get to choose what her mind wanted to obsess about.

She tried to change gears in her brain, to simply narrate her experience as it was happening, to help keep her oriented to the present.

Alex was rolling with the waves of life again.

She was at the festival with JT. She was going to walk around in her hometown and hope nobody asked her *what happened.*

She was closing the door of the Jeep and taking a step toward the festival.

Children and families laughed, and a carnival song played somewhere in the distance. In front of them, a dunk-tank held a brave resident on a pedestal facing a line of kids with softballs in their hands ready to throw them at a bullseye.

There was the smell of hot dogs coming from under a tent

and the scent of popcorn and cotton candy coming from an old county-fair food truck. There were hula hoops, kids with water balloons, a horse-riding ring, and people carrying strings of orange raffle tickets. Green port-o-johns lined up against the wall of the school.

The Greenview Falls Fourth of July Festival was one of her oldest memories. As kids, she and her brother would run around with their friends, beg their mom for money for snacks, beg their dad for tickets to play games, and run around some more. They were always safe here, safe almost anywhere in town, and the whole town usually showed up for at least one of the three days of the festival.

Local churches set up fundraising stands of chicken and dumplings and barbecue pork, and the high school sports teams sold candy bars and sodas to raise money for their uniforms. The fire department sold beer. During the day there were games and food and laughter, and at night there was a DJ or a local band, then a fireworks display. The kids ran around, the adults danced. She had sung here one time with her dad's band.

New thought.

Where are your feet?

JT strutted next to her, and she felt safe in his familiarity. The instinct arose to grab his hand, but she dismissed it.

Though they hadn't spoken in so many years, Alex had forgotten how comfortable of a presence he had. He hadn't even asked her about her dad, hadn't asked her why she quit drinking, hadn't asked her about the on-again-off-again, hadn't pried into her life at all. Yet here he was, standing next to her. Smiling.

"There's Gracie," he said.

Since she quit drinking, Alex went to work, went to meetings, went home. And in all those situations except for recovery rooms, she played a part. Waiting tables was an act she had perfected. She was nice and friendly, stayed on the surface of things, and brought people food and drinks. At school, she followed a bit of a different script, though specific and intricate. She didn't share anything personal with her students, she only talked about reading and writing and college.

She was most authentic in meetings. Otherwise, she preferred the comfort of staying on the surface. She didn't always want to talk.

She could just pass Gracie and say *hi,* and keep walking.

"Here she comes," JT said.

Gracie Dailey, best friend from middle school turned mean-girl in high school. Gracie Dailey, who always had the name-brand clothes, the popular boyfriend, and led the clique of popular girls that looked down on band geeks and girl athletes. Gracie Dailey, who had teased even the boys whose families didn't have enough money or the right clothes. Gracie Dailey, who had stolen Alex's long-time crush at the senior prom and then married him two years later.

Her hair was fire-red with unruly bangs, and she wore her signature hot-pink lipstick. She had a tanned face and a larger bra size than Alex remembered. A white tee-shirt with a v-cut. She didn't just walk up to Alex and say *hi,* but she got right into her personal space and then hugged her.

Flowery perfume stung Alex's nose and Gracie's oversized chest smashed against her ribs.

"Alex!" Gracie said. "Were you just going to walk right by me without saying *hi?*"

Alex thought about how many times they had walked by each other in the hallways of high school without saying *hi.* Before Alex could answer, Gracie stood on her tippy toes and smashed her chest against JT's. A twinge of jealousy, almost territoriality, rose in Alex's stomach, and her mind didn't know what to do with it.

JT, always charming, said, "Hey," and took a step back, glancing at Alex from under his hat, from between his long eyelashes.

"What are you doing home!?" Gracie said. "Why didn't you call me?"

Why didn't she call her? After fifteen years of never calling each other? Why didn't she call her?

Alex adjusted her brain. Their dads had both passed away. Alex could at least be sensitive to this.

"Yeah, I'm . . . um . . . sorry to hear about your dad." She hoped she sounded sincere, because she meant it. "I've been kind of disconnected from everything, and everyone." Alex nervously gripped the top of her own baseball cap with her palm.

"Grief really sucks," Gracie said.

For a moment, Alex liked her.

"My dad had colon cancer." Gracie set her eyes at her white Reeboks and then looked back up. Alex felt sorry for her then. Maybe they had more in common now.

Gracie pulled a bag of popcorn from her purse and opened the top, offering the bag to Alex and JT who both declined, before she popped a piece of popcorn in her mouth, and began crunching.

"What happened to *your* dad?" Gracie said.

JT cocked his head. Alex tried to take refuge in the shelter of his calm, and searched his face for a response. He did not answer with words, but held a safe space for her panic.

Gracie continued, "I heard a bunch of different things. That it was drugs, that it was suicide, that he was murdered—you know how people talk around here. Kevin Wolfe even said that he heard there were some strippers." She continued to crunch on her popcorn as Alex processed the feelings arising. "I thought I should go straight to the source."

Alex's heart sank. Her arms tingled. Her vision blurred, and she was dizzy. She was chest-deep in a wave now and losing her footing.

It was tugging her under.

The infinity of grief could drown you.

Her mother's words rang out in her mind, but they wouldn't come out of her mouth . . . *undiagnosed* . . .

"Excuse me," Alex mumbled. She made her feet move as fast

as they would toward the green port-o-johns and pulled on the first door that said *vacant*.

The smell hit her. That medicine pee smell in this heat, and her stomach turned once and she threw up right into the never-ending hole.

What happened?

She wretched again, sour, and braced herself against the plastic. Gross, the plastic. Her eyes watered. Her stomach flipped and pieces of bacon came out. She was full-on sobbing. She heaved again.

She didn't f-ing know what happened.

Alex steadied herself on the plastic wall. She had to get out of here. The fumes mixed with the heat. She wiped her eyes and her mouth with the scratchy excuse for paper towels, pumped some sanitizer in her hands, and looked only once at her swollen eyes in the mirror.

She'd stopped wearing mascara this year. She'd stopped even buying it.

She didn't know if she could do this.

Chapter Seven

When she emerged from the port-o-john, Gracie had wandered away and Diane was standing next to JT, right where Alex had left him.

"Mom," Alex said, not wanting to crumble in front of JT, but wanting to crumble into her mom's arms. "Gracie—" she couldn't get the rest of the words out. Alex broke into tears and hugged her. "I'm sorry. I thought I could do this and be social, but I can't. It's too much."

Diane hugged her tight. "Okay, honey. It's okay." Her mom's scent enveloped her.

Where are your feet?

Alex was in a public place. In her small town. Crying on her mom's shoulder. In front of JT.

She stared at the star on her flip flops. She tried to focus on her breath. The Ohio heat. She pulled back and tried to gather herself. Diane wiped Alex's eyes.

Alex didn't have room in her body for embarrassment. She looked at JT.

"Can we get out of here?"

"Sure." He put his hands in his pockets and jangled his keys.

Diane said, "Andrew just landed. He said he'd be here in forty-five minutes." Alex's brother. She would love to see him. But not here. Diane continued, "He said he would come straight here. The Yamahas are playing tonight, and they were going to do a special thing for your dad. I'm hoping your aunt Skylar makes it in time."

The last thing she wanted to do was be around more people who wanted her to think about her dad. Even if they loved him. Even if half of the band were his bandmates for years. Even if they were his old friends.

What if one of *them* asked her what happened?

"I just don't think I can." She started to cry again. She was fighting another grief wave. "I—it's just too hard."

"Okay, Alexandra." Her mom only used her full name when it was serious. "I'll tell anyone who asks that you're not feeling well."

"Tell them whatever you want."

JT stood there calm and gentle and cool, as he always was. Quiet. She latched her hand under his arm, like she used to when they were younger.

"Can we go?" Alex asked.

"Of course," he said. "Whatever you need."

As they walked together toward the exit, Alex hoped she wouldn't see anybody else she knew. The Jeep was in sight, and she had her eyes on the pavement when she heard a familiar voice. A mixture of deep and high tones.

"Hey, Al!"

Al. Only her teammates and her coaches called her "Al." She turned to see her softball coach waving from the Lemon Shake-up stand.

"How are you?"

She guided JT toward her softball coach, Dean Banks.

She felt herself smile. "Hey, Coach."

"I thought that was you." He wiped his hands on his pants and then waved a bee from a giant metal juicer. As she and JT got closer, she saw concern in Dean's eyes.

Of course, he could read her. He'd spent most summers and

four years of her best athletic life teaching her and her friends how to hit line drives, catch fly balls, and steal bases. He'd selflessly spent hours and hours on the field with them, watching and critiquing their softball skills, and guiding the girls to be better athletes and humans. He and his brother, her volleyball coach, had practically raised her.

Dean took a white towel from his shoulder and wiped his forehead.

"It's a hot one today," he said. "How about a shake-up?" He began juicing a lemon into a giant plastic cup and then shaking it with crushed ice and sugar. "Coach Torrez, you want one?"

Alex had heard JT was coaching little league, but she hadn't asked him about it. She still had her hand wrapped into his arm; she was not going to let him go until they got away from here. Somehow, it seemed so natural.

"Sure," he smiled.

"Maria won't let me work the beer stand anymore," Coach Banks said. "But she loves lemon shake-ups." He handed Alex a tall plastic cup, and for the first time since she arrived in Greenview, she felt like she was *home*. "I'm working on getting the girls new uniforms."

"They deserve it." Alex took a drink through the straw. The girls always had to compete with the guys for financial backing from the sports boosters, even though the guys were never as good. Maybe JT coaching the young boys would help them with their averages as they got older. "Awe, man. I needed this." She didn't know how thirsty she'd been. The refreshing lemon took over the vomit taste lingering on her tongue.

"You two staying for the band tonight?" Dean asked.

"I don't think so," Alex said. "I don't feel very festive."

Dean handed JT the other shake-up and JT pulled a five out of his pocket.

Dean said and waved JT's money away. "On the house for my star left fielder." He looked at Alex. "I don't blame you for not feeling festive."

Alex nodded and sipped another sour, sweet bit of liquid through the straw.

"For the team," JT said, and handed Dean the five-spot anyway.

Coach took it gratefully and plopped it into the pitcher labeled *uniform fund*. "Tiphanee is around here somewhere," he said. "She's probably going to go All-State this year." Tiphanee, his daughter. "She's not quite as good at diving for fly balls as you, but she's got an arm on her."

"That's really great, Coach. I bet she can hit, too." Alex could catch anything in the outfield, anything, but she could get psyched-out so easy at the plate. "Tell her I said hello and good luck, will you?"

"She's got a strong line drive to the middle." He smiled proudly. "I will. Don't be a stranger, okay? We're practicing every Tuesday through the summer if you want to come out and chase some balls with us. We have some good talent this year."

"Thanks, Coach." Alex looked down at her feet. "I'm only in town for the week."

"Well, it's always good to see you. Stay out of trouble." He grinned.

He'd told her team every Friday night after practice, before the Saturday morning games. *If you girls get in trouble and one of you can't play, then we'll have a* situation. *Stay out of trouble.*

JT said, "Thanks, Dean," and then placed his free hand over hers and escorted her to the Jeep.

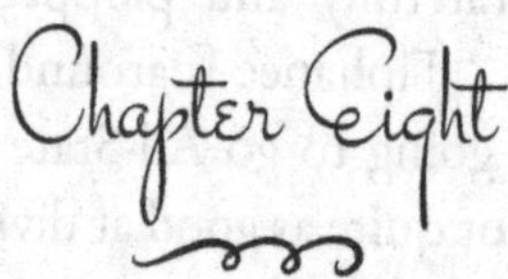

Chapter Eight

When the engine cranked on, Tom Petty sang out of the radio.
Breakdown.

"What station is this?" Alex released the flip-flops from her
feet and put her toes on the dashboard. She wished she still
smoked. Instead, she put her hands on her knees.

"The new Ace FM," JT said, putting the Jeep into gear.
"They play *whatever they want whenever they want.* Radio really
went downhill here for years, you know, after Crap Communica-
tions took over, but these guys play all kinds of stuff."

Alex smiled. The corporate radio conglomerate. "And that
Nickelback song!" They'd played that "Rock Star" song until Alex
couldn't stand it.

"We can listen to country if you want," he said.

She was a big country fan in high school, but lately country
songs were either sad stories, love stories, or beer stories, and she
didn't have the emotional capacity for any of them.

"Tom Petty is good."

JT looked at her then, like really looked at her with his copper
complexion and his chiseled jaw, and his kind and gentle soul.

"Where do you want to go?" She felt vulnerable. "What do
you want to do?"

She didn't have any idea. She wanted this day to be over and there not to be any fireworks and for nobody else to remind her that her dad was dead.

And for nobody to ever again ask her what happened.

She wanted the Fourth of July not to exist anymore. She wanted to go back in time to last June. To do something different. To say something different.

"Somewhere where nobody else is going to ask me about my dad," Alex said. "You have any ideas?" She chewed on the straw. "I haven't been able to make any kind of rational decision for months." She took another drink of lemonade. "I'm lucky I've been able to hold down a job."

It was a miracle she had decided what to wear today, except she had packed exactly three outfits for a one-week trip, and one hooded sweatshirt. She put her cup in the console next to his.

Fewer choices lately had helped.

He scratched his chin, set his eyes on the rearview mirror, and started backing up.

"I have an idea," he said.

He drove them out of town and wound down the old country roads surrounding Greenview. They passed the old red barn of her babysitter's where she rode horses as a kid, and saw her first litter of kittens, then past the pond where she learned to swim, after Drew had thrown her in.

The Jeep bumped past the rock wall by the Amish houses, past the Old Brethren Church. Corn spiked up through the fields, and she had forgotten how certain sections of town smelled, like natural fertilizer, then pine trees, like lilacs, like home.

He drove them to the south side of town where the Indian River wound through the forest and between hills and small valleys, where the true country people lived. This was the most beautiful place on earth other than the ocean. At the stop sign by Dr. Miller's house a blue butterfly swept past her face and fluttered on. Madonna's song "Holiday" came on.

"I always thought this part of town was magical," she said.

"There's just something about it." On top of the hill to their right was the old Brethren Cemetery. Around the corner in front of them, they crawled over the covered bridge. A tiny spring and a corresponding waterfall nestled itself next to an old well in someone's front yard. Not a man-made spring, but clean water just bubbling out of the earth.

"You said that every time we drove out here as kids." He half-smiled.

"*Like fairy land,*" they said in unison.

They drove out into the country where the houses became fewer and farther between. He took a left on the old River Road. It was a winding path set between lines of trees, that curled along the river and led to a clearing everyone called Makeout Cove. They never came out here as kids. Unless you were going to make out with someone who had a car, this place was off limits.

Because they were friends.

The air felt ten degrees cooler on her skin. "You taking me out to Makeout Cove to make out?" Alex joked.

"So, what if I am?" JT shot back. "You afraid to make out with me?"

Every once in a while, a hint of his family's accent came out. There was something sexy about it, but like everything else about him, it was incredibly subtle.

Alex laughed. The first time she'd laughed in days. It almost startled her.

"JT, *come on.*" She punched him in the shoulder. He smiled. It was an understanding between them: their friendship always came first. Before everything. He tapped his fingers on the wheel to the beat.

They wound around through the canopy of trees lining the river and the air cooled and caressed her shoulders. They passed Makeout Cove and drove deeper into the woods where the river narrowed. If you kept going on River Road, the trees would open again to the sky and more farmland, then lead into Middle Falls, the next town over.

They emerged to the next clearing and JT slowed down.

She hadn't thought about the falls in years. The road changed into gravel, and then into a dirt path between trees just wide enough for one vehicle to get through.

"Greenview Falls," she whispered.

It was a five-story rock cliff where the river cascaded over a gray limestone wall and into a clear pool below. A suspension bridge stretched over it; the blue paint faded to gray in some places. Wild daisies spurted up in clumps around the tall grass at the bottom. A stone path led out into the pool.

He tucked the Jeep between the bottom of the cliff and the water and turned off the engine.

"Nobody here," he said. "You want to go swimming?"

Chapter Nine

She wanted to go swimming.

Alex had her bathing suit in her bag. Florida prepared her for everything fun.

"You bring your suit?" She eyed JT's camo shorts.

"Boxers." He brushed his hand against her leg as he opened the glove box, tucked the keys and his phone inside, and closed it.

What was she doing at Greenview Falls on the Fourth of July with JT?

She noticed her mind racing and stopped it.

Going swimming. She knew where to change.

She jumped out of the Jeep.

Behind the wall of water was a small cave. As teenagers they would steal wine coolers from her mom's fridge, drive out here, and sit back behind the water and talk about school and their dreams. What they would do when they grew up. Back then he wanted to play music or baseball professionally, and she wanted to join the Peace Corps.

Life just kept happening. None of those things had happened.

She wouldn't have really needed the comfort of the cave, having learned how to suit up and suit off with only a sundress to cover her on the beach. But JT. She wanted to respect him. She was not trying to seduce him. She knew exactly what that was like from her last fifteen years of being around men, and exactly how to seduce someone.

But *this* was not *that*. They were friends.

The water fell in front of her, leaving a fresh scent in the air as it dropped. The stones smelled damp and familiar. When she came out in her basic black bikini top and skirt, she felt like a nine-year-old at the pool for the first time. Geeky and awkward, like a Cabbage Patch Kid. He took a double-take at her.

"Damn," he said.

"What?"

"I don't want to get weird." He took his shirt off with one fluid movement. She hadn't seen him with his shirt off since they were kids. Defined shoulders carved over his collarbones, and lines drew down his arms like a chalk sketch. Her insecurity disappeared. She held her lips together.

A faint scar about the size of a cigarette stretched above his left hip. He'd been so kind not to pry into her private thoughts, so she didn't ask about the scar. But his body was . . . structured. Not bulky; just incredibly fit.

"Weird," she said. "We're all grown up, I guess." She needed to say something else because this was, in fact, weird. "You look great."

He walked straight toward her with an intense look. She trusted him, but she froze. He opened his arms, and she thought he might pick her up and kiss her, but instead he picked her up and she felt his strong body between her knees and suddenly they were in the water cold and then warm and she was coming up for air, laughing.

She wiped the water out of her face and splashed him.

"Sorry." He smiled, scooped her up with one arm, and wiped the water out of his eyes with the other. Both of their hats were floating away. He held his arm under her legs, and she cradled him around his neck as he swam one way, and then the other, to fish their hats from the water. "I thought I might as well rip the bandage off. Save us the awkwardness."

The water felt *divine*. Refreshing on her skin. Alex tilted her head back, craned her neck, and blew water out of her nose while she situated her hair. It flowed behind her when she came up for air. JT shook his head from side to side and his black hair spurted in all directions, tiny drips of water coming off the tips.

He kept her in his arms, swam over to one of the rocks and sat down, holding her close. He placed their hats next to them on the rock. She sat on his camo shorts and loosened her arms around his neck. Aware of her wet skin touching his wet skin.

"I can't remember the last time I went swimming," she said. A white bird swooped down over them, perched in a birch tree, and then flew away. Droplets of water clutched his eyelashes.

"You live in Florida, and you can't remember the last time you went swimming?" The *e*'s of his accent came and went.

"People have to work, JT, even in Florida." She tucked one finger underneath the leg of his shorts. "You forgot to take your cargos off."

"I am trying to be respectful since *we're friends*," he said.

When anybody asked them, and everybody asked them, in high school if they were dating, that's what they said. It came up so much that they answered in unison and made an inside joke about it.

If things became awkward between them—and even the night on the hammock with the Strawberry Boone's Farm when they talked about it the one and only time—if they should date, why they never dated, if they could date, that's what they come up with. Their default.

Alex repeated, "*We're friends.*"

They sat shoulder to shoulder, their legs dangling into the water.

"You want to talk about today?" he asked.

Today. She had forgotten about today, for just a few minutes.

"Not really." She stared at her toenails and wondered when

she had painted them last. The turquoise paint was chipped. "I cry a lot. It comes out of nowhere and sometimes I can't stop."

"Same," he said. "I feel like I've been crying for a week straight."

Alex was so self-centered. She'd also forgotten about his situation.

"You want to talk about that?"

"I dropped everything when she got pregnant, you know? For the last fifteen years I've just been working. And working." He shook his hair out again, and a bit of water landed on Alex's bottom lip. "I did everything I thought I was supposed to do. So, what am I supposed to do now?" She cleared the drop of water from her lips with her tongue. A faint taste of moss.

"What do you *want* to do?" Alex asked.

He turned to her with a deeper intensity. Had she said something wrong? It was an honest question, right? Asking someone what they wanted to do?

He softened.

"Nobody has asked me that in *years*. I don't even know."

She kicked the water around with her toes.

Alex knew this all too well. Nobody ever asked her what she wanted to do.

She learned as a young female she had to do what she wanted *without* asking permission, because for small-town girls in the Midwest, one thing people didn't want to do, was give them permission. Even strong ones. Even athletes. Even intelligent girls, who people thought could truly do what they wanted if they set their mind to it.

What people really wanted girls to do in Greenview was get married and have kids. Go to church. Live in a box. Alex had climbed over and climbed through an endless gauntlet of pressure to get married, and pressure to have kids, and pressure to settle down and be someone's secretary or someone's housewife. She'd felt the pressure of these expectations all her life.

She had always known what she *didn't* want.

JT put his hand on her knee, which aroused her curiosity more than her suspicion.

"My friends from college are getting together this week at a lake house in Tennessee," he said. "Coach's house. I wanted to go, but it's a couple's thing."

He took his hand from her knee and looked at her. "My parents were going to watch Jared, since baseball season's over. Doesn't matter now." He steadied himself and stared up toward the sky. A few puffy clouds had drifted in front of the sun.

"That's what I want to do," he said. "I want to go to the lake house to see my friends." He turned to Alex. "It's a place called Serenity Lake. Do you want to go?"

The other thing about grief was that sometimes it was like living in the old science fiction television series, *The Twilight Zone*. Weird things would happen, and you would find yourself questioning what was real, and what wasn't.

The real seemed too strange.

Alex had been saying the Serenity Prayer every day for over a year. Now JT was inviting her to a place called Serenity Lake?

Surrender to your higher power, they said.

"Sure." She kicked at the water. "I'll go."

Chapter Ten

On the drive home the air was almost chilly. Alex kept her sarong wrapped around her shoulders and took in the scenery and aromas. They drove next to the river through curves of tree lines, and past the tiny front yard waterfall, up the hill around the cemetery, and back past the red barn where she had spent so much time with horses and kittens and swimming in the pond.

When they pulled up to her mom's house, a white truck sat out front.

"Drew," Alex said. "Mom said he was going to the festival first."

"Guess he's home." JT turned off the engine. Alex strapped her bag over her shoulder, slipped on her flip-flops, and they went inside.

The scent of cinnamon lingered from Diane's morning baking. The cold air conditioning hit Alex's arms, and she shivered.

"I'm going to go up and change," she said.

Drew was standing in the kitchen with the refrigerator open.

"Hey!" His big and booming voice reminded her of their father's.

Alex smiled and ran to him. "Drew, it's so good to see you!"

She squeezed him tight. His black hairline had receded.

"You look good," she said. He was tan, too tan, for a guy who lived in Chicago.

He placed his hands on her shoulders and studied her. "You look skinny. What are you doing?"

"Grief," she said. "I guess."

"These arms, though. You're *cut*." Drew had been a dedicated member of every local gym, and at one point, had bought one, but the deal had fallen through.

"Walks and push-ups," she shrugged. She walked thirty minutes every day now to quiet her mind. Sometimes it worked, and sometimes it didn't. "I wear a lot of tank tops at the beach." He nodded and turned to JT.

"Sup," he said. "The best friend is back. How are you, man?" He shook JT's hand and then moved in for a quick guy-hug. They patted each other on the shoulder blades, made a couple of slapping sounds, and then pulled away.

"Good," JT said. "Fine."

"You don't look fine, but I get it."

Had Drew heard about Emily, too? Alex looked closer at Drew and saw the bags under his eye sockets.

"How's Florida?" Drew asked Alex.

"I don't know, it's okay." She was being honest.

"You live by the beach and it's just, okay?"

"I live in a city that has beaches. But yes, I don't know. It's okay." This year had taken a toll on her. What was she doing with her life and why couldn't she be happy at the beach, of all places, her happiest place?

"I've been meaning to come and see you," he said. "But real estate is booming right now."

"My futon isn't all that comfortable, anyway. How are Elaine and the kids?"

"They're good." He turned back to the open refrigerator door and pulled out a stack of deli turkey and Swiss cheese. "Samantha is ornery, and Sebastian is mouthy, but they're doing well in school. Sebastian's playing soccer."

"At least they're giving you a run for your money."

Drew was younger, but as soon as he'd passed her in height, he'd started treating her as if she were the younger one. As if he were her father figure. He had been the mouthy one, and Alex had stayed quiet, the peacemaker, doing what she was supposed to do, and learning from Drew's mess-ups. Right up until she'd gone to college.

Alex wondered if this conversation might be tough for JT.

"Mom said you were going straight to the festival from the airport."

"I went," he said. He closed the refrigerator door, then opened it again to retrieve a jar of pickles. "There's nothing to eat there for chubby kids-turned body builders." He smiled. "It's all fried food and junk." He started stacking the sandwich elements between two pieces of gluten-free bread.

"True," Alex said. Healthy meals were hard to come by unless you were cooking at home. Diane came in through the garage door. She carried an elephant ear and a bag of sugar waffles.

"Both of my children are home at the same time," she said. She took off her shoes, set her purse down by the door, and kept talking. "I made an apple pie this morning, and there's salad mix in there, and Steve is coming tonight so we thought we'd make some shrimp kabobs on the grill before we went back to the festival." A strawberry-blonde curl dangled in front of her face.

Alex did not want to go back to the festival. She was not sure how her mom was going to react but prepared herself to hear disappointment.

"We're going to drive down to Serenity Lake for a few days," Alex said.

JT chimed in. "My college friends and I meet there for The Fourth every year. I haven't been in a few years."

Diane had stopped lecturing Alex since their dad passed; Alex wasn't used to it yet.

"Okay, honey. Are you planning to leave after the fireworks? You should take a sweatshirt, because it's supposed to be in the sixties at night."

Alex shrugged. "I think we're going to just go now," she said. They had talked about it at the falls. Alex didn't want to see the fireworks, didn't want to hear a tribute from The Yamahas to her father, and didn't want to run into Gracie or anyone else who wanted to ask questions.

She mostly didn't want to cry.

JT didn't care either way; he'd always been so easy to hang around with.

"Okay." Diane hugged her. "Be careful."

"We will," JT said.

"Always running," Drew said.

Usually, he would save his uncomfortable comments for when they were alone.

"What?" Alex wrapped the damp sarong farther over her shoulders. She took a side glance at JT.

"Nothing," Drew said. "I hope you have fun." He took a huge bite of his sandwich and chewed with his mouth open.

"I'm going to go and change," Alex said.

Diane wiped her hands on a towel. "When will you be home?"

JT said, "We have the house until next Friday. I told Alex we could come back whenever she wanted."

Alex shrugged.

"Okay, honey. Aunt Skylar is staying for seven days, so try and get back before she leaves, will you?"

Alex nodded. She did really want to see Aunt Skylar. She had to catch her flight home, anyway. Diane slipped five twenty-dollar bills into Alex's hand.

"For gas," she said sweetly, and then hugged her one more time.

"Mom," Alex said, "I have money." But the truth was, she had a credit card with five-hundred dollars left before it hit the max.

She'd lost some money this week by taking off from the restaurant in Florida, but she was supposed to get paid this Friday by direct deposit from the college.

"You're poor," Diane said. "You can pay me back when you're not. Have fun."

Alex struggled financially, but she wasn't *poor*. She lived by the beach, for goodness sakes, and she went with her friends from work on Sundays out to Sunfish Beach Drum Circle where they danced and watched the sunset. Magical moments of sky and music. Those moments she hardly felt poor.

She'd stopped going into debt when she stopped drinking, which was something.

She remembered the conversation she'd had with her mom during tax time. Steve had done her taxes, and when it finalized, Alex had owed the IRS fifteen-hundred dollars for having just barely crossed one tax bracket. Alex had cried over the phone. "I have *money*," Alex had said, "but I don't have, like, fifteen-hundred dollars lying around to just send to the government."

Her mom had wired her the money the next day and sent her a text that said, *"Early Birthday Present."*

Alex had to get her life together.

Diane said, "I love you. Be careful," and went downstairs.

Drew had almost finished his sandwich in three bites and was rummaging around in the snack cabinet. He pulled out some Oreos. This was the irony of Drew. He wouldn't eat fried food from the festival, but he would polish off this whole package of Oreo's before the night was over.

"You can't just always run from everything," he called after her, as she climbed up the stairs to the guest room.

Chapter Eleven

JT lived behind his parents' restaurant on Main Street. They hadn't driven this way yet, and Alex studied the ways her hometown had changed. Some of downtown Greenview was the same—the police station and the library. But some of it was different. The bank had closed, and the video store, and the general store. Large, beautiful buildings made of gray and white bricks sat with lights off and boards over the windows. They pulled up to the restaurant and JT parked in the spot right out front.

Carnitas had been the first and only Mexican restaurant for miles when they were younger, and people would come from three towns away to enjoy his father's cooking and his mother's colorful decor. The multi-colored block lettering in front of the restaurant spelled out the name in blues, greens, reds, and yellows.

"You want to go in?" JT asked. "My parents would love to see you."

Tropical flowers had been specially placed between the signs. Hibiscus, peace lilies, and some kind of orange flower with a hardy stem, like the orchids her friend Layla grew in Florida, but hardier. A line of small American Flags was placed thoughtfully between the sign and the street. Alex had missed the Fourth of July Parade without even thinking about it.

"Is that a banana tree?" Layla also had a banana tree in her front yard.

"A hardy banana. We dig it up every year and bring it inside for the winter. My mom is gonna be stoked to see you."

JT opened the door and held it for Alex. A wall of air conditioning hit her, and the mariachi ringing through the atmosphere brightened her spirits. The hostess was a small, muscular blonde girl in a red shirt and black leggings.

"Welcome to Carnitas," she said.

"We're not eating," he said. "We just came to see Mom."

Ukuleles hung from the walls, along with some unique stringed instruments, maracas, and some hand drums. The place looked the same as she remembered, green floors, red walls, yellow wooden trim. Two tables of older customers sat in booths by the windows to their right, and the bar lined up against the back wall to the left. Alex tried not to look at the liquor bottles.

Sonya came around the corner wiping her hands on her apron and scooted across the green tiled floor into Alex's arms.

"¡Mija!" she said. "My daughter, how are you?" Alex opened her arms and embraced Sonya, who smelled like spicy perfume. Sonya's head only came up to Alex's shoulder. "Te extraño, I missed you!" Carlos came quickly behind her.

"Hola, Alexandra. Bienvenidos a casa. Welcome home." He pronounced her name with the 'x' sounding like an 'h.' Respectful like JT, he allowed her personal space for a greeting. She hugged him, anyway.

"What are you up to?" Carlos asked.

"We're going to take a ride down to the lake house." JT favored his father—the same strong jawline, the same curled eyelashes. A spatter of freckles over top of his cheeks.

"Ah," Carlos said. "Con tus amigos de colegio. Muy bien."

Alex glanced toward the bar and had a flashback of JT's wedding.

He'd gotten married here at Carnitas, and Alex had started in on the margaritas early. She hadn't brought a date, so she spent most of the night by herself, palling around with the Luis the bartender, only chatting with the attendees here and there.

She'd sat in the back closest to the bar and JT's Aunt Teresa. *Tía T,* they'd called her as kids. Tía T had turned to Alex while the couple recited their vows, looked her straight in the eyes as if scolding her and whispered, "That could have been *you.*" She didn't even speak much English, but she had said it plain as day, as if she'd been practicing it.

Emily had worn a princess dress that hugged her body in all the right places. JT still had his boy-face, and his shiny black hair was parted down the middle in a perfect line, the ends of it hanging around his eyebrows. He'd gotten laser surgery on his eyes.

The couple seemed like the All-American couple. Like they were perfect for each other and they'd have a perfect marriage.

Alex sat back and observed. The most poignant thing she remembered from the reception was her parents together . . . dancing. Her mom was in between boyfriends and her dad had split with his second wife by now.

Alex sat at the bar in her long navy-blue dress, legs crossed, and watched Curtis approach Diane. Her mom wore a red dress, shiny under her strawberry curls. Curtis had actually dressed up, although he wore Vans tennis shoes with his blue suit. He'd spiked his black hair up with mouse.

"Lady in Red" was playing by Chris de Burgh.

Curtis reached his hand out to Diane. She stood up, and took it, and he slowly led her out onto the dance floor. He said something and she laughed, and then she put her face against his, and they danced the whole song together, moving in small circles under the disco ball that spun white lights around them, both of their eyes closed and smiling.

He held Diane's hand against his chest, the other hand respectfully on her waist.

Alex had sipped her margarita in awe, sucked at the salt and lime, and then ordered another.

Curtis had kissed Diane on the cheek, and they'd parted ways.

To this day, it was the only memory Alex had of her parents together, looking like they were in love.

After the reception, when everyone else was cleaning up, JT walked over to her at the bar. She wasn't accustomed to seeing him without his ball cap on. *His eyes.* She'd long switched to beers by now, and after watching all of the happy couples dance all of their happy dances, after seeing her best friend in love with a girl she'd never be, she was feeling no pain.

She had wanted to tell him how much he'd meant to her, how good of a friend he'd been, how she wouldn't have made it through their childhoods or teenage years without him. After this, she wouldn't have a wingman anymore—someone to ride around town with, pal around with, hang out by the falls with.

She knew this was the end for them. Their inside jokes. Their silly little notes. She'd wanted to send him off and wish him well, to put her feelings all into words. She had wanted to say goodbye.

Instead, she'd stood up, grabbed him by the collar of his tux, pulled his face close to hers, slurred her words and said, "I think she's . . . too good for you and you'll al . . . ways love *me* most." Then her knees had buckled, and she'd dropped her beer bottle, so it shattered with a popping-gush-sound all over the tile floor.

Alex had woken up on Diane's bathroom floor the next morning, still in her dress, with a bruise on her forehead from the toilet rim.

She'd seen his face while she was falling, though. A flash of his eyes, as if he thought what she'd said was *funny* for an instant.

The last flash of memory she had before she blacked out was everyone rushing over to her. She didn't think it was funny the next day, or any day after. She didn't even remember if she had paid her tab.

She cringed every time it crossed her mind. It was another amends that she owed. She was supposed to be doing that this week. When was the last time she had called her sponsor? She hadn't looked at her phone since this morning.

The bartender Luis waved to her.

She snapped back to the present moment, nervously waved, and focused on JT's parents.

"Mija. Yo lo siento sobre tu padre. Estaba un hombre gran." When Sonya didn't translate, Alex turned to JT.

"She said she's sorry about your father . . . he was a great man."

"Oh, thanks," Alex said. "Gracias." It was the one Spanish word she knew. The only one other than hola she could use with confidence.

Sonya reached out and held both of Alex's wrists. "Creemos que el alma es eterna." Tears welled in Alex's eyes, but she held them, and Sonya's arms, in gratitude.

JT rolled his eyes. "*Madre*, it isn't nice when you don't translate."

Carlos turned to Alex. "She thinks the real meaning will get lost in translation. She said, 'We believe that the soul is eternal.'"

Sonya appeared pleased, squeezed Alex's arms again, and then released them. She put her hands together in front of her chest, made the Catholic sign for the trinity, and then clutched the purple rosary hanging around her neck.

"Diane says you are teaching in a prison," Carlos asked. "¿Por qué? Is it scary?"

Alex hadn't thought about teaching for a few hours, which was an improvement. "It's just the job I got." She knew she could be honest with them. "It was kind of scary at first, but now it's not. It's actually really fun." She tucked a piece of hair under her baseball cap. "Challenging and rewarding."

"Okay," JT said, and clapped his hands together as if he wanted to end the conversation. "We're going to get Charlie and pack a bag. We'll see you sometime next week," he said.

"Tienes cuidad," his father said.

Alex followed JT through the back of the restaurant, past a couple of guys and a woman who stood over the grill-line stirring giant pots. Wafts of onion, garlic, and sizzling steak mingled in the air. Alex waved at the cooks. "It smells amazing in here," she said, as they walked out the door and into his backyard.

She understood then: his quiet, and the stress, and his just showing up at her mom's house today with no particular agenda. There was a swing set in the backyard, and water guns and nerf guns strung about. A bicycle laid over on its side. A treehouse in one giant oak tree, that he must have built himself. But something was missing. No kid running around.

The small cottage overlooked Lower Main Street and the old water treatment plant. When they were little, they would play in the river. There were enough rocks for them to get from one side to the other without getting their feet wet.

"What did I work so hard for?" JT asked.

He'd come back home to Greenview right after college, gotten his Commercial Driver's License, ran a regional route during the week, and worked at Carnitas on the weekends. Even though his degree was in percussion performance.

"I just did what I thought I was supposed to do," he said. "And out here, it was either work in construction, get my CDL, or work with my parents." As a teenager, he'd sworn he'd never work at the restaurant.

Alex hated when she was working through something and venting, and somebody else gave her some unwarranted piece of well-meaning advice or pointed to another option for her path. So, she listened.

"She and I grew apart, but I thought she had what she need-ed." He shook his head and stared at his back door as if he were seeing his life through a different lens, a different past. "I could have kept playing drums *and* baseball."

JT had gone to South Ohio University on a baseball scholarship. Alex had never once gone and watched one of his games. She was in Florida, though, a sophomore when he was a freshman. He wasn't the star of the high school team, but he was the best catcher they'd ever had. She'd heard he'd been pretty good in college, too. And he'd turned down a chance to play in the minors.

They walked up two cement steps and reached the back door. People didn't lock their doors in Greenview.

"Brace yourself," he said. "You like dogs, right?"

Alex had never had a dog, but she had friends who did and had gotten more used to them. As JT opened the door, a giant Rottweiler leapt out at them, almost knocking them down as he bounded down the steps.

"Meet Charlie," he said and smiled.

Alex was taken aback. The dog ran around in a circle in the backyard, sniffed at things, and then ran back to Alex and licked her hand. He sat back on his hind legs, just briefly, let out a puppy bark, licked her hand again, and took off running again.

"Oh my gosh," Alex said. "He's *huge*." The dog's head was bigger than Alex's, and he had a silver-linked chain around his neck.

JT smiled his real smile, the one she hadn't seen since the falls. "The vet says 125 pounds."

"How old is he?" Alex asked.

"Four. Kind of a teenage puppy, if you didn't notice the puppy-like bark."

"He looks full grown."

"Indeed," JT said, and laughed again. He opened the door further and said, "Awe, man." His whole body drooped.

"What's wrong?" Alex asked.

Chapter Twelve

Alex looked around inside. Gray wood paneling, laminate floors with green rugs placed about, and hardly any furniture. There was a lamp on the floor, plugged in, where a mark on the rug suggested a table used to be. "*Fuck,*" he said, quietly.

JT flipped a switch and turned the light on. The white curtains were closed, but the light helped illuminate the emptiness of what must have been a room full of furniture and toys. "My stuff is gone."

He dropped down to his knees. Alex wasn't sure what to do or say, so she knelt down next to him and rubbed his back. The laminate floors didn't feel great, but she wanted to comfort her friend. Muscles bristled beneath his tee shirt, and she ignored an electrifying feeling. It had been so long since she felt anything but sadness; other feelings were dull and stayed on the periphery.

When Gracie stole her boyfriend in high school, she didn't get out of bed for a week except to go to school and to softball practice. He was beside her every day, trying to get her to watch a movie and trying to get her to eat. He had shown up with her favorite movies: *Dirty Dancing* and *The Bodyguard*. *Empire Records* and *Good Will Hunting*. VHS tapes of *The Karate Kid* and the old Michael Jackson *Thriller* video they'd recorded from MTV. And pizza, and tacos.

What could she say to make this hurt less?

Charlie ran in behind them, licked JT's face, and knocked him over. Alex scrambled not to fall over herself and stood up. A giggle escaped her.

"Charlie!" JT said, and then he laughed. He got to his feet, wiped his eyes with his thumb and his forefinger, then petted Charlie on his head. The dog sat down and panted, the brown markings on his face distinct like warrior paint.

"Fuck," JT said. "I'm sorry. My mom would slap me. But that's the only word I have that makes any sense." Sonya and Carlos all but dragged him to mass every Sunday, and sometimes on Wednesday nights. "Emily must have known I'd go to the festival."

Alex put her hand on the small of his back. "I'm here."

"What is happening?" JT asked. "I don't understand anything anymore."

Alex recognized the thought as if it were her own. She had spent every day for the last year asking herself those same questions. The answers hardly ever came, except for the narration she could make up in her mind about her motions.

Going to work. Going to eat. Going to bed.

Putting on my shoes.

She'd been praying, too. After she started recovery and going to meetings, it's what her sponsor and the women had told her to do. Even if she didn't believe anybody was listening. Especially, they said, if she didn't believe anybody was listening.

Lately she'd been praying for *acceptance*. For whatever higher power there was out there to help her understand what was going on in her mind and her heart.

He wandered into the kitchen, and she followed him. The cabinets had been left open and mostly empty except for one plate, one cup, and one bowl. The rest of the doors were splayed open and the shelves clear.

"Fuck," he said again. He opened the silverware drawer to one set. "I paid for all this shit, and she just takes it? And my kid?"

He sat down on the lone chair and settled his eyes on a piece of paper on the counter. His head moved from side to side in disbelief.

"*Please don't call me,*" he read. "*We are fine. I will call you when I am ready to . . .*" JT's voice cracked. "*Come and get the rest of Jared's toys and Charlie from you.*"

He ripped the paper up, threw it on the floor and abruptly stood up.

"She's not taking my dog, too."

Alex hadn't looked at her phone since this morning. The text messages, the condolences, she wanted to avoid them. She opened JT's front door, and found Emily had at least left the front porch swing.

Before she took her cell phone out of her bag, she promised herself she would not open any messages from anyone who wasn't in her family or her trusted friend group. It was a small list. There was a message from her sponsor, Kara.

How are you? Call me soon.

She would call her tomorrow. She was supposed to call her every day, but today she didn't have it in her. The sun was still high in the sky at 7 p.m., and Alex could barely hear the festival, a band playing from afar.

The street was quiet, and Alex plopped herself on the porch swing and looked over toward the river. It was quite beautiful here, in its own way. The houses across the street were humble, but well-kept, and the trees were tall and healthy. An ash tree provided just enough shade in JT's front yard.

A message from Randy.

I miss you. Did you land safely? This one had come in the

morning, and she hadn't seen it. Another one, from 5 p.m. *We need to talk.*

This one boggled her mind. We need to talk? On the anniversary of my father's death while I am home, and you are in Florida? On the Fourth of July? We need to talk?

He had a show tonight; he should have been loading in.

JT emerged in a pair of army-green shorts instead of camo, backpack wrapped over his right shoulder. He stopped abruptly, eyes wide.

He leaned his left shoulder against the blue paneling of his house, as if he needed to take the weight off his knees to steady himself. The screen door slammed behind him.

His dark eyelashes clapped up and down.

She took in his face, freshly shaven. Gentleness and masculinity had imprinted themselves on his skin in faint lines. She raised her eyebrows while new feelings swirled around in her chest. He smelled like high school, like Cool Water cologne.

Alex tried not to fixate on thinking about his abs from earlier, and the way his biceps seemed to be carved by a sculptor.

Instead, she focused on his eyes.

"What's wrong?" she asked. "I mean, aside from the obvious. You look startled."

"I was going to ask you the same thing. You look like you saw a ghost." JT adjusted his backpack.

"You first," Alex said.

"Nah," JT shook his head. "You don't want to know."

"Same," Alex said. She still had the panic running through the back of her wild mind in Randy's words.

We need to talk. We need to talk. We need to talk.

JT lowered his backpack and sat down next to her on the swing. His leg just barely touched hers, and she hadn't noticed how strong and lean his calves were, as if he were also now a soccer player. They flexed as he gently pushed the swing back and forth.

He stared over at the water toward the stones they used to run across when they were kids. When their lives were easy and carefree.

"I guess we can either keep skating around the surface of things, and be cautious with each other," he said, "or we can do like we did when we were kids and just tell the truth." He adjusted his gray baseball cap.

This was the JT she remembered. Never prying, always respectful, but honest.

And handsome. The handsome part was new.

Honesty had been the topic at the last meeting she attended with Kara.

"We are only as sick as our secrets," someone had said.

Right after the funeral, she had stopped talking altogether. She spoke only at work, and sometimes on the phone. She realized how often people use words just to use them, when silence would fit just fine.

"I mean," he continued, "we can go to the lake and not talk at all. I'm glad you're here. It's been too long." He lowered his head. "I haven't been on vacation for five years. The last four I've told the guys we were too busy, but the truth is, she didn't want to go, and I felt too guilty to go without her. I couldn't really afford to take off work, anyway." He sighed, planted his feet, and stopped the swing. "I didn't want her to *have* to work, though."

Alex stayed quiet. A drop of sweat rolled down his cheek.

"I think you'll like my friends." He continued to stare across the street and over the water. "They're going to like you."

She nudged the concrete with her own foot, so they moved back and forth again.

"My boyfriend just sent me a text from Florida that says, *We need to talk.*" She accidentally brushed her leg against his. Or did she? She thought it was an accident.

He sighed audibly. Loudly this time, like he was trying to blow out a thousand invisible candles, like he'd been punched in the stomach and was trying to breathe through the pain. Alex watched a leaf fall from the ash tree, dancing back and forth on the imperceptible breeze before it settled in the grass with no sound.

"You have a boyfriend. In Florida?" He laughed a sarcastic laugh. "Of course you do."

"Yeah." She adjusted her bra strap. It slipped out of her fingers and snapped back into place.

"What's his name?" JT asked.

An uncomfortable silence stretched out.

"Randy."

A car puttered by. Somebody in the driver's seat waved, and JT waved back.

"That sounds like an old man's name. What's he like?"

Alex tried to dodge the question. Lately Alex had a thing for older men. "Are you trying to decide if you like him or not?"

"Don't, never mind. You're right. I don't really want to know if I might like him or not. I don't really want to know you have a boyfriend in Florida named Randy who needs to talk."

A fly landed on his face, and he waved it off. "What does he *need to talk* about?"

That was the question, wasn't it? Her mind didn't have space for any more questions. She leaned her leg against his, this time on purpose.

"I don't know," she said. "I don't really care today."

"Look," he said. "I don't want to cause any static in your relationship. We don't have to go to the lake."

"No," she said. "It's already staticky. I want to go. He'll be fine."

Her curiosity kicked in. Why had he seemed so startled when he came out of the door?

"What were you going to say?" She wished she hadn't left her lemon shake-up in the car. Her mouth was dry.

He stared thoughtfully and shook his head.

"I don't think we're ready for that yet," he said. "It's too much. Are you ready to go, though?"

"No, come on." She tapped his shoulder and smiled. "You just gave me that whole talk about how we might as well be honest with each other. Honestly. What was that look on your face when you came out of the door? Why did you stop like that?"

He turned his head toward her, and his kind and gentle eyes sparkled. A depth of compassion arose, something a wounded man would only show to someone he trusted.

"That look on my face when I came out of the door was a memory I had."

He seemed to want to leave it at that, but she didn't, and so she pried. It wasn't like her lately, but it was like Alex-the-teenager had been with her friend.

"What memory?" She nudged his sandal with her toe and smiled. Maybe she could cheer him up.

He cleared his throat. "The memory I had when I knew I wanted to buy this house. The vision I had about it."

"Vision?" Why was he being so cryptic? "What vision? I thought we were being honest."

She knew she was pressing him, but she didn't care. He kept his eyes on hers, peering at her in slits from between his curled eyelashes. She saw loneliness and hope and sadness and desire, as if each tiny fleck of yellow had its own unique feeling. She lowered her eyes to his lips. A moan came out with a sigh, then her name. A hesitance.

He breathed her name like a whisper from far away.

"Alex," he shook his head from side to side and stopped the swing again.

She made a point to keep her knee against his.

The next sentence came out louder and deeper, like a bass guitar riff underpinning a song. But slowly. With rests. Like half notes.

"Honestly. The vision I had . . . that it would be you . . . sitting on my front porch just like this and raising our kids . . . not someone else."

A tingling rose up her spine and spread out at the base of her neck. She stayed silent while those words reverberated and replaced, *we need to talk* in her head.

. . . that it would be you . . .

Alex pressed the concrete with her toes, and the swing jutted sideways, then regained its back-and-forth momentum. She carefully folded her hands in her lap, trying to ground herself. The swing rocked back and forth; the two friends suspended in the moment with their legs touching.

She searched for words but there were only questions.

"I told you," he said. "It's too much. Let's go to the lake."

Chapter Fourteen

They went back through the restaurant to get to his Jeep, and Sonya stuffed two to-go boxes in their hands. "Some snacks." She hugged them both one more time. "For your trip." Charlie sniffed everyone's hands, ate a treat from Carlos, and then tugged at the leash until they arrived out front.

"I'm going to hit the bathroom before we go." Alex rushed back inside, turned the corner and swung open the door that said *Señoritas*. Flowers and musk permeated the air, surrounded by mauve paint. A palm tree shined green in the corner. Everything was spotless.

As she squatted in the stall, Alex thought she heard sniffling from the next stall over. She peeked down beside her but only saw two black tennis shoes. Someone was in there crying.

She went to the sink to wash her hands and looked at herself in the mirror. How many times this year had she snuck into the bathroom at work to cry? More times than she had fingers and toes. She scrubbed her hands with the flowery soap, turned off the water and grabbed a paper towel, but she couldn't bring herself to leave.

She tapped on the door of the stall.

"Hello? My name is Alex. I'm a friend of JT's, and the owners? I just wanted to check on you."

The stall door creeped open, and the hostess stepped out. Her mascara ran down her cheeks in spidery lines. Alex dipped a paper towel in water and handed it to her.

"Thanks." The girl sniffled and meekly accepted the towel. Alex noticed her name tag.

Tiphanee.

"Are you Tiphanee Banks?"

The girl nodded and dabbed at her eyes.

"Oh, God, hi. I'm Alex Ward. Your dad was my softball coach." Alex watched Tiphanee's expression through their mirror reflections. She had her dad's eyes.

"I remember you." Tiphanee pulled at the waist of her leggings. She was small, built strong. "My dad still talks about you. There's a newspaper picture of your team on our refrigerator."

Alex returned her smile. "I think I went to college the year you were born. How old are you?"

"Seventeen." She held her cell phone in one hand, and the brown paper in the other. "I'm going to be a senior this year."

"I just saw your dad at the festival. He said you might go All-State. *That's* pretty cool." Alex wasn't sure how to talk to teenagers. "You'll probably get some college offers?"

"I've got a full ride to UC Berkley," she said.

"California?"

"I don't know if I'm going. It seems so far away."

"California is rad." Alex looked at Tiphanee's expression and decided to tone down her excitement. "You can always come home. Not everybody gets to go to college, though."

"I know," Tiphanee said. Alex realized she sounded like she was lecturing.

"I don't want to get into your business, but I was just crying in the bathroom earlier. Well, the port-o-john at the Fourth of

July Festival. Which smelled way worse." Alex managed a laugh. "You want to talk about it?"

Tiphanee shook her head. "My boyfriend just graduated. He's going to UNC this fall. Today he broke up with me by a text message." She wadded the paper towel into a ball, then made a fist. "And now the girls in my class are shame-bombing me." A whimper came out, and then a triple-breath inward puffed up her chest. She put her fist to her mouth and her face tightened.

"I'm so sorry." Alex squeezed her shoulder with one arm. "That really sucks."

Alex pulled another paper towel and handed it to her. "What's shame-bombing?"

Tiphanee held her phone out to Alex. "Group messages. One after the other after the other. Saying I'm fat, saying I'm ugly, saying I'm a lesbian." She blew her nose into the new paper towel. "Even some of my teammates."

Alex didn't need to look at the phone to remember how cruel high school girls could be. She still remembered all the times anyone had called her *fat*. Especially, the head of the mean girls.

Third grade, Gracie had puffed out her cheeks and called Alex chubby. Sixth grade, Gracie had made fun of her for having to wear her mom's jeans. Eleventh grade, she had told Alex her prom dress made her look like a sumo wrestler.

How quickly the other girls jumped on the insult-train because they were trying to stay in a cool-girls group. It had deeply injured her self-image.

"You're *not fat*." Alex studied Tiphanee's blonde hair and rounded face. "You're *beautiful* and *strong* and, if you're Coach's daughter, you're kind. And tough as bricks." If high school girls knew how crazy the outside world could get when they got out into it, they'd maybe try and lift each other up and stick together, rather than tear each other down. "Can you ignore your phone for a day? Just focus on what you're doing in the present?"

Tiphanee lowered the paper towels from her face and looked at her reflection in the mirror. She nodded and tucked the phone into her pocket. "I know I'm strong. But sometimes I *feel* fat. And I just don't always feel pretty. Why are they being so *mean?*" More tears appeared on the rim of her eyes. "I'm sorry," she said.

Alex remembered the awkwardness of her own body filling out. How getting her period made her feel like a whale sometimes. How turning from a girl into a woman could feel so damn uncomfortable.

Alex let out an audible sigh. "Ugh. Don't be sorry. High school girls can be ruthless. All girls feel fat sometimes. And *nobody* feels pretty." Alex thought of Layla, how unapologetically herself she was. "You know, being a lesbian isn't a bad thing."

"But I'm not!" Tiphanee said. "And *it is* a bad thing in Greenview. The girls in my group are so mean to the girls who came out."

Maybe you need some new friends, Alex thought. But that was hard in a small town. There were only so many people to choose from.

"You know what? You have one year left, and then you can get out of Greenview, make new friends in California, and get on with your life." Tiphanee pulled out the waistband of her leggings, hiked them up, and they snapped back as she released them.

"You're not fat," Alex repeated. "You're a softball star! I bet they're jealous of you." She was trying to sound cheery, and realized she probably sounded fake. Alex lowered her voice and rubbed Tiphanee's back. "I was chubby in high school. One of my doctors actually wrote *obese* on one of my physicals. But when I got to college, I realized almost all the girls thought they were fat. Or too this or too that. Eff-that!" Alex didn't want to cuss in front of Coach's daughter. "We only get one body. We can learn to take care of it the best we can, but there's no use in obsessing about it. Especially to fit into some stupid box created by mean girls."

Tiphanee rinsed the paper towel in the sink, added some flowery soap, and used it to dab the mascara smears from her cheeks. She looked down at Alex's legs, and then back to her eyes in the mirror.

"How did you lose so much weight?"

There were a lot of ways Alex could answer this. It had taken thirty-five years. Yo-yo diets, obsessing, addiction and then . . . recovery, fiber, probiotics, and walks.

"I went to college, took a nutrition class, and I started running." Her own reflection in the mirror was determined. "And I made all new friends."

Tiphanee straightened and put her hands on her hips. "Do you still run?"

"I walk now," Alex said. "But I'm comfortable in my own skin."

I'm comfortable in my own skin.

"I'm sorry about your dad."

It caught Alex off guard. It always caught her off guard.

She took the paper towel from Tiphanee's hands and tossed it into the trashcan.

He wasn't that great of a dad. I wish I would have had your dad.

"Thank you," Alex said. "You gonna be okay?"

"I think so. I feel better, I guess."

"Hang in there," Alex said. "College is pretty cool once you get there." After she opened the restroom door, Alex turned back to her. "Give your dad a hug for me, will you?"

"I will," Tiphanee said.

She wiped her eyes one more time in the mirror.

Chapter Fifteen

"Are you sure you want to do this?" he asked.

JT and Alex put the top up, and Charlie jumped inside like he belonged there in the back seat. He laid down with a huff. JT stuffed the dog food in the small trunk behind the tailgate, threw their bags onto the back floorboards, and placed a small cooler in between.

They put the back windows in and left the front windows down before they rode through town toward the interstate. He had brought his old CD case, a black zip-up thing with four CDs tucked inside every page.

Alex said, "I want to get out of town, and I can't think of anybody else I'd rather go with." His comment on the front porch had left her speechless, so she'd let it roll into acceptance like every other thing that happened lately. The sun was beginning to set, the heat was beginning to dissipate, and then eventually, it would be tomorrow, and she would have made it through her first Fourth of July without her dad.

Hopefully, without losing her marbles.

"I ran into Tiphanee in the bathroom." Alex put her right hand out of the window and let it flop and flow in the wind. "Why didn't you tell me Coach's daughter was the hostess?"

"It's been kind of a weird day." He lifted his ball cap off his face and then lowered it back over his eyes. "She just started. I guess I didn't think about it."

They rode through the country in silence and stopped at the gas station where Alex had worked one summer. Some people had made fun of her for it, but she had always wanted to call her own shots and make her own choices, and it was where she wanted to work. It wasn't a dream job, but there were paychecks. And that first summer back home, she still had a few friends and wanted to have fun with them.

It was very little responsibility. Low expectations.

As JT pumped the gas he said, "Will you choose a CD?"

She unzipped the black case and found a treasure of old CDs inside.

"I can't believe you have all of these. You still have all your CDs from BMG and Columbia?"

Music subscription services had become popular in the late nineties when the two friends were still in high school. Every month they would send you a new CD for free. It's how they had discovered Dave Matthews Band, Nirvana, Alanis Morissette, Green Day, and all the music they had listened to on repeat for years. Her own CDs had gotten all chewed up in her travels: dropped on the floorboards, lost in moves, or scratched. She had one small CD case left, and it mostly held her dad's music, some percussion stuff, and some piano instrumentals.

She flipped through page after page in awe.

"Silverchair? I forgot about them! Toad and the Wet Sprocket? Just . . . wow." She caught one side of his face smiling. He replaced the gas pump and climbed back into the driver's seat, just as she noticed a burned CD with her name on it.

In the early 2000's, when music got to the internet, you could load your CDs into some computers and "burn" them to make a modern-day mixtape. Her dad hated when that happened, because it had crushed his own CD sales.

But you could make a *mixtape*.

Alex said, "What's this? It's got my name on it." In JT's handwriting, *ALEX* was scrawled across the front in purple marker.

"Oh," he said. "I must have made it for you and never sent it."

He revved the engine. "You want to go in and clock in? See if they still owe you a paycheck?" He nodded at the front door and laughed.

"Shut up," she said. "I always hated how it smelled like melting plastic in there. If I wouldn't have worked there, I would have never started smoking." It had been harder to quit smoking than to quit drinking, which was hard.

"I'm kidding," he said.

She had just stopped going in one day. It was before you needed to authorize a credit card to pump gas, and they told her she would have to start paying for people's gas who just gassed up and drove off. She refused.

They had never even called her to see where she was.

"Put your CD in," he said.

The first song started ringing through the Jeep and then into the night. John Mayer's "Why Georgia."

"How did you know I loved this song? John Mayer didn't come out until after we graduated and lost touch." He turned the Jeep onto the on-ramp and sped up.

"I *know* you," he said. "I knew you'd be fawning all over John Mayer." He glanced at her and laughed.

"I don't fawn over him." She wrangled a bottle of water out of the cooler and looked at Charlie, now sleeping soundly. "But okay, I might have played that *Gravity* CD over and over again and asked my musician friends to cover it at their shows."

"See." JT lightly tapped out the rhythm to the song with his fingertips. "I knew."

Next, Jack Johnson's "Flake" played. She couldn't believe he still knew her musical taste. Jack Johnson had come out after they graduated, too, and she loved his beach-vibe voice and how he used congas and shakers in the tracks.

"Remember when we went to the Dave Matthews Band

concert at Riverbend, and we couldn't figure out where we parked at the end of the night?" She smiled.

"You made me carry your purse, your drink, and then your high heels, and I thought we might never find it." He laughed. "Who knew there were so many sections of gravel in that parking lot, and so many oak trees."

"Not really great landmarks," she said. "Also, the last time I wore high heels to a concert. And anyway, they were chunks. They made me look tall."

"I remember," he said. "They were heavy."

It was like so much time had passed and then, no time at all.

She thought about that summer, how he had been the good-boy baseball player, always around, never drinking too much, never smoking. And how she had gone a little wilder than that, trying anything once, trying some things more than once. Falling in with a group who partied all day, then being so lucky that she'd come out of it unscathed.

She'd lost most of her high school friends, her reputation, dropped out of college for a while, made her mom crazy with anger, and then finally found her way. After a good talk from her brother, and a scolding from her dad.

Only finding solace in the encouragement of Nana Kate, who always said, "*Watch your back, but follow your heart.*"

"I was really worried about you after that summer," he said.

"You were?" She didn't remember him being around much after that. After the night she and her party friends left him at Diane's to go to a rave. He wasn't 21 yet, but the rest of them had fake ID's.

"But you were always going to do what Alex wanted to do, and I wasn't going to try and stop you," he said. "You wouldn't have listened to me, anyway."

"I don't know where I got my stubborn independence," she said. "But I thought I was always on the right path."

"You aren't sure where you got your stubborn independence?" JT said. "Did you just say that out loud?" He laughed at her and tilted his head.

"Where do you think, JT, since you seem to know me so well."

"Umm . . . from Curtis?"

From her dad. Never doing what he was supposed to do but always doing what he wanted. Part of the reason she had so many feelings about how he was as a father. Part of the reason she had so many feelings about his death.

She had considered she was like her father, many times, but that meant she had these parts of her that her mom didn't like. The stubborn hard-headedness—she would absolutely always do what she thought was best for her, rather than what anybody else told her to do—no matter what. Which might have border-lined on, as Kara and the girls called it, a *character defect.*

The Jeep was loud and bumpy. There wasn't much traffic, but lightning bugs dotted the darkening horizon on both sides of them and then the fireworks began. Clusters of colors rang up into the night on all sides of them, some to the east, and some to the west.

They couldn't hear them, but as they drove south down I-75 they saw every fireworks display in every city from there until the bridge to Kentucky, and then some. Reds and greens and blues and whites. Different shapes and burst patterns, like artistic fire in the sky.

Maybe there was a higher power somewhere, because this is the only way she could imagine spending the Fourth of July without her dad.

Without crying.

One of her dad's songs came on, "Imperfect." JT studied her, as if to see if she wanted him to change it, or if she were going to.

She let it play.

"I'm sorry about all that. That year, you know?" She fidgeted with the latch of the glove box. "I'm still learning how my actions affected other people when I was in active addiction, or whatever.

That's what they call it in recovery." She was making amends. Was she making amends? She was supposed to plan it, but these words were just coming out of her mouth. "Since we're being honest, I always felt really bad that I broke away from you. Or I maybe might have, I don't know, hurt you in some way. I wasn't always really *with* it. I was always going with the flow then, and I didn't really have a handle on what the flow was or where it was taking me."

He adjusted his arm on the steering wheel, propping it up so his elbow rested on the console. "It's okay. It seemed like you were kind of lost, is all. My dad says sometimes we have to get lost to be found." He scratched his chin with his other hand. "Emily and I were happy at first. We had some really good times together." The CD restarted, and he pushed the button to eject it. "We all have regrets, Alex. No sense in feeling guilty for something that happened fifteen years ago."

She still felt an anchoring in her body, a certain guilt. "I'm really sorry about your wedding," she said.

"My wedding?"

She shifted in her seat.

Like he didn't remember?

"Getting so drunk I couldn't stand up and then . . . that thing I said about . . . her being too good for you."

"Right," he said. "That." The look came back, the last flash of his eyes before Alex hit the ground and realized she was on the tile floor in a puddle of beer and glass, in a dress.

The look like he thought it was *funny*.

It was *humiliating*.

Shame crawled all through her body.

He smirked. "I forgive you." He studied her, cocked his head, and rested his tongue on one of his canine teeth before he looked back at the road in front of them.

How had she never noticed how pink and full his lips were? Or that he had perfect teeth? She was at a loss for words again.

Sometimes there were just too many thoughts in her brain at one time to speak.

"How did you two meet?" Alex finally asked.

He huffed. "Emily and I?"

"Yeah, she seemed perfect for you. *That's* what I should have said that night."

He put his hand on the bill of his hat and breathed a loud breath. "Your dad brought her to one of my college games junior year. He introduced us." How had Alex missed so much? "Curtis had a lot of good friends who were girls, you know?" His eyes did a guy thing.

She knew.

All of them were gorgeous. Emily included. She didn't want to talk about her dad. Alex rolled her mind back to childhood.

She and JT had met before they had memories.

Both of their moms had taken them to the community park when they were toddlers. According to Diane, when Alex saw JT on the slide the first time, she walked over to him and stared.

According to Sonya, if they didn't go to the park after that—if it were raining or something—JT would cry. As Diane told it, Alex would watch the clock after lunch in the summer, and drag her out the door at 1 p.m. So, their moms took them every weekday and they became first friends. When Alex went to kindergarten a year before him, JT waited at the bus stop every day for her to get home.

They both played little league, and they would meet at the concession stand in their dusty ball uniforms after their games and buy gummy fish and creme sodas and then sit on the bench and talk about if they had good hits or good catches, whose team won and whose didn't.

When baseball season and softball season were over, they'd play pitch and catch on their own, in one of their backyards, talking about everything, or nothing.

In high school she had talked him into joining the drum line. He'd practiced more than she had, and he'd gotten really good. In all her happy high school times, he was there somewhere, with a ball glove in his hand, or twirling a drumstick.

They always had so much fun together.

Alex's first *conscious* memory of JT was at the playground on the swings.

The day Diane told her that Curtis and she were "going to live in different houses from now on" and "be friends." Alex hadn't really understood, but she'd felt something was really wrong. Drew was only four, but he'd started immediately crying.

Alex was in kindergarten, and she'd opened the front door, and made a beeline to the playground down the street. She'd gotten on the swingset, steadied herself through tears, and started to swing as high as she could, imagining she was flying into the sky. Flying into the clouds, flying away.

She got as high as she could, then let go of the handles, and jumped, landing in a thud on her feet in the grass.

JT had come over from the slides where his mom was sitting.

He had thick, round glasses then that made his eyes look big, which reminded her of bugs. The glasses were strapped to his head with a black strap.

"How do I do that? Can you teach me?" he'd asked in a small voice.

Six-year-old Alex had said, "You just kick your legs back and forth and pretend like you're flying. Then, you let go and think about your feet."

"What if I *fall?*" JT had asked incredulously, his bug-eyes larger than his whole face.

"Falling's just the bottom part of jumping," she'd said.

And he'd gotten on his own swing.

"What's your first memory of us?" Alex asked. "When we were kids?"

His eyelashes curled closer together, then flapped up and down.

"The day my sister died," he said.

Alex soaked this in. So long ago, now. Sonya and Carlos had been expecting another baby. They had her name picked out, the room ready, and JT was going to be a big brother.

"I remember your mom picking me up at the hospital. You and me in our booster seats in the back, Drew in between us in his car seat. I remember the adults all crying. Me not understanding. Then going to the store. Diane bought us ball gloves that day, remember? And she took us to the park and taught us how to throw the ball back and forth. We were out there for hours while your mom said, *"Good job,"* and *"oops!"* And *"It's okay, let's try again."*

Diane had watched JT for a week while Sonya was recovering, so Carlos could keep the restaurant going. Alex's mom had rallied her Methodist Church friends together, and they'd surrounded Sonya and Carlos with love, support, and casseroles until she was on her feet again. Diane had done all this with three kids in tow, piling them in the back of her old Cutlass, going to the church, going to the hospital, then JT's house, then the playground.

The memory was faint for Alex, but it was there. She wondered if the altar was still set up at Sonya and Carlos's, where they kept Rosa's ultrasound picture next to a pink baby blanket, white candles, and a painting of the Virgin Mary.

"What's next?" he asked.

What's next?

She stared at the black sky above the road in front of them.

She didn't want to think of the future at all.

This was a part of her that was just like her father. A part she embraced in her twenties.

Did he mean what was next for she and him?

Oh, God. She couldn't let herself go there.

"A CD," he said. "Pick a new CD," and he laughed.

Chapter Sixteen

They crossed the bridge into Kentucky and the sky darkened completely into night. Crossing the blue suspension bridge over the Ohio River always made Alex feel like she was officially on vacation.

She only came this way when she was going to the airport or headed south. The hills started to rise around them after the bridge, large rock cliffs covered in vegetation, sparse and unruly.

"You're cool with diversity, right?" JT asked.

"I'm sorry?"

He laughed at the face she was making. "I'm not sure exactly how to say this, but when I went to SOU, they put the athletes together in the multicultural dorm. So, my friend group is . . . diverse."

"I love that," Alex said.

"Well, and with a name like Torrez, that's probably the only dorm I would have ended up in, anyways."

"I forget about your name," she said. When she first got to the University of Southwest Florida, she was surprised you could have almost drawn a line down the middle of the main lunch-room in the student union. Black students on one side, white students on the other. Part of what she'd done intentionally was make friends with people who didn't look like her. She'd made good friends in college, although she'd lost touch with many of them, too.

The beach was full of all types of people, from all different backgrounds and places. Her friend Layla was biracial, and Layla told her that most of the time she moved pretty easily through the world, but every once in a while, some old, entitled white guy would make a comment about her skin or her hair, or ask her if she was black.

"Was that weird for you?" she asked. "Coming from Greenview with all the white people to going to college and being in the multicultural dorm?"

JT shrugged. "Not really. We were all there together for the same reason, so we clicked pretty much right away. A couple of the guys on my team hardly spoke any English at all, so I got to help them with their English, and they helped me speak better Spanish."

"But you grew up speaking Spanish."

"Yeah, but there are different dialects, and different slogans and stuff depending on where you grow up. My parents came from Mexico, but there was a guy on my team from the Dominican, and one guy from Puerto Rico. It's pretty much the same thing, with some different slang. We could communicate, anyway, and they kept their grades up."

"Will you teach me Spanish?"

"You took four years in high school, smart girl."

"Yeah, but I failed Spanish Literature in college—okay, I stopped going because it was so hard, like reading *Romeo and Juliet* in Spanish, and I didn't know I was supposed to talk to my academic advisor about it."

JT laughed again. "You're a trip."

"Okay, and maybe one time I showed up to a Spanish exam just a little bit drunk from the night before and I think I only got a 'C.'"

"You're still defining yourself by your worst grades in

college?" he asked. "Over a decade ago? You should probably let that go. I didn't pass all my classes the first time."

"You didn't?"

"Nah, I failed first-year Geology, and I ended up having to take it again."

Alex stared at him. "You failed rocks for jocks!?"

"I failed rocks for jocks. The seniors played a prank on us and told us that we didn't have to go to class, but that we would still pass. Turns out that's not true," he said. "They were just messing with us. You have to sign in, every week. And take the tests."

Alex giggled.

"My mom was pissed," he said.

"I bet."

"Luckily, I got A's and B's in all of my other classes and I didn't get put on academic probation. I could have lost my scholarship."

"I didn't even take rocks for jocks because everybody said it was so easy. Now I kind of wish I would have," Alex said. "I have some kind of weird thing about rocks since my dad died. I think it's something about trying to stay grounded. So I don't get so lost in my head I float away. On my morning walks, I keep finding these really cool stones."

"You've hardly talked about your dad today. Do you want to?" he asked.

"I don't," Alex said. "I want the clock to turn to midnight and I want to have made it through a year without him, without going nuts."

"Okay," JT said. The clock read 10:45. "Pick a new CD."

Chapter Seventeen

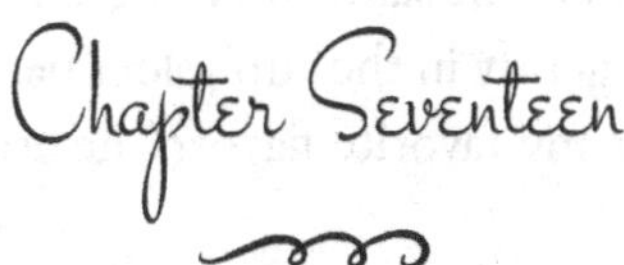

Alex found a Sarah McLachlan CD in the book and slid it into the radio. Her sweet, airy voice sang "Angel." The piano music almost put her to sleep. Around 11:15, Charlie woke up and nudged JT's ear.

"We need gas, anyway," he said. They pulled off the interstate at the next exit and up to a Pilot Station. A couple of semis were parked around the outskirts of the lot surrounded by hills. There was nobody inside but the attendant.

Alex used the restroom while JT led Charlie out to the grass on the leash and filled up the tank. She bought a diet soda and a lemon-lime sports drink, and when she got back in the passenger seat, she ruffled around in the cooler for the to-go boxes from Sonya.

Inside were steak and shrimp fajitas, chips and salsa, and homemade guacamole.

"Your mom makes the best guacamole," Alex said. JT helped Charlie into the backseat and climbed into the driver's seat.

"Do you want to drive?" he asked Alex.

"Not really," she said, stuffing a fajita into her mouth. "Are you good?"

"Yeah, I'm good. Just thought I'd offer."

Alex wrapped a fajita in a napkin and handed it to him as he guided them back onto the interstate. The sky was black, and traffic was sparse.

"I got you a drink," she said, and twisted the cap off the bottle for him, then put it gently in the cupholder between them.

"You remember my favorite flavor?" he asked and lifted it to his lips.

"It's still your favorite?"

"It's the best," he said. "Thanks." They ate and drove in silence. The CD had ended, and when Alex finished her fajita, she wadded up the paper and tucked it into the side of the cooler. Charlie had curled back up on the backseat, in a surprisingly small ball of fur for his size.

After some silence, JT said, "Why'd you stop drinking?" He reached into the box between them and took out a tortilla chip.

"Kind of a long story." Alex wrapped her hands back around her knees.

"I've got time," he said, adjusting his hand on the wheel.

Alex took a deep breath. *Honesty.*

"I woke up after an argument with Randy, where he grabbed my arm and pulled me back. Nobody had put their hands on me before, and it scared me." She sighed. "I kept thinking that all I needed was vodka, that nobody cared about me, and I sat at my desk drinking in the morning thinking vodka was my only friend." She took a drink of her soda. "Thank God there was some little part of my brain that chimed in and said, *this is the most dangerous thought you've ever had.* I never wanted to be a washed-out, sad alcoholic; you know? But that's where I was going. If I didn't quit drinking, I was going to die that way, all alone at my desk, with an empty bottle of vodka as my only friend."

She'd been telling this story for a while now, but mostly to her recovery friends. "I'd been trying to quit, for years, you know. I'll just quit tomorrow, or next weekend, or after this vacation, and I never did . . . I never really could."

She went back to that morning at her desk and thanked this higher power, or whatever, that she'd been brave enough to call the Alcoholics Anonymous hotline and find a meeting that day. She'd gone to 86 meetings in 90 days after that, to get over the hump of the first few months.

JT stayed quiet for a while, then he said, "What were you arguing about? With Randy?"

Alex fiddled with the cap of the soda bottle. "The real shit of it was I couldn't remember at first." She took her mind back there. "I finally put the pieces together after a while. The same old things. I was jealous and insecure. He was *not* comforting." She didn't say she'd had the same argument with every other man she'd dated.

"I don't like that at all," JT said. "That he put his hands on you."

The thing was, though, Randy had grabbed her arm and held her, trying to get her not to leave.

Was she in danger?

What was happening?

Whose fault was it?

These questions she'd asked herself over and over since that night. Even through the fog of sobering up. The encouraging phone calls with women she hardly knew. Sober women, who helped her get sober and stay sober.

"I thought about it for a long time," Alex said, sipping her soda again. "In the moment, I couldn't tell whose fault it was. I thought it was my fault, then I thought it was his fault." She stared out at the pavement before them, the white and yellow lines guiding their path. "Turns out, it was vodka's fault."

It had taken her a long time to see that. Like most of the things in her life, she didn't really understand what had actually happened until much, much later.

It was vodka's fault.

"Did he quit drinking, too?"

"No," Alex said. "The girls say recovery isn't really about

changing other people. It's about changing yourself, or letting God change you."

One golden firework exploded in the sky in front of them, and its sparkly ends trickled down in tiny strings of light.

Chapter Eighteen

"We're here," JT said. Alex had fallen asleep. She woke up to darkness and adjusted her eyes to orient herself in time and space.

"Where are we?"

"Tennessee. You missed the last round of curves through the mountains." He turned off the engine. "It's probably good you did."

"Why?" She stretched her legs. She wanted to get out of the car. Charlie stirred behind her and then whined.

"It was pretty curvy. Not very many streetlights." He opened the door, and the overhead light came on. "We're in the mountains."

She wished she had a map. "I thought we were going to the lake?" She wiped a bit of sleep out of her eyes and still had the taste of guacamole on her tongue. Garlic and lime. She found her diet soda and took a sip.

"We're at the lake," he said. "Well, it's more like a group of rivers, but they call it a lake." She hopped out of the Jeep, onto the gravel and looked around. There was a steep incline behind them, and an A-frame house in front with an American flag hanging over wooden steps to a door. She looked up at the sky. There were a million stars, and a full moon casting light over a steep hill. The echo of a fish jumping was the only sound, and then it was pure calm and quiet.

"It's gorgeous out here." She felt as if she should whisper. "What time is it?"

"One-thirty a.m." As he led Charlie to jump out of the back-seat, he said, "You made it. It's July fifth."

It was *July fifth*.

The door burst open.

"JT!" a man's booming voice said.

"Pauly!" JT and Charlie ran toward him. JT dropped the leash and hugged Pauly in a bear hug. Charlie licked Pauly's hand and sat down and panted.

The two men separated, and JT turned to Alex.

"Alex, this is my roommate, Paul. Paul, this is Alex."

"Alex," he said. "Nice to finally meet you."

Nice to finally meet you? Finally?

He approached her in a bit of a strut and clasped her hand, in one of those grips where he held the back of her hand upwards and put his other hand on top. It was disarming. Dimples framed his smile from under a ball cap.

"It's nice to meet you, too," Alex said.

"All right, man," he said to JT. "You made it back."

She hadn't heard anything about Paul, had she? How had he heard about her? For the first time since she agreed to come on the trip, she wondered if the guys might have been expecting Emily instead of her.

But maybe not.

A tall and thin blonde came out of the door behind them, also wearing a baseball cap. "This is my wife," Paul said, "Jessica." She came down the steps and first greeted Charlie.

"Oh, hey there, big guy!" Charlie stood up and licked her hand, and she petted him on the head and then patted him on the side, making a bass drum sound. "I love dogs," she said.

Paul said, "Jess, you know JT." JT reached out to shake her hand, but she pulled him into a hug.

"Hey, JT, long time," she said.

"Yeah. This is Alex," he said.

"Alex," she said. "I've heard a lot about you." She gave the same warm handshake that Paul had, with both of her hands encompassing Alex's.

"I'm glad to finally meet some of JT's college friends," Alex said.

She'd seen them at his wedding, but she hadn't met them. She'd tried to stay in the background of things, and she'd gotten really hammered. She did remember thinking she was glad to see some Black people in Greenview.

"Come in," Paul said. "We've been waiting on you. Can I help you with your bags?"

Alex and Jessica let Charlie inside and the guys carried the bags in behind them. Charlie almost pulled Alex over from the leash, so she let it go, and he bounded into the house and sniffed around.

"Hey, doggie!" The sliding glass door opened, and two more people came inside, a guy and a girl.

"Yo, JT!" The guy, also wearing a baseball cap, danced around JT and Paul and hugged them both. The guys all laughed and poked each other, punched each other in the shoulder and the stomach. It was almost too chaotic for Alex to keep up with.

Jessica leaned over and said, "They do this every time. They'll calm down in five minutes or so."

"Wanna beer?"

"Sure," JT said.

"Alex, beer or wine," one of them said. Then he stopped and said, "Sorry," and walked over to her. "I'm Todd. They call me Bingo." He reached out his hand. "You must be Alex."

Alex shook his hand. Light, curly hair sprung out of his hat. "My wife, Vanessa," he said.

"We're glad to finally meet you." She had a strong handshake and a warm smile. When she embraced JT, she pressed her cheek against his, and then pulled back with a fond up and down study of him, as if she were assessing his wellness.

"Nice to meet you all," Alex said. "I have a water in the cooler."

"Water," Todd said. "We heard you were a party girl."

Alex could have been offended, but she wasn't. She had indeed been a party girl. In college and right up until last year.

"I, um, used to be," Alex said. "I'm just not drinking tonight."

"Okay!" Bingo clapped and handed JT a beer.

JT smiled at Alex with an air of confidence she'd never seen. Maybe she had caught a second of it when they were at the falls earlier, like some of his boyish insecurity had disappeared, but now he seemed ... cocky?

Attractive.

He was in his element.

He adjusted his hat down further over his eyes and laughed at his friends' antics and comments.

They talked so fast and were so bombastic, Alex couldn't keep up with what they were saying.

Jessica took Alex by the hand.

"Let's show you around," she said. "Come this way."

The women went outside and into the night. A deck stretched across the front of the house and a table for six sat to the right. The moon hung between two tall trees, and the girls walked up to the railing.

"Don't look down too fast," Jessica said. She tossed her ponytail over her shoulders and stuck her head over the railing. They were four stories in the air. The house was built on wooden stilts against the side of the hill.

"Wow," Alex said. It was beautiful; but they were very high up. A wrap of wooden stairs wound all the way down the side of the house in sections, to a dock where a red and white boat floated.

Vanessa said, "I'm not big on heights, but you get used to it."

She sipped her wine. "There are 109 steps all together. If you go down to the dock, don't forget your sunscreen."

"We can go downstairs and check out the water after you get settled in," Jessica said. Some Jet Skis were parked on a lift next to the dock.

"Todd and Paul have been trying to get the Jet Skis working, but there's something wrong with them," Vanessa said. "Maybe tomorrow."

The guys came out and sat down into the chairs. "Alex," Bingo said. "What do you think?"

"Pretty cool," she said.

"You ever been out here to Serenity Lake?" he asked.

"No," Alex said. "First time."

Todd finished his beer and squeezed the can. "We've been coming out here since the early 2000's. We haven't seen JT here in a while, though. Thanks for bringing him."

JT lifted his hat up off his head and stared at her.

"It wasn't me. He wanted to come, and I just happened to be home from Florida."

"You still live in Florida?" Pauly asked. "You went to school there, didn't you?"

"I did," Alex said. She was surprised they knew so much about her.

"Our friend here talked about you nonstop freshman year," Pauly said.

JT seemed resigned to just listen. He didn't look embarrassed; he looked happier than she'd seen him all day.

Charlie came out and licked Alex's feet. It tickled, and she lifted her right foot. A yawn and a shiver overtook her. She was enjoying herself, but she was so tired. And suddenly aware of the garlic on her breath.

"I don't mean to be rude," she said, "but I've had a long day."

"Yeah," Pauly stood up. "We'll show you to your room."

Chapter Nineteen

JT insisted on carrying Alex's bag, and they wound down inside the house, downstairs through the different levels, following Pauly. The level below had a couch, a television, and a refrigerator between two bedrooms. Charlie hesitated on the steps at first, but then he bounded down around them and checked out the new atmosphere, sniffing at curtains and the furniture.

"Bingo and Vanessa are in here," Pauly explained. This floor had its own balcony, too. They climbed down another level. Alex was amazed at the size of the house. Because only the top two floors stuck out from the driveway where they parked, she had no idea how big it was.

"Six bedrooms, four-and-a-half baths," Pauly said. The next level also had a couch, two bedrooms, and a kitchenette.

"And, finally. We thought you two might like to have the beach room." Pauly turned on the light in a large, beautiful room with whites and creams and blues, shells decorating the curtains. "For my flawless catcher and his Florida girl." He set the bags down, opened the curtains, and pointed through a sliding-glass door. "Closest to the water. Best bathroom. Also, there's a hot tub to the left." A king-sized bed with a white, fluffy bedspread, and sheer white curtains surrounding it.

JT said, "We're getting the special treatment, huh?" He opened the bathroom door and revealed blue-gray marble tile and a walk-in shower with a bench on one side.

"Only the best for my long, lost brother and his best *friend* from childhood." He winked at Alex.

It occurred to her there was only one bed in here.

"I'll leave you two to get some rest, and I'll see you in the morning. Whoever gets to the coffee pot first makes a big pot." He double-punched JT in the stomach once and hugged him, gripping his shoulders when he pulled back. "It's really good to see you, man," he said. "Not so long next time, okay?"

"Okay, man," JT said, and then Pauly closed the door behind him.

They were alone again.

Alex needed to wash her face and brush her teeth, but first she wanted to go outside and stare at the water. The moon lit subtle moving ripples of blue and green. She stood at the rail and rested her elbows. JT came up behind and stood beside her, resting his own elbows like a mirror gesture.

It was so quiet out here. They could hear the others chatting upstairs, but their voices weren't decipherable. Charlie sat down next to them. Alex patted his head.

She smiled. "I don't think I've seen you in your element before."

"I love these guys," JT said. "They're my second family."

"I get that." She felt that way about her girlfriends from Florida. They looked out for her and gave her advice when she asked, and they were kind and smart and funny. She started to miss her friend, Layla. Maybe she should text her. No, she didn't want to text anybody. She didn't want to look at her phone.

"Hey," JT said. His eyes. "What I said earlier? On my porch?"

"Yeah?" Alex felt the tingling up her neck again.

"You can forget it," he said. "I was feeling kind of . . . off."

"No, I'm sorry I pried." She didn't dare tell him how many times she had thought about that night on the hammock drinking strawberry wine before her freshman year of college, and how many times she had asked herself if she should have done something different. If she should have said, *Yeah. Let's give it a shot. Maybe we can make it.*

She would have screwed it up with him. She was not the kind of girl who wanted to settle down. And he wasn't so, grown-up back then.

Back then he was her geeky younger best friend. Now, he was like—

"You wanna go skinny dipping?" he said.

"JT!" she laughed. "Too weird."

"Just thought I'd throw it out there. Don't let me forget to get you into the hot tub, though."

He was smiling again, and she noticed one dimple over the left side of his mouth she hadn't seen in a long, long time. The side of his face that smiled halfway, like a smirk. She thought about their drive, and how this, at least, today had taken her mind off her dad.

She hadn't thought about wanting to drink today, and that was something. She hadn't thought about dulling the pain or trying to run from anything. She hadn't had to think too much about anything. Except for the incident at the festival with Gracie, it had been an okay day. Better than she could have planned for herself.

He broke her thought train. "I've been thinking about today at the falls. About when you asked me what I wanted?"

"Yeah?"

"Well, I was watching you sleep in the passenger seat of my Jeep, and Charlie curled up in the back and I realized, I just want to be happy. And I don't know, it might sound cliché, but I can't remember the last time I felt, happy." He smiled. "Except today."

"Well, yeah," she said. "We're here with your friends on vacation."

"*We're* here," he said, rubbing a hand over his chin.

She smiled. It was nice to feel appreciated. Like someone cared about her more than they cared about their next beer or their next show or their next boat ride.

"But I didn't ask you what *you* wanted," he said. "I don't know what Alexandra Ward, thirty-five years old, swimming at the falls with me and now here at the baseball lake house with my friends, like an old dream I used to have, wants out of her life now."

A white moth flew by, touched the top of JT's hat, and then flitted away into the night.

Alex sighed. When she woke up this morning, she just wanted to get through the day.

"The truth is, I don't really know what I want anymore."

He nodded, and she could tell by the way his cheek moved, he was grinding his teeth.

"Didn't the dentist tell you grinding your teeth could give you cavities?"

"Last I checked, I left my mom in Ohio." He slapped at a mosquito on his arm.

"I brought some bug spray," she said. "I can dig it out of my bag."

"Maybe tomorrow. I don't want to go to sleep smelling like chemicals." He added, "I can sleep on the couch if you want." He took his baseball cap off and rubbed his eyes.

She thought about how many times they had slept in the same bed when they were kids, and then the summer before college when they were with their friends and saying goodbye to their childhoods. After parties where the parents took their keys so they couldn't drive home. Always innocent. Nothing ever happening. Sometimes they cuddled, and sometimes they didn't. She missed sleeping next to someone.

"It's okay," Alex said. "The couch doesn't look very comfortable."

He opened the sliding-glass door for her, and she noticed again how he carried himself differently, how much stronger his body was, how he had grown from a boy into a man. Charlie went in first this time and JT dug a treat out of his backpack.

"You've been a good boy today, Charlie," he said.

She ruffled through her bag to find her nightshirt. It was a soft and simple black thing with slits up both legs. She went into the bathroom, brushed her teeth, and while she was washing her face she looked into the mirror.

Her hair had pulled from her braid under her hat and was flying in all directions. Alex was embarrassed she had walked around meeting JT's friends like this. She took her hat off and unravelled the braid with her fingers.

She didn't look as sad as she felt, though. Something glimmered in her own eyes that she hadn't seen in a while.

Maybe it was hope.

Chapter Twenty

Sunrise flowed into the window through the sliding glass. Her leg was twisted around JT's bare calf, so the arch of her foot was tucked against it. She'd fallen asleep as fast as she had hit the pillow. His body was perfectly spooned with hers, in the most respectful way it could be, his knees tucked inches from her legs. Charlie was sprawled out at the foot of the bed—taking up half of it—and one of Alex's feet rested against his back.

JT's arms held her around the stomach, his palms were politely placed on her waist. It was gentle and comfortable. Though she had fought tooth and nail for her independence as a young woman, she'd never liked sleeping alone. This, she thought, was nice. She could stay here for a minute.

The sheer bed curtains were pulled back toward the headboard. She felt safe.

A dream was on the periphery of her mind. She had been in a room full of writers, sitting in the audience. And then she had been on some kind of boardwalk at dusk, looking over the ocean. A man in a red cloak had given her a blue jacket with a frog on it. She knew she was dreaming, but she couldn't control anything. Randy had been there, driving his car too fast, and when she asked him to slow down, he had sped up and driven through fences and barriers before she could get her seatbelt on.

She had asked in her dream, if she could wake up, but she couldn't. Often her dreams were strange, but this one was *vivid* and strange. A vague scent of coffee drifted into the room.

Alex moved JT's arms and tried not to wake him. He opened his eyes immediately and seemed disoriented. She caught herself looking at his bare chest, the way his muscles were carved in perfect lines. The sheets were tangled around his knees, revealing his green mesh shorts.

"Hey," she said. "I didn't mean to wake you."

"Where are we? Am I dreaming?"

Alex giggled. "We're at the lake house. With your college friends."

"Oh, yeah," he whispered, opening and closing his eyes just slightly. "Baseball lake house vacation." Had his eyelashes always been this long? His face was childlike.

Charlie lifted his head and yawned, so his big teeth and his pink and black gums showed. If she didn't know this dog, she would be afraid of him.

"I'm going to go upstairs and write," she said. She found her notebook, slipped on her blue sundress over her nightgown, then slipped her nightgown over her shoulders and off. Charlie bumped off the bed as if his big body were a drag, and he was relearning how to maneuver it.

JT watched her. "Would you let Charlie out for me?"

"Of course. Where's the leash?"

"Upstairs, in the kitchen."

Charlie followed her up the stairs and finally onto the main level where a full pot of coffee sat next to the sink. She poured herself a cup, found the leash, and led him out the back to where their cars were parked. A giant pink tropical flower bloomed next to the deck, and she wondered how she had missed it last night. She tried to give the dog his privacy, staring at the vegetation, and down the gravel path at the other houses lined up against the river.

The water was the color of raw emeralds, like a million green rocks had melted into liquid. Tall oak trees surrounded them, and pine trees lined the lake. She hadn't thought about a plastic bag, so when she let Charlie back inside, she removed the leash and found a bag in the pantry to clean up after him. She tossed it in the dumpsters lined up against the side of the house, then went back to her coffee and took her notebook outside. Charlie climbed back down the stairs to JT.

Birds sang morning melodies, and she heard a couple of crows cawing. The sun glistened off the green water below. She found a seat on a cushioned metal chair and opened the notebook to the first empty page. She hadn't written yesterday. Maybe part of why she felt so off-kilter. She'd been writing every morning for years, even if it was drivel. She'd read a book by Julia Cameron a few years back, who encouraged her students to write morning pages. Three pages of whatever came to mind.

"In the dream," sometimes her pages began. Sometimes they started, "Good morning pages." Sometimes they just started.

Today she wrote about the dream. She'd been writing regularly for years but had only published a couple of things. She loved writing for the simple act of it, not because she wanted to sell anything. But selling things had become more important, now with this student loan balance hanging over her head and two jobs barely covering the bills. She'd done some freelance journalism work, but it always paid peanuts, and sometimes she had to fight with the editors of small publications to pay her those peanuts, which she'd grown tired of. There was this novel manuscript she had only told her dad about.

She pushed the thought out of her head and kept writing.

It felt good to get her thoughts onto the paper. Something about it lowered her stress level. There was nothing earth-changing about any of the words she wrote down this morning, except she wrote, "Woke up cuddled next to my old, best friend and his dog. It's nice to have an old, best friend." She wrote a little bit about the festival and running into Gracie, but then she stopped the train of thought when it became too painful. It was July fifth, she wrote. She had made it to her first July fifth without her father. Well, the second.

A noise behind her stopped her pen. Paul emerged from the house with his own cup of coffee. "An early riser," he said. "Mind if I sit with you? Jessica's still sleeping."

"Sure," she said. "Same with JT."

He settled into a chair facing the water and sipped his coffee before setting it down.

"It's so pretty out here," she said.

"One of my favorite places in the world."

Alex closed her notebook. She had written her three pages and that was enough.

"Where do you and Jessica live?" Alex asked.

"New York City. Lots of noise, and lots of people. We love it."

Alex had been there one time. "My dad played there at the Apocalypse back in the early 2000's."

"Oh, yeah." Paul said. "I think JT mentioned that."

"Really?"

"He was totally into your dad's music in college. We listened to that live CD over and over. I liked that song, 'Imperfect.' The guitar riff on that one was tough."

"Yeah," she said. "I liked that one, too."

"I was sorry to hear about him. His passing."

"Same. Thanks." And she stared at the water hoping he would not ask her any questions.

"I lost my dad in '08. I know what that's like."

Okay, this was okay. It was better when someone knew how hard it was to lose a parent. If he asked her what happened, maybe she could try and answer. Diane had sat Alex and Drew down and told them their dad passed suddenly from an *undiagnosed heart condition*. When she'd said it, she'd closed her eyes, so Alex knew she was lying. Her mom was a horrible liar.

But that phrase was better than all of the other gossipy stories people were telling. And the never-ending questions. Everybody close to her had been so weird about it. He was young. He went for regular checkups. He was healthy, like Drew. Why had there been police and detectives? Even Aunt Skylar wasn't telling her something.

Alex was so devastated, had she been in denial? Stages of grief confused the mind, shocked the system. Like a catapult into a different dimension. What was true now? What was real? How to get through a day? *Twenty-four hours at a time. Sometimes, one minute at a time.* She'd stopped asking questions. *Acceptance.*

She couldn't form the words *undiagnosed heart condition.* Her mouth wouldn't do it; the phrase made her sick to her stomach. So when people had questions, she didn't have answers. She was an addict, but she wasn't a liar.

Something about his heart.

Alex clutched her coffee cup. "What do you do in New York?"

"I'm a cop." Alex pictured him in uniform.

"Really? That must be a hard job."

"It is, but it's worth it. My dad was a cop, and so was my grandfather. It runs in the family."

"I bet you had some interesting conversations around the dinner table growing up."

"We would have, maybe," he said. "But he wasn't around a lot, my dad. He and my mom didn't get along."

Alex understood that, too. She'd never quite reconciled her feelings around how everyone everywhere loved her father, and how she'd only gotten part of a childhood with him. He'd had a second family after her parents split up. Two more boys. She and her brother had taken a back seat to them. As well as both of his careers.

"What does Jessica do in New York?"

"She works for a literary agency. It doesn't pay a lot, but she loves what she does. Reading books and making deals. She really looks out for her authors."

"Oh my gosh," Alex said. "I'm not good at sales, except for

beer and food. But I love to write, and I love to read. I bet that's such an interesting job."

He smiled. "She works long days, but she never complains."

The door opened behind them, and Jessica came out with her blonde hair piled on top of her head and wearing a long white sundress and black sunglasses.

"Good morning." She kissed Pauly quickly on the lips and sat down next to Alex. "Did you sleep okay?"

Alex remembered how safe and comfortable she felt waking up. "I did. I was pretty much asleep before I hit the pillow." She smiled. "Paul was just telling me that you're a literary agent. Is that fun?"

"It is." She slurped at her coffee. The prim and proper impression Alex had gotten from her last night was more down-to-earth today. She liked her.

"I mean," she continued, "agenting has changed a lot since I first started, thanks to the internet and self-publishing. My day-to-day is completely different from five years ago. But I've managed to roll with it."

Alex noticed a slight accent. "Where are you from?"

"North Carolina, originally."

"She's the original Southern Belle," Pauly said and smiled.

"How did you two meet?" Alex loved hearing the answer to this question from both partners in a working relationship. She *did* have a slight interest in romance, though it had never really worked out for her.

She had come to believe she wasn't good at relationships.

Pauly smiled. "I was pitching a game at UNC, and I noticed this *beautiful girl* behind home plate. I couldn't keep my eyes off her. I could barely focus on the signs JT was giving me, because all I could see over his head was this luscious blonde girl in this white tank top and Daisy Dukes."

"I was not wearing Daisy Dukes." Jessica laughed.

"Short shorts," he said. "Legs for days. I didn't have my best game that day, but afterwards I went straight to where she was standing near the opposing team's dugout and asked her what she was doing for dinner. I think I fell in love with her accent right then. After her legs."

Jessica smiled warmly. "My brother played for North Carolina, and my mom and I went to one game. They had a hot pitcher, but I didn't think he was my type. Too cocky. He waltzed right up to me after the game as if nobody else was around and said, 'I'm taking you out tonight.'" She laughed. "My mom was completely floored and thought he was rude. He opened all the doors and paid for dinner and then we walked around talking and I realized the cockiness was just a front."

"Hey." Pauly sat back and shrugged. "My mom told me when I was ten that girls liked confident guys who opened doors. Turns out she was right. But, speaking of cocky, I'm going to go down and tinker with the Jet Skis before it gets too hot."

He stood up and kissed Jessica on the cheek.

"Go tell JT to get his ass out of bed," he said to Alex, and then headed down the steps.

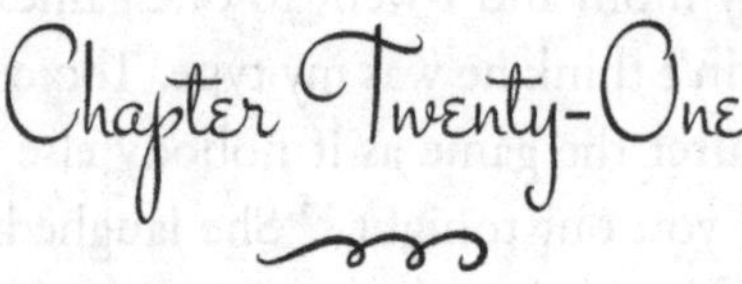

Chapter Twenty-One

"That's a cute story," Alex said. "I love hearing stories about how couples meet."

Jessica seemed sporty now that Pauly was gone. She put both of her hands on her knees.

"When I found out how good of a person he was, I told myself it would be stupid to try and resist him. My parents weren't so cool about him at first. They had some outdated ideas about what my husband might look like, you know. But when they got to know him and learned he wanted to be a cop, they slowly started to accept him. They're all really close now. So, here we are." She adjusted the ponytail on top of her head. "I would ask you about how you and JT met, but he's talked about you pretty much constantly since I met him."

"Really?" Alex was embarrassed to admit she hadn't thought of him much over the years while she was out in the world having adventures, falling in love, and falling out of it. Mostly falling out of it.

"Oh, yeah. My best-friend-from-high-school, this, and my-best-friend-Alex that. It sounds like you guys had a special friendship."

"We did," Alex said. "We grew up together." She thought of young, chubby JT. How different he was, but still the same.

"What do you do now?"

Alex used to hate this question, too, but she didn't so much now that she was teaching. It sounded like a real job. "I teach English composition at a community college, and I wait tables on the weekends. I played some hand drums in college, but I haven't played lately." She hadn't played since she was playing small shows with her dad, after the band broke up the first time. Years ago.

"Oh, wow," Jessica said. "So, you must also write?" Alex hardly ever told anyone she wrote. It was one of the magical things, like drums had been, that she was afraid would lose its magic of she told too many people.

"I do," she said. "I've done some journalism work, some free-lance editing." And then it came out of her mouth before she had the chance to stop it. "I'm working on a novel."

"You are!?" Jessica said. "What about? I'd like to read it!"

Oh, gosh, oh gosh, it wasn't done yet. It was never done yet. "Umm, yeah," Alex said. "It's not quite done yet."

"Okay," Jessica said. "Well, when you're done, I'd like to be the first to read it."

She felt the familiar fear at the thought of other people reading her work. The thought of mean girls waiting in the nooks and crannies of the internet, ready to criticize every typo and every perceived flaw, and then flouncing their unsolicited opinions on social media, trashing the work so sacred to her.

She caught her mind racing. Maybe the coffee had kicked in.

Charlie emerged onto the deck and licked her legs, and then Jessica's. She pulled her knee back and patted him on the side. "What genre are you writing in?" Jessica asked.

"What genre am I writing in?" Alex didn't know. She reminded herself to look the word up later, *genre*. What genre was she writing in?

"I'm not sure yet," she said. "It's fiction."

"What's it about?" Jessica asked.

"Morning," JT said. "Excuse my dog." His coffee cup clinked on the glass, and he used his biceps to lower himself into the chair and settle in with the girls. Alex stared at his arms. "He doesn't have good boundaries. He's a licker."

Jessica laughed.

Charlie sat, and Alex busied her hands by scratching behind his left ear.

"Qué día bello," JT said. Alex looked up at the sky. Only a few wispy clouds drifted over the trees in front of them. She tuned back into the birds. The crows had settled into a tree on their right and quieted down for the moment. It *was* a beautiful day.

"Pauly up yet?" he asked.

"He's down working on the Jet Skis," Jessica said.

JT put his hand on Alex's bare knee.

She thought she should brush it off, but it sparked an excitement in her stomach, so she didn't.

She put her hand on top of his. And he moved his fingers around just slightly, so their fingertips were brushing in random strokes.

"Alex was just telling me she's writing a novel." Jessica tilted her coffee cup all the way back to finish it.

JT slid his hand up slightly on her leg. "She is?" He raised his eyebrows, and Alex noticed his accent coming up again. A drip of sweat forming on his temple.

She didn't want to talk about it, couldn't talk about it, wasn't ready to talk about it.

"What's it about?" JT asked.

They were holding hands. And it was, *weird*, but it was also, *nice*. "It's about a girl trying to figure out life," Alex said.

Jessica's expression was welcoming and knowing. "Some of my authors aren't ready to talk about their books until they're completely done."

"I think that's where I'm at," Alex said. She turned to JT. "Did you sleep okay?"

He moved his hand back down toward her knee. She kept her

fingertips just barely intertwined with his, feeling the callouses and the lines on his skin, following his lead for touching her. His index finger moved playfully against the very tip of her ring finger.

"I did." He turned his eyes toward her, and the golden flecks carried something mischievous. "I slept better than I have in weeks."

Alex had to remember that she had a boyfriend, and he had a wife. Or ex-wife. And a kid, or teenager now. He was married. And she had a whole life in Florida to go back to.

But his hands. There was this electricity-something happening.

Jessica glanced down at their hands and said, "Eggs, anybody? I'm going to fire up a skillet."

"Sure," Alex said.

JT stared into her, and she felt vulnerable again.

"I'm good with whatever," he said.

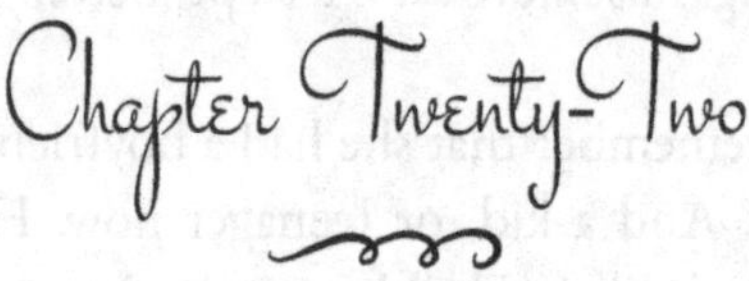

The sun hovered over them in a giant yellow ball and the air was heating up. Alex guessed it was nine o'clock. Charlie laid his head on his paws and panted. Jessica brought him out a bowl of water and then went back inside. "Almost done," she said.

JT turned his chair straight toward Alex and took both of her hands in his. He bent down and kissed the back of one of her hands, then stayed bent over, so his elbows rested on his knees and his head was lower than hers. His supple bottom lip and his perfect white teeth. The way his canine teeth were slightly longer than the others. The left dimple showing again. His eyes.

She was so uncomfortable being vulnerable, she searched and grasped for any kind of shield. Any kind of wall she could put up between them. She had not meant to fall in love this week. This was not her intention. A feeling welled up in her stomach, an openness, and she tried to stop it, tried to quiet it, before it moved up into her heart and lodged there. She could feel it rising above her ribcage.

Her friends in recovery said, *"You have to feel to heal,"* and talked about how they used to numb their feelings with alcohol. One girl whose name she couldn't remember had encouraged her to try and name her emotions. If you could name them, she said, then they would have less control over you.

Nobody had told her about *this*.

Alex had spent the year unable to feel the intensity of her father's death. It was too hard and too heavy. She always tried to outrun it, tried to protect herself from it.

But this was a pleasant feeling. Light and airy.

A little spark of desire anchored in her body, and it scared the hell out of her.

Her mind was reeling and confused.

"What do you want to do this week?" he asked.

This seemed like a loaded question. What did she want to do this week? He rubbed his fingertips gently over hers and studied her eyes. *What did she want to do this week?* Forget about her life and who she was and her day-to-day and that her father had died and her mother wouldn't talk to her about it, and ignore she was a general failure, and behind all her classmates in everything because her dad had encouraged her to go against the grain, and she wanted to write and maybe she wanted to be here with JT and let him touch her ever so slightly as not-friends, and do this?

Oh, no.

Not this.

She was always better at what she didn't want to do.

She didn't want to feel this vulnerable. She didn't want to have feelings for her best guy friend. She didn't want to get tied up in a one-week affair and complicate their already complicated lives. She didn't want to talk about her dad. She didn't want to embarrass herself in front of JT's friends. She didn't want to be seen as a girl who stole another woman's husband. Or even had a relationship with someone who was married.

She didn't want to cheat on Randy.

"It's not meant to be a loaded question," he said.

He released her hands and turned his chair back around and put both hands around his coffee mug.

She'd faltered. She'd stumbled, and waited too long, and the moment, the opportunity to make a choice and say what she truly wanted had passed again.

Drew had told her once that the combination of her hesitation and her impulsivity were going to trip her up every time. As if he were the rational one.

She wanted to do more of this.

JT seemed annoyed, and his cockiness came back. Just a slight raise of his shoulders.

He drank his coffee and looked down toward the green water.

"Maybe we could go swimming," she said.

It was the only thing she could think of to say.

Honesty was eluding her.

He nodded and smiled his comforting half-smile from under his baseball cap and blinked his long eyelashes a few times.

"Okay," he said. "We can go swimming."

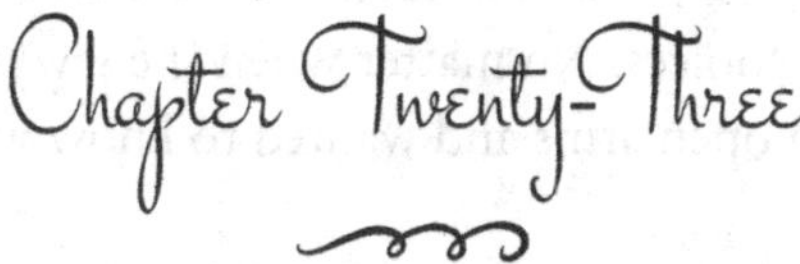

Chapter Twenty-Three

Jessica came out wearing a white baseball cap over her ponytail and hung her elbows over the wooden railing.

"Pauly, babe!" she yelled down. "Eggs are ready!" Charlie bounced to his feet as Alex and JT stood up.

"None for you," JT said to Charlie, and the dog cocked his head and lifted his ears as if he were trying to decipher JT's words. "Okay, maybe one piece of bacon."

It took a couple of minutes for Pauly to join them. He was sweaty and out of breath when he came into the house.

"If I go up and down five times a day," he said, "there'll be no reason for my morning run." He went straight to Jessica and kissed her on the cheek. "Smells great, babe. Thank you for cooking." He washed his hands at the sink.

"Yeah," Alex said, wondering how couples did that. "Thank you for cooking."

How did couples just seem so happy and kind to one another? It was a foreign concept to her. Respect, kindness and love. It wasn't something she'd grown up with.

She was kind of mesmerized by it.

Not even her grandparents, who were married for forty years, acted like they were ever *in love*. They respected one another and spoke kindly of one another, but when it came to love, it seemed they merely tolerated each other.

Nana Kate had been religious, the church-going-every-Sunday type, and she'd showed a special fondness for Alex, especially after she'd gone to college, and even after she'd started making a string of questionable choices. No matter when she saw her, Nana Kate greeted her with open arms and wanted to know what she'd been up to.

Her grandfather, on the other hand, had been quiet and sort of grumpy. Both had passed already, her grandfather first, and then Nana Kate.

There were her mom's different boyfriends, her dad's different wives. She didn't exactly have an example of devotion and stability at home. She loved to see it in others, though. She just never could quite get the hang of it. It was one of the reasons Alex had told herself she was never getting married. Regardless, she made a mental note to study the happy couple this week.

JT put his hand on Alex's back.

"Go ahead," he said. "Ladies first." She hardly ever felt like a lady around him. She had always, especially in high school, felt like one of the guys. But she was starting to feel . . . differently.

Maybe she could pretend she was someone else for the week. Like a girl . . . like a girl with a guy she liked. Oh, God. Did she like him? Not like a girl whose father was dead, who dated a guy she didn't know if she liked back in Florida.

Like a different person with a different life altogether.

Here we go again. Her thoughts could get so out of control. No wonder she drank so much before. Her own mind was exhausting.

Where are your feet?

She tried to rattle off a prayer. Something to turn the volume down. The Serenity Prayer was the only thing that calmed her sometimes.

She listed off the words in her mind, with the familiar rhythm of them.

God, grant me the serenity . . .

"Got the one Jet Ski running," Pauly said. "The blue one."

JT picked up a plate and high-fived him with the other. "Nice," he said. A line of plates and silverware sat next to a stove with eggs, bacon, potatoes and toast.

"Coach is coming in tonight," Pauly said, and gestured for Alex to go first.

Jessica put her hands on her hips. "Yes, please," she said in her Southern hospitality voice. "Guests first."

Alex filled her plate with eggs and potatoes, two pieces of bacon.

"I can't wait to see coach," JT said. "I haven't seen him in ten years."

Pauly put a piece of bacon in his mouth while he spooned eggs onto his plate. Alex found a place to sit.

"Because you haven't been around," Pauly said.

JT looked guilty. "It's cool," Pauly said, reassuring him. "You're here now. Think his wife's coming, too."

Todd and Vanessa wandered in. She was wearing a pink robe and green pajama pants. Her long braids were pulled back at her neck.

"Morning, team," Todd said.

"Bingo," Pauly said. "Good morning. You made it just in time. If you didn't show, I was going to finish off the bacon."

Todd had a ring around his curls from a hat, and his eyes were groggy. "Think I had one too many beers last night." His complexion and his hair were the same color, like the golden color of corn tassels in September. Alex didn't miss being hungover. The prayer had grounded her.

"We have any aspirin in here?" Todd rubbed his eyes. Pauly pointed to the cupboard above the sink. Vanessa picked up a plate and began filling it. Charlie sat at her legs and sniffed at the air.

"Why do you call him Bingo?" Alex asked JT, as he sat down next to her.

He subtly wrapped his leg around the back of her calf. His

skin on her skin was so very, nice. She pulled her sundress down a little to make sure her upper legs were covered, and to maybe hide the new sensation she had, as if somebody else could see it.

Maybe she *would* pretend she was someone else this week. Without a past, without the baggage. Just a girl on vacation with a handsome guy. Who used to be her friend and was now, also, kind of, hot?

JT seemed calm as ever, as if he knew what he was doing to her. He picked up a piece of bacon licked his bottom lip.

"Todd can *hear* a home run," he said.

Pauly chimed in. "Before you even see the ball, from the crack of the bat, Todd knows when it's going over the fence."

"There's a certain song to it," Todd said, reaching into the cupboard and finding the white bottle of pills. He shook it until it rattled, then he twisted open the cap.

"So," JT smiled. "Todd would sing out BINGO, whenever he heard a homer."

"We started calling him Bingo after the first game."

"A home run has a specific frequency," Todd said and shrugged, popping three aspirin into his mouth.

Vanessa reached into the refrigerator and pulled out a bottle of Champagne.

"Anybody want a mimosa?" she asked She retrieved the orange juice, unwrapped the coil and popped the cork.

"Sure!" Jessica said.

"Is there a diet soda in there?" Alex asked.

JT released his leg from hers and said, "I'll get you one." He pulled open the top. "You want a glass of ice?"

She was not used to anyone waiting on her. She was used to doing everything herself. Waiting on other people.

"No, thanks." Although she did want a glass of ice. She just didn't want him to have to go to the effort for her. She didn't want to be high maintenance. He stared at her, then filled a glass with crushed ice and brought it to her.

Nobody else noticed.

"Pop is better with ice," he said. She always said that when they were kids. He sat back down and put his toes against the back of her ankle.

Todd and Vanessa sat at the table and Vanessa sipped on her mimosa and started asking questions.

"So, Alex," she said. "JT talked about you a lot when we were in school, but it's been a while. What do you do now?"

Alex hated this question, but it always came up. She used to say, "I live by the beach" and leave out the part about waiting tables. But now she said, "I wait tables, and I teach English. And I live by the beach." For her, living by the beach was an accomplishment.

"Cool," Vanessa said. Alex noticed how she daintily used her fork and her knife to cut her food. She became a little self-conscious of her own table manners and reminded herself not to eat with her hands. "Where do you teach?" Vanessa asked.

Alex hesitated, because she didn't like to tell everybody, but she was on vacation. "I teach English through a community college, at a correctional institution."

"Whoa." Vanessa used her left hand to lift a piece of potato with her fork to her mouth. "What's that like?"

"Educating the criminals," Pauly said. "Yeah, what's that like?" She wondered if she should feel defensive. But his smile was honest and disarming, so she didn't.

"It's actually fun," Alex said. "I mean, I'm still getting used to it. But my students are just like, regular guys who made a mistake." Which was true.

She had gotten really attached to this last class. They were brilliant and kind and super-disciplined with their work. If they weren't her students, but her coworkers, in her younger, wilder years, they might have been in her circle of friends.

She definitely didn't tell people *that*.

Depending on what they'd done to get in there, anyway. Alex never looked up their crimes, because she wanted to see them as students, not as criminals. It was her job to see the best in them.

When she'd parted with this last class, she'd been praying for them every morning. She worried sometimes, that she cared too much about them as humans.

Jessica put her hand on Pauly's to stop him from saying something. Alex continued, "Inmates who get a college degree are eighty-five percent less likely to commit another crime." That's what the guy had told her in her orientation, anyway.

"Let's hope so," Pauly said.

Alex changed the subject. "What do you do, Vanessa?"

"I'm an assistant to the vice president at Chicago Financial," she said. "I run numbers and calculate investment risk. I do some HR, and some administrative stuff. Kind of boring," she said.

"No," Alex said. "I think that's interesting. I should have studied something practical instead of creative writing." She thought this sometimes, when she was having to pick up an extra shift to pay rent or pay the latest student loan bill, which was always changing. She thought this almost all the time, except when she was writing. She had fallen in love with poetry in her twenties.

She had wanted to travel and fall in love, and to write. Which, she supposed, she had done. Not much to show for it, though.

"I really look up to creative people," Vanessa said. "I always wanted to paint—to be an artist—but now, I'm looking at retirement and stuck in my position until then. I think it's brave of people to choose creativity."

Alex really needed to hear that. She pictured Vanessa's life: waking up early, going to the office by nine, not getting home until dinner time. It reminded her of Drew. It didn't sound like all that much fun, but it probably paid well. "My brother lives in Chicago," Alex said.

"Nice," Vanessa said. "We're neighbors, then."

Jessica sipped her mimosa and said, "Alex is also working on a novel."

Under the table, JT ran two fingers up the back of her calf and then scratched the back of his own leg, as if he had done it on accident.

"Alex got all A's in high school," he said, proudly.

She never really told that to anybody, either. In fact, she never mentioned it in her twenties, even at job interviews. She thought it made her seem uncool. Or uppity.

"The valedictorian," Bingo said. "Nice."

"How about you, Todd?" Alex asked.

"I'm a defense attorney," he said. "I work for the state. I think it's cool what you're doing in prison. I know some guys who could use some hope and direction. Sometimes we get offered plea deals that we can't really turn down, even if we think the guys are innocent. A lot of times, they're just guilty by association. Wrong place, wrong time, with the wrong people," he said. "But a jury is hard to convince without the right evidence. And sometimes, five years is better than an unknown choice between not guilty and twenty-to-life. It's hard." He lifted his ball cap and adjusted it back over his curls. "But I don't want to talk about work."

Alex was feeling more like herself as she ate. More comfortable here with JT's friends.

"How did you two meet?" she asked Vanessa.

Vanessa and Todd looked at each other fondly.

"I'll take this one," Vanessa said, and set down her fork. "I went to SOU on a math scholarship, and Todd and I met in Future Business Leaders of America. It was mostly white people in the club, which, we'd been getting used to in the hills of Ohio. But whenever there was a volunteer project, our mentors put us together. I hated working with him at first." She smiled. "He was too *cocky*." She laughed a big, surprised laugh, and her voice got more serious. "But after I got to know him—"

"She couldn't resist me," he finished her sentence.

"I was going to say *he wasn't that bad*." They stared at each other and then quickly kissed. She smirked at him. "Once I met the other guys on the team, I realized that it wasn't *cocky* as much as it was *confidence*. As you've probably noticed," she smiled, "they're all like this."

"We were the best team in the league all four years we played together," Pauly said. "Coach says confidence and humility both have a time and a place. Wait until you meet him," he said to Alex. "You're going to love Coach."

They finished breakfast and JT stood up. "You said that blue Jet Ski is working?"

"Yeah," Pauly said. "Might need gas, but it's good."

"My girl here wants to go swimming," JT said, picking up Alex's and his plates.

He went into the kitchen, and she helped him load them into the dishwasher.

My girl?

She tried not to let her mind race.

Chapter Twenty-Four

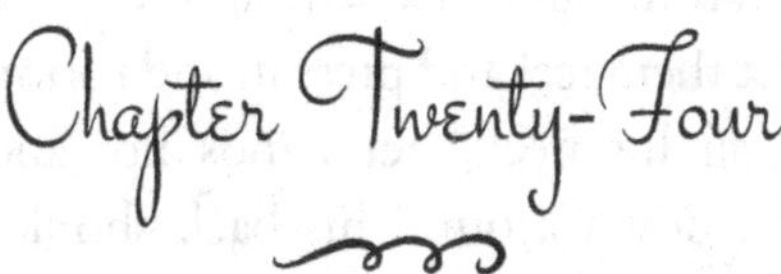

Alex cleaned up and put her bathing suit on while JT gathered their things. She thought to check her phone and then didn't. She was going to let herself be on vacation. Anybody who wanted to talk to her could call her later. She found JT on the balcony when she finished getting ready. He stared at the water with misty eyes and held his phone at his side.

Confident now, yes. Sensitive also, like her old best friend. The old JT was quiet, and though always quick to say what was on his mind, he never really talked about his feelings.

"I checked in with Jared," he said.

"You wanna talk about it?" she asked.

"Not really." He grabbed her hand and interlocked their fingers. "Let's go swimming."

She had put on coconut sunscreen and braided her hair. She felt pretty, like a woman on vacation with an attractive guy. Maybe she would just make the best of it. Maybe she could let her guard down and not be so worried about the consequences of thinking about JT as more than a friend.

Maybe this was the final stage of grief.

Maybe she had finally, absolutely, gone crazy.

"Will you put some sunscreen on my back?" he asked.

Oh, gosh. "Sure," she said.

He sat down on the bed and pulled his tee shirt off. She squeezed some of his sunscreen into her hand, a banana-coconut scent, and studied the lines of his muscles. She tried to keep her hands flat and platonic and mechanical, but she wanted to relax her fingers and let them feel and press in and rub around.

She started on his neck, her hands hot and nervous, and pulled the lotion down around his back shoulder blades, then down to the small of his back by his waistline.

"Make sure you get it in all of the crevices, will you?" he said. "I hate getting burned."

Her eyes widened; she was glad he couldn't see her face. She tucked the lotion down around his swim shorts, the trail of his spine, his smooth skin, and then finished with another spread over his shoulders, down his arms, his triceps.

"There." She patted him with flat palms three times on the side of his arms and put her hands on her hips.

"Thanks," he said. She stared at the floor then turned around, so he wouldn't see the look in her eyes.

After JT fed Charlie and the friends said they'd keep an eye on him, the couple stood at the top of the steps and looked down. The steps were rather steep and didn't seem completely sturdy.

"Come on," he said. "I've got you." She kept her hand in his. Alex was strong and agile, but the steps were precarious, wooden things, worn with moisture and sun. They stopped two stories down, as Pauly had suggested, and pulled two life jackets out of a shed on the middle level. JT shook off the dust and slung them over his one arm, while he led her with the other.

The sun was high in the sky now as they walked out onto the deck by the boathouse. The emerald color of the water reminded her of Florida.

"The water is so pretty out here," she said.

He stared at her, then looked down and smiled.

"What?" She couldn't read the look on his face.

"*You* are so pretty out here," he said. "Your eyes are the same color as the water right now."

She felt her cheeks turning pink. "I don't know how I'm going to get used to this," she said. She chose the blue and black life jacket, patted off some remaining dust and cobwebs, and buckled it around her.

"Get used to what?" He released her hand and pulled the blue Jet Ski over with his foot, his long, lean calf muscle defined. His jacket was yellow and black.

The words again. How was it that her mind could be completely full of thoughts racing around, and she could not find the right ones to let out of her mouth?

He climbed onto the Jet Ski and motioned for her to climb on. She stepped on easily and slid behind him. She was glad her bikini had a skirted bottom. Just in case they bounced over any waves, it would keep her covered.

"Hold this." He handed her his phone in a waterproof case. He turned the key and pushed the button. The engine rumbled.

"You brought your phone?"

He unhooked the bungee cord that attached the machine to the dock and pressed on the accelerator. They eased forward.

"It should sync up with the speakers. You didn't answer my question." He steered forward. "Choose a playlist."

As they entered the channel, she felt the breeze on her face and remembered how she loved the water so. It's the main reason she had moved to the beach. The water calmed her spirit. It dissolved all the tension in her body, all the anxiety and stress.

Her mind had stopped racing for now.

She kept her knees pinned against the seat and her feet anchored on the surface of the Jet Ski, while she tried to focus on the playlists. There was one called *Workout*. One called *Work*, one called *Kids Bop*, and one called *Pissed Off*. She laughed.

"What's this one about pissed off?"

"For when I'm pissed," he said. "Limp Bizkit, Insane Clown

Posse, some Rage Against the Machine, you know. The angry nineties classics."

She laughed. "Seems like Bob Marley might help on a playlist called *Pissed Off*," she joked, and kept scrolling.

At the very bottom she found a playlist called *B-Sides for A*.

"What's this one?" She read it to him.

He glanced behind them, then turned forward and steered the Jet Ski to the middle of the channel.

"I forgot it was on there," he said. "You can play it."

She pushed play. The first song, *The Karate Kid* theme song came on. "The Glory of Love," by Peter Cetera.

This was her *first ever* favorite song.

She remembered listening to it and thinking that men could be knights in shining armor. They would stand up for her and fight for her. Sing her songs. And then they would live happily ever after, forever.

The song had gone along nicely with her first crush on Ralph Macchio, *The Karate Kid* actor. Whom, now that she thought about it, was not what JT looked like growing up, but maybe who he looked like now. His dimpled half-smile and his perfect teeth.

He guided them forward. "It's been a while, but I think the marina is up here on the right."

On the left a line of pine trees grew against the cliff of a small mountain. The house they were staying in felt surprisingly private for how many houses there were strung up against the cliff on their right, and how many people were out and about playing in the water.

Their neighbors were on the dock fishing. JT waved and a man waved back. The next house had a waterslide attached to their boathouse, and a gaggle of kids in life jackets climbing the ladder and splashing down into the green, with a swarm of orange and yellow inner-tubes and floats around them.

As they got closer to the marina, they passed a fishing boat and a small speed boat. In the middle of the river was a houseboat. Just floating out in the water.

She handed the phone back to him and he set it inside a small cubby under the handlebars. Then she scooted up against his back, so their life jackets were mashed together, and her knees were straddling his thighs. She wrapped her arms around him.

"They have a restaurant and karaoke at the marina," he said over the song. "And a gift shop."

He put one hand on her knee, and then slid it up to her hands, interlocking their fingers again, and steering with one hand. "You wanna stop there?"

"Sure," she said.

Alex moved her fingers around his hands and felt the rough texture of his skin.

A small, green brick building sat across from the parking lot of the marina. The marquee out front said, "Serenity Lake Chapel. Sunday Services, 10 a.m."

"You never answered my question," he said. JT navigated them past a line of sailboats and small speed boats docked at the marina.

"What question?" Peter Cetera kept singing.

She thought she had adequately changed the subject.

"You said you didn't know how you were going to get used to this. What do you mean? Get used to what?"

He squeezed her ring finger, then teased it with his thumb and forefinger, and let it go. She stayed quiet, watching the people meandering around the marina. Thinking about how nobody knew them here.

Liking the feeling of her body against his.

"Are we still being honest?" he asked. "At some point, I'm hoping you're gonna let your guard down and let me in. You used to be able to tell me anything."

They puttered toward the guest tie-ups, and he eased the Jet Ski against the dock. She wrapped the bungee cord around the metal cleat, and he turned off the engine.

She didn't really want to let him go right now. She had just gotten used to her body pressed up against his. Used to his energy mingling with her own. Used to being so calm while she was touching him.

He helped her with a hand as they climbed onto the dock. She straightened her bikini skirt and hoped there wasn't a no-shirt, no-shoes policy, since they'd left their sandals at the A-frame.

He grabbed her hand and twisted her around.

"Before we go in, I want to tell you something."

He pulled her close, put his lips to her ear and said, "Nobody knows us here."

Then he put one finger under her chin and the other hand on the small of her back and kissed her.

Right there in front of everyone and no one; she couldn't help but feel like somebody was watching them.

Panic turned to sensuality.

He was gentle and solid at the same time.

Yearning and resistance melted together in her body, and she stepped forward and brushed against his swim shorts. His lips were full and soft and strong, and his tongue glided against hers, ever so slightly, and then his smile.

He tasted like spearmint toothpaste.

She smiled. He laughed then. And pulled back.

"I've been wanting to do that since the falls," he said.

He ran his hands down her arms and let them rest at her hips. His voice dropped its usual tenor to pianissimo, to quiet.

"What don't you know if you're going to get used to?"

"That was nice," was all she could say.

"Come on," he said, then grabbed her hand again, pulling her along. "Let's pretend like you and I just met, and we fell in love at first sight, and that you're my girlfriend." His voice was musical. Teasing.

She caught up to him, and he began swinging their arms back and forth. "But we're going to have to part ways at the end of the week, and so we only have this one week together, for the rest of our lives."

He scanned the boats and the people outside of the marina

and stepped over somebody's fishing pole. "So then maybe, you can see if you can get used to thinking of me as your boyfriend instead of thinking of me as your geeky best friend from childhood." He laughed at his own words. "But only your one-week vacation boyfriend, no strings attached."

Her mind was blank. "How did you know—"

He didn't let her finish but turned and smiled at her with that cocky new confidence she found equally charming and alluring.

"I know you," he said. "I've always known you."

A sparkle of wisdom flashed from behind his eyelashes.

She thought of all the ifs, ands, and buts as they walked into the gift shop, but the fears were outnumbered now by a sheer feeling of desire. Not just in her heart, but the rest of her body was coming alive to him. She resolved to try and at least enjoy it. Even though she was equally confused and not just a little scared. How long had it been since she felt like this? A band in the corner played "Knee Deep" by the Zak Brown Band with Jimmy Buffett.

A cluster of older folks were holding Bloody Mary's on the dance floor and singing along to every word. "They're getting it early," JT said. "You want some ice cream?" The tinny guitar part sounded exactly like the juke box version. To the left of the dance floor was a small ice cream stand, which also had hot dogs and soft pretzels on the menu. He tapped along to the swing beat against his stomach.

"No thanks," she said. "I saw Zak Brown Band a couple of years ago before they were big. Their show was so fun."

"That sounds like a blast. Where at?"

"They played at this small Food Truck Festival in Tampa." She lost herself for a second in the memory. Sam, the guy of the year, had paid for her ticket which came with a free basket of fried grouper, and he had dragged her up to the front row.

She had been so impressed they had a fiddle player and an upright bass. It was a fun day, that one. But of course, she drank too much in the sun and blacked out at the end of the night.

"How about a piña colada . . . a virgin one?" He led her to the bar in the corner and ordered two virgin piña coladas. "We'll at least stay hydrated for our Jet Ski ride."

He thanked the attendant and put two dollars in the tip jar. They wandered through the gift shop, looked at over-priced tee shirts and souvenirs. She stopped at a jewelry stand displaying small white rings made of shells.

She remembered these from her vacations with her dad when they were little. Before he had another family and stopped being a dad to her and Drew. She still had a small one in her old jewelry box, with a heart carved into the top. Her mom would always let her bring one home for Gracie.

"You want one?" he asked. "I'll get you whatever you want." He kissed her again, quickly this time, the sweet coconut taste on his mouth. He pulled back and stared. "Anything for my girlfriend."

"No, thanks." She squeezed his hand. "I don't know if I am going to be able to get used to thinking of myself as your girlfriend."

There, she said something honestly, finally. Even though her body was curious now about what it might be like to think of herself as his girlfriend.

"We only have one week to practice," he said. "Let's get out of here."

He led her by the hand, and they walked side by side down the dock. She felt strangely like someone was watching them, but nobody paid them any mind at all.

He was right, nobody knew them here.

They left the rest of the tourists to dance their day away.

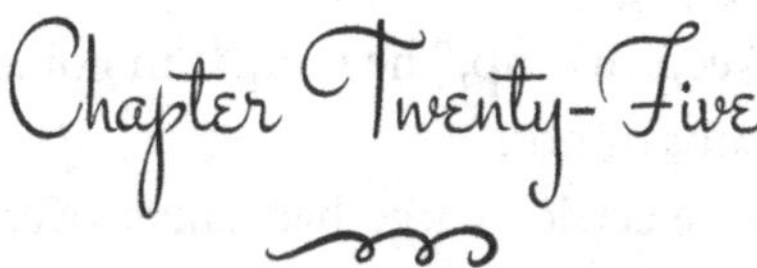

Chapter Twenty-Five

Alex and JT settled their drinks into the cup holders, and he drove them out of the marina, past a few more houseboats.

"It's Fourth of July weekend," he said. "Everybody's out."

They ambled for ten minutes or so. Families had tubes and water skis trailing behind their boats, with random brave souls in life jackets at the end of the lines. He navigated around them, waving here and there, and then they floated toward a section of river that was narrower, and less crowded.

She pushed play on his phone, *B-sides for A*, and Jimmy Eat World came on.

"I forgot about this song," Alex said.

"Can You Still Feel the Butterflies" started slowly. In her early twenties, Jimmy Eat World had been her favorite band. How had she lost this CD, too? They had the prettiest vocal harmonies, like Blink182, but kinder, and more mature. She'd seen them before their hit album, as well. Her early twenties had been so full of adventures. Maybe the good memories did outweigh her regrets.

They passed a few boats and waved at some folks who waved back, then they were surrounded by trees, cliffs, water, and the sky. Everything was different shades of green and blue, except for one gray cloud covering part of the sun.

"It might rain," he said. "If so, we can pull off on one of these islands and take cover until it passes." He turned the music up.

She had her body completely against his now, and her hands on his thighs, playing with the bottom of his swim trunks.

She teased her fingers under the edges.

"But if you keep that up," he said, "I'm going to have to pull over whether it rains or not."

Some kind of electric charge had taken over her. Instead of fighting it, she thought, what would be the harm in following his lead? In pretending that she was his girlfriend for the week? Here, where nobody knew them. Where nobody knew they were only friends.

Feeling the courage start to swell, she said, "Let's maybe just sit on the beach out here for a minute." The part of her that knew and loved seduction was taking over.

He steered them into a little cove where a willow tree hung over just enough sand to tie up the bungee cord and anchor up the Jet Ski. They bobbed up and down slightly on the calm water. She scanned the trees behind them and in front, looking for any sign of other people. They seemed to be completely alone.

A desire and an excitement welled up in her stomach. Then something clicked in her heart, and it started to burn, and she was overtaken by an almost kind of magic.

A self that didn't really feel like herself, but the braver, bolder version.

Her mind quieted, and she decided.

Before he dismantled, she said, "Wait."

She stood up, stepped over his leg on one side, and stared at him so they were face to face. He put his hands on her waist and raised his eyebrows while she balanced and then adjusted her other leg, so she was straddling him, but with enough space to let their energy mingle in between. She had surprised him.

"Honestly," she said, and she edged herself closer to his lap, her back to the handlebars. She wrapped each leg, one by one, over his knees, so the underside of her own knees rested on his lower thighs. She tried to read what the yellow flecks in his eyes were feeling.

She studied his bottom lip, the way his canine teeth showed as half of his mouth raised gently. The Jet Ski bounced in the water but stayed balanced under their weight. She grabbed the front of his life jacket with both of her hands.

"I don't think this is a good idea," she said, and she slid herself closer on the soft bench seat. "You know I'm not good at relationships. I don't want to hurt you."

"Alex," he said.

She shushed him with her lips. Then put her index finger there, and he touched the tip of it with his tongue, then took it into his mouth. She slid closer still, so their bodies were lined up together. Just right, just barely touching. She lifted the bill of his baseball cap and put her forehead against his. He closed his eyes and let her overtake his mouth and slide completely against him. His hands squeezed her waist, clutching her and pulling her closer. She moved her hands to his.

"I don't want you to hurt me, either," he whispered. "But you can be as rough as you want." He closed his eyes and laughed, his mouth still on hers. "We can make a safe word."

She laughed out loud. "JT, I'm serious." She pulled back and put a gentle fist to his padded chest. She knew her words were not matching her actions. "I'm not—" The song changed, and Usher's "Nice and Slow" came on. She laughed again. "Usher, really? What is this playlist?"

She tinkered with the straps of his life jacket and considered unbuckling them. She secretly loved this song, but she didn't think she'd ever told anybody.

He nonchalantly took his hat all the way off, hung it over the handlebar, and shook his black hair out. She watched his tongue anchor on one of his canine teeth.

She began unbuckling her own life jacket. His eyes moved to her hands, and the click of the buckles coming undone, one by one.

"This playlist," he said, and brushed his lips against hers. "Is called *B-sides for A*."

He sighed, and directed a smile to the sky, "Ah, Dios," he said. "Honestly." Then he drilled his eyes into hers. "B-sides for Alex." He lifted her by the waist, scooted himself toward her, and guided her body back down to his. "I made it when I was nineteen, on a mixtape, and I never sent it to you." He took a long, deep breath, and blew it out so it was audible. He smelled like banana-coconut sunscreen. "I made an electronic version, just in case."

She didn't have words, and her mind wasn't racing. Some kind of clarity came over her, and she felt suddenly young, and vulnerable, and aware.

"JT—"

"Hey," he said. And he pushed her back just slightly. "Okay, honestly." His breathing was deeper and louder. Her heart aligned with the rhythm of it, and the electric guitar of the song intro. It had started to drizzle, but there was this invisible static between them. "You always wanted to run away, right? To explore, and live a life of excitement? That's what you wanted when you ran away to college and then you ran away to the beach, and you were always running somewhere to do something that nobody else thought you should do, but that you really wanted to do."

He took a break from words to kiss her vigorously now. She was completely turned on. His mouth tasted like the tropics. Then he squeezed her just above the hip bones, his thumbs pressing into her muscles. He removed one hand to adjust the leg of his shorts.

She slid back up toward him. She wanted to slide closer. "We've both run away for the week. I'm starting to see what you like about it." He laughed again.

A this point she was done with words, and she just wanted him to stop talking. "Nobody thinks we should do this. Not even us." She put her hands on the back of the jet ski, trying to hold them steady. "I've got you," he breathed into her ear. "I'll keep us balanced."

He put his mouth on her neck, and she felt his tongue pulling at her skin. Then he panted into her ear and the back of her arms tingled. "Just this week," he said. "Run away with me." She took a deep breath. Her body couldn't quite quench all the air that it needed. "If you want to."

At that, she unbuckled his life jacket and let her hands slide up and down his chest until it fell behind him onto the sand. He kissed her hard, and then softly, leaning into her, and then leaning back. His biceps flexed as he untangled the jacket and wrapped his arms all the way around her, cupping her body into his chest, while she lifted herself all the way onto his lap, so there was no space between them. He grabbed her ankles, and held her behind the calves, until she felt him resolve to let her closer. His hands grasped her from behind the knees, then her waist, and he pulled her all the way into his chest.

Raindrops fell around them, in small spurts at first, and then a heavy downpour began. She opened her eyes once to see the blue of the sky beyond the clouds and a glance of his warm, glowing eyes studying her as she breathed harder, and a sensation like the sparkling wick of a firework started at the base of her spine, and then slowly rose up and out toward her arms.

Then she lost all sense of space and time.

Chapter Twenty-Six

When she had rational thoughts again, they were lying under a tree on the sand, her sarong underneath them and the rain still pouring down in sheets.

They were mostly dry now, and JT had covered them both with his towel as they huddled underneath their cover, and watched the water fall all around. He'd laid the lifejackets at the top of the sarong to rest their heads on. Their suits were in a neat pile on the Jet Ski, getting ever more soaked.

Dave Matthews Band, "Lover Lay Down" came on.

Her mind was clear.

"You made this playlist when you were nineteen?" She toyed with a freckle on his shoulder. "It's like you picked the songs this morning, just for this."

She loved the saxophone solo in this one, weary and full of desire.

He smiled and kissed the top of her head.

"I may have listened to it one-hundred times since then and fantasized about this very day. I've been practicing my gratitude prayers." Opposite the water, a rainbow faintly stretched from the horizon into the middle of the sky. "It's a bit different than I pictured," he laughed, "but the bones of it are here."

She pointed to the rainbow. "Look! Gratitude prayers?" She felt safe and warm, like she was exactly where she was supposed to be. He kissed her gently on the shoulder blade and said, "Didn't you read *The Secret* or *The Magic*?"

She hadn't, but Kara had asked her to write out gratitude lists her first few months of sobriety.

"Your body is beautiful," he said.

She wanted to believe him. "I mean, you were always pretty, but womanhood looks good on you."

Womanhood.

She didn't feel much like a woman most of the time. But the way he'd just touched her and then ravished her senses with his gentle movements, his muscles all-encompassing her, surrounding her like a shield and dissolving her insecurities. She ran her hand up his thigh and traced his abs with her forefinger. She'd felt like a woman as she dominated him, although he had taken soft care to watch her pleasure before he let himself let go.

"Careful," he said. "I'll be wide awake again."

"Your body's not so bad, either," she said. "You've taken good care of yourself."

You've taken good care of yourself? She laughed at her own words.

His teeth teased her earlobe, which sent tingles down her arms again. She was not thinking about him as her friend, at all, but was thinking of him as her mysterious new boyfriend, whom she'd met and fallen in love with at first sight, on vacation.

Without words, he turned her over, so she was on her back on the sarong, He studied her before he kissed her on the left, then the right shoulder, and all the way down to her inner thighs. She let her neck arch back and felt his elbows on either side of her, propping him up to line up their bodies.

She felt softer now, and more like herself, as he lowered his weight on to her, and she let herself take him in. Her eyes met his one more time before she closed them and let go of her mind and allowed her body to think about the gentle confidence and pure strength of her new boyfriend for one week.

Sounds of rain pattered on the water, and the occasional squall of a bird mixed with the music.

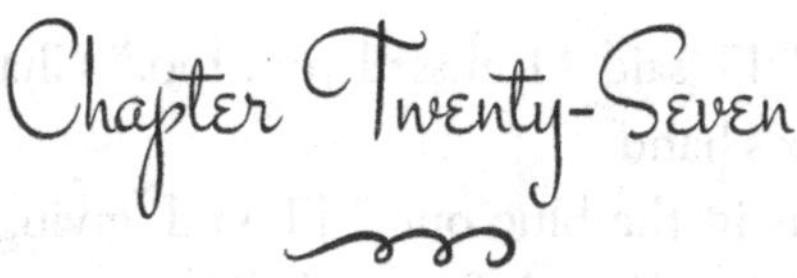

Chapter Twenty-Seven

She mounted the Jet Ski behind him and held him close while they swung by the marina and gassed up, then idled back to the A-frame in low gear.

Norah Jones played over the speakers, "Come Away with Me," and then Billie Myers, "Kiss the Rain." Any time doubt or fear came up, she brushed it off and latched her hands tighter around JT's lifejacket.

They listened to Tonic's "If You Could Only See," and Vertical Horizon sang "Everything You Want," as they navigated the channel past vacationers and waved. He drummed on the jet ski handles, and she sang the harmony parts. Like all was right in the world.

When they pulled up to the A-frame, "Summer Girls" came on by LFO. Alex had declared herself too cool for boy bands after junior high school, but she loved this song, too. JT lip-synced all of the words as he tied up the jet ski, and helped her pull off her life jacket. She laughed at his goofiness and he tapped her back side playfully, then they ascended to the house.

"That was a long ride," Pauly said, after they climbed back up the stairs. He was holding a beer. Alex was ready for lunch and air conditioning. "Have fun?" he asked. The smile on his face directed toward JT was mischievous. "Gotta little spring in your step."

JT winked at him and opened the sliding glass door for Alex. Charlie bounced toward them, prancing on his front feet in excitement.

"Hey, Boy," JT said. "I missed you, too." Charlie sniffed and then licked Alex's hand.

"We put gas in the blue one," JT said, giving Pauly a quick low-five handshake. "What's for lunch?"

Jessica was lying on a beach chair in a simple white and pink bathing suit with her headphones on. Vanessa sat next to her rubbing sunscreen over her arms.

Pauly turned to follow them in.

"Ham and turkey in the fridge," he said, "bread in the cupboard." He tilted the beer can and emptied it into his mouth, then he squeezed it and tossed it into the recycle bin. "Jessica bought enough chips and crackers for an army. Help yourself."

"What do we owe you guys?" Alex asked. "For our share of the groceries and stuff."

Her suit was still damp, so she resolved to go downstairs and change into something else.

Pauly said, "We'll figure it out at the end of the week, and we'll send JT a bill." He laughed and pulled another beer from the fridge. "Help yourself, really."

"Thank you," Alex said. "Will you make me a turkey sandwich?" she asked JT.

He was only wearing his trunks, cargo-looking with pockets lined down the sides of his legs. She approached him and thought of kissing him but then wasn't sure she should in front of Pauly.

He pulled her in anyway, grabbing her by the hand and then the waist, holding her in a fast kiss with his back up against the counter. Maybe she could get used to this.

She smiled.

"Okay, okay," Pauly said. "It's a good day. I'm gonna go down and see if I can get the boat running. You two, make yourselves at home." He slurped some fizz off the top of the beer can. "Coach should be here around five. We're having a concert tonight." He shut the door behind him and headed downstairs.

Alex was confused. "A concert?"

JT pulled her in again. "Sometimes when we get together, we have a jam session." She liked the feel of his lips on hers, the cocky accomplishment on his face when she pulled back.

"Okay," she said. "I'm gonna go change really quickly."

"You need any help?" he asked, opening the pantry door.

"No thanks," she grinned. "I'm good."

She felt the smile spread over her face again as she walked down the steps and wound around below to their room.

Her hair had stayed mostly in place, but she tucked some stray strands and then put on the black tennis dress she had bought at the discount store. It was a little tight. She should have gotten a large instead of a medium. But it was so hot outside, she decided to wear it anyway. She had to remember to put on some sunscreen.

Alex caught a glance of her phone plugged in by the bed stand. Maybe she should check her messages. She'd been the last one of her friends to get a cell phone when they came out. She couldn't see the point in somebody being able to reach her at all hours of the day.

In her mind, if she didn't answer the house phone, whomever was calling could leave a message. And then she would answer the message when she wasn't busy doing something. She didn't like the idea of being at everybody else's beck and call, all hours of the day. Here she was, looking at it anyway.

It wouldn't take long.

She laid down on the bed, relishing the air conditioning, and picked up her cell phone.

Sixteen new messages?

Her first thought was to put it back down and forget she even looked at it.

Kara: *How are you. Are you okay?*

Awe man, she'd forgotten to call her sponsor.

She sent back a quick text: *Hey! I'm okay, thanks. Took a road trip with a friend. Spotty cell service.* On second thought, she deleted the last line before she sent it. Honesty.

Randy. Oh, she really didn't want to open this one from Randy. She had not replied to the last one, *we need to talk.* She opened the one from her mother instead: *Did you get there safely?*

She replied. *Hey Mom, here safe.*

Layla, her friend from Florida: *Hey, miss you. Call when you can. I was thinking about you yesterday. Sending all the love. Need to tell you something.*

Alex wanted to call her, but her stomach rumbled. She would call her later.

The other thirteen messages were from Randy. Thirteen messages? She did not want to open them.

Where are you?

Why won't you answer me?

Are you with another guy?

We need to talk.

The messages grew longer. *I know what you're doing. I always knew you were a whore.*

I thought we had something special.

Are you trying to embarrass me on purpose? You'll never be anything special. Can't believe my heart is broken like this. By a waitress.

She called and told me everything. Don't bother calling me or texting me again. Or coming to my shows.

I got my stuff out of your apartment.

I'm sorry about the couch . . . no, I'm not sorry. I saw this coming.

You need to grow up.

Good luck being poor and alone.

You were nothing when I met you and you'll always be nothing.

Alex was stunned.

She didn't hear JT come in behind her.

"Hey," he said. He flopped down on the bed. "Sandwiches are ready. Whatcha doing?" He put his arm over her back and let his hand linger on her bare shoulder. He kissed the other one and tucked his chin in the space between her neck and her arm.

She shook her head, trying to latch onto a thought, any thought, that made sense. No words again. Tears stung her eyelids.

"I don't even know."

She handed the phone to JT.

"Randy."

He rolled away from her and propped himself on his elbows.

He clicked on the messages.

"*Jesus,*" he said. "What in the—" She watched the anger turn his copper skin mahogany. He stood up. "Fuck *this* guy. Who the hell does he think he is?"

Alex started crying, let the tears stream down.

He adjusted his baseball cap on his head and put one hand on his hip.

"Oh, man," he said. "Alex." He lay the phone down on the table in the corner and crawled back onto the bed next to her. The anger in his face turned to concern. "Hey," he said. "Hey, it's okay."

She couldn't help it, she started bawling. Ugly crying in front of her best guy friend turned one-week boyfriend.

Maybe she'd never wear mascara ever again.

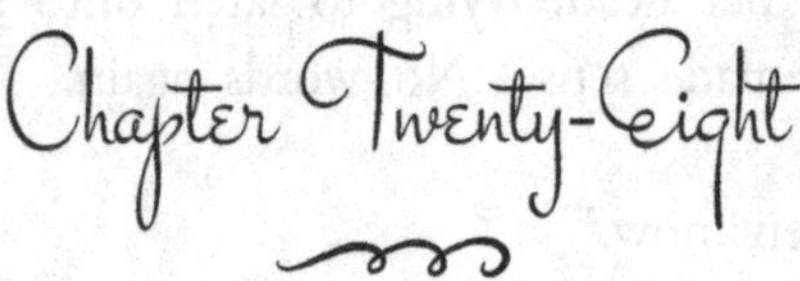

Chapter Twenty-Eight

"He's an absolute *dick*," JT said. "And if I ever see him, I will be glad to tell him that, and more." He put a finger on her cheek and caught one of the streams of water coming out of her eyes. "He obviously doesn't even know you."

She couldn't speak for a moment, and when she calmed the shaking in her chest, she said, "No, he's right."

She turned over on her back and stared at the ceiling. The pattern reminded her of clouds. She wiped at her eyes and folded her hands over her stomach.

"I'm a failure at everything. I probably *am* going to end up broke and alone." The tears poured over her face now and dripped into her ears. "I'm thirty-five, and I have absolutely nothing to show for my life, except for sore feet and knees, a student loan bill that the lottery wouldn't pay off, and a long list of failed relationships."

"Nah," JT said. "Come here." He sat up and put his back against the pillow-padded headboard. He spread his knees and pulled her up, so she was sitting between them, back to him, and he wrapped his arms around her like a bear hug. She let herself cry.

She'd been able to run from the tears yesterday, but here they were, catching up to her. She settled back into his body.

"Why did he have to say all of that?"

He squeezed her closer and cupped her elbows with his hands. She took in his familiar scent, musty and sweet. Coconut sunscreen. Spearmint.

"He's *not* right," he said. "One, he's not right to talk to you like that. Two, he's not right about whatever he thinks he knows, and three, he's completely wrong about who you are and what you're capable of." Her body relaxed a little.

The tears stopped so much pouring, as they were trickling now. She wiped her face again.

"Alex," he said. "You're the most independent, and intelligent woman I've ever met." She wasn't used to hearing nice things about herself; she wasn't used to thinking them. "You've always lived life on your own terms, and you've always been capable of doing and getting what you want, when you focused on it." He sighed. "Hell, you got out of Greenview, you got an education, you travelled, you live by the beach . . . now you're writing a book, you're teaching . . . you do all of this cool stuff that some people would love to do but are too afraid to. Being rich isn't always about money," he said. "Your dad taught me that. Being rich is about doing what you want when you want and not letting anybody tell you that you can't."

Maybe he was right. She sucked in a breath and held it.

Then she exhaled. "He called me a *whore*."

"Fuck him!" JT said. "Obviously he doesn't know you at all." He started to pull her in tighter by the stomach, but a bit of rage came over her and brought her abruptly to her feet.

"No, I *am*," she said. It washed over her.

"I am at a lake house on vacation with somebody else's husband."

The words *somebody else's husband* echoed in her brain.

What was she doing here? Her mind was going to a dark

place, but she was so out of sorts and lost in her emotions, she couldn't get herself out of it.

It was like a tropical storm swirling in her stomach. It was getting bigger, and the bands of rain were lashing out.

"What just happened was a mistake," she said. "I shouldn't have done that. We shouldn't have done that. I already regret it. I'm sorry." She started stuffing things into her bag. "I should go."

"Uhh. . ."

Pain poured out between his lashes. He folded his hands together. "I think we've established I'm not going to be married much longer. Please, don't regret what just happened."

He said her name again like a whisper.

"Alex."

She couldn't stop herself.

His rational voice made her crazy.

"You think she's just gonna let you go like this? Emily will be crawling back to you next week, and you two will make up, and I'll be alone again, just your regular, independent traveling hooker." She paced. "Randy's right. What just happened was wrong." She stormed into the bathroom and retrieved her toothbrush and her shampoo.

"What just happened was beautiful, and you know it. Don't run from me right now. Alex," he pleaded.

Why was he always so level-headed?

If she could make him mad enough, then maybe she could get him to leave her alone before she ruined his life, too.

"You'll realize your kid needs a father, and that's the only way to see him, and you'll do whatever she wants because you're *Jason Torrez, Mr. Always-Do-the-Right-Thing.*"

Alex saw the mahogany crawl into his cheeks again. Magenta.

"Fuck you, Alex! That's a shitty thing to say." His bass guitar voice rose an octave. "So, I did what I thought was the right thing by marrying Emily and trying to be a good father and a good provider. You can't blame me for that, and I won't feel guilty about it. You were off doing whatever the hell you wanted to do, with whomever the hell you wanted to do it with. I never blamed you for it. I looked up to you, traveling around, falling in love. I *had* to marry her, do you understand? My family would have disowned me if I would have left a girl who was pregnant with my child high-and-dry to fend for herself. There's no honor in that, anyway. That's not how I was raised."

Alex hated to argue. God knows, she'd heard enough of it as a kid. She wondered if the others could hear them.

But Alex didn't like her anymore, didn't want to hear her *name* anymore. *Emily.* Everybody's dream girl. Her perfect legs and her perfect smile. The blonde bombshell all the guys wanted to date. The girl who had a crush on her dad but married her best friend instead.

The swirl of Alex's feelings was a category three.

"You know what I hate about her the most?"

"Who?" JT asked. "What are you talking about?"

"Your wife," she said and put her hands on her hips.

JT bent his head back and shook it from side to side. "The one who just took my kid and my stuff and everything I ever worked for my whole adult life, and left me with a note? Don't go there. *Please,* don't go there."

"No," Alex said. "Let's go there."

He stood up and took a step toward her. "Stop," he said. "Before you say something you'll regret." Both of his palms were up in front of him, but she was far past saying anything she would regret. She would regret almost all of this for a long, long time.

Alex gritted her teeth. "Emily," she said her name like a growl, "fucking had a crush on my dad, and she married you to get closer to him."

She watched JT in slow motion. He cowered as if the wind had been knocked out of him. His knees weakened, and he sat back down on the bed. A single tear came from his left eye and settled in that dimple she loved. She watched the tear gather there and fall down his chin and onto the floor.

She wanted to kiss him.

To hug away the curveball she'd just thrown.

"I'm so sorry," she said. "*Oh, gosh,* JT, I'm sorry."

She rushed over to him and put her body between his knees, grabbing both sides of his face.

"I didn't mean that. I'm sorry, I didn't mean to say that. *It's not true.*"

He removed her hands, gently dropped them to her sides, and stood up.

"But you did." He lifted his baseball cap, rubbed his forehead, and then walked toward the door.

The color had drained from his face, and now his eyes were the only part of him that were red and swollen. Before he walked out, he put one hand on the door frame and turned to her, his bicep flexing in a perfect line.

"If you want to point fingers at someone who wants to be with somebody they love, but settles for somebody *less,*" he said, "then maybe you should look in the mirror."

He turned around and walked out.

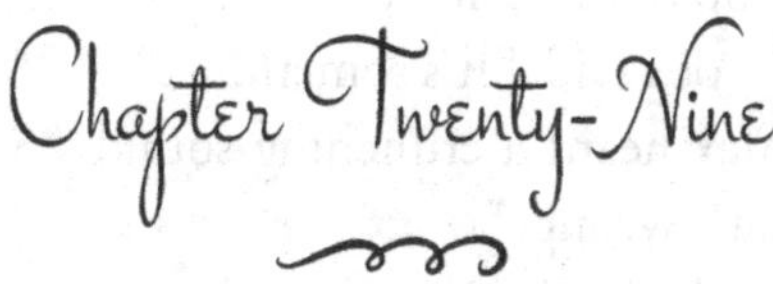

Chapter Twenty-Nine

Alex didn't know how long she'd been on her knees, face on the bed, hands folded in front of her. What had she done? What had she said? She didn't mean to kick him when he was down. She hated when people did that. Why had she done that?

Her emotions had gotten the best of her. The message from Randy had torn her apart, and then JT's reaction, to be so protective and reassuring?

It had torn her in two and left her split on the inside.

She had taken it all out on him. The grief of her father's death she didn't have a place for, and the long list of failures she'd added up over the years. She'd wadded up all her anger and disappointment and pain and thrown it at the one guy who always had her back.

She'd been here praying for a while now. *I'm sorry* and *forgive me* on repeat. Eventually, she prayed for *the next right thing*. What should she do? She had no idea what to do with herself. She picked up the phone and called Kara.

"Hey!" Kara was one of those people who was always cheery. Alex hated it about her at first, especially when she was first getting sober and trying to work through the fog. But there was something else Kara always had, which was more important. This thing Alex wanted.

Kara had hope.

"How's your trip?" Kara asked. "I was worried about you yesterday when you didn't call me."

"Yeah, well," Alex said. "It's something."

"Oh, no." Alex heard a crunching sound. "Sorry, I'm eating some cereal. What's wrong?"

She started at the beginning. Yesterday, the anniversary of her father's death. How JT had shown up at her house, how they'd gone to the festival. About seeing Gracie and then crying in the port-o-john, about going to the falls, about seeing his parents. About JT finding the note. About getting to the lake house. She told her everything except for the part about being alone with him on the Jet Ski.

She told her about their fight, about Randy's text message. About saying that awful thing about Emily. Kara listened through most of it, with some *"hmms,"* and *"oh's."* She was a good listener, and Alex felt better telling somebody.

And then Kara said the thing Alex hated.

"Did you do a fourth step about it?"

Alex hated when she was venting or trying to figure something out, and Kara came back at her with 'program.' Plain old wisdom from the *Big Book of Alcoholics Anonymous.*

Something really sucked about it all.

"No, it just happened."

Kara was still crunching on the cereal. "Well," she said, "do a fourth step about it and then call me back when you're done."

The fourth step, where you identify your feelings around whatever it is that is bothering you so much with another person, and then you identify your part in it, and where you may be wrong.

The first time she had done the fourth step, most of her answers had come down to pride and fear. With a hefty dose of emotional codependence connected to sexual attraction and men.

The last part, Alex knew, was going to take some more time to unravel. Maybe a lifetime. But she had followed the directions in the book on the fourth step the first time around, and she had felt better afterwards.

"Can I ask you something?" Kara said.

"Sure." Kara had been her friend for the better part of a year now, and though they only met up once a week or so, Kara had become something of a best friend. She didn't always tell Alex what she wanted to hear, but she was usually right.

"When's the last time you were single?"

"I'm sorry?" Alex heard her, but she was buying time to think about it, and to compose an answer.

Kara laughed. She had this guttural, belly laugh that ended in a *heh, heh, heh.* "When's the last time you didn't have a boyfriend, or, like, a guy you were talking to?"

Alex counted. This year it was Randy. Before that it was Sam. Sam was fun, but he also had a long list of other girls who thought he was fun, too.—who weren't shy about having her know it. Before that was a guy named Joel. He played hockey and worked on airplanes, but he'd gotten mad at her one night and punched the refrigerator, which was a deal-breaker for her. Before that it was the helicopter pilot. He was *really* fun, but he was only in town on leave. And before that was . . . she kept on going. She couldn't remember how long it had been.

"You there?"

"I'm here," Alex said. "It's been a while."

"Okay, so why don't we do this," Kara laughed again. "Sorry, my dog just jumped on my lap. You've done a really good job of not making any big relationship changes in this first year. It sounds like Randy is bailing on you, and that's probably good, because I don't think he's good for you."

"You don't like him?"

"No," Kara said. "He treats you like shit, drinks in front of you even though you quit, and there are always a million girls waiting for him after his shows. He's *toxic* for you, Alex. I'm sure he has good qualities, but, really, I've only been nice about him because you like him. So, let's figure that out. You guys are gonna have to talk, but then what if you try and be single for a year?"

Alex did not love this thought, but why didn't she love it?

"For a year?"

"Yeah, I mean, you're not going back to Randy after he said all that awful stuff to you, right?" She hadn't really thought about it all that much. She'd been thinking mostly about how she'd just hurt JT, and how she was ever going to make it up to him. "What did Randy mean about *sorry about the couch*,' anyway?"

"I'm not sure," Alex said. "I can't really wrap my brain around it."

"And what did he mean about *she called and told me everything?*'"

"I don't know."

"Okay," Kara said. "Anyway, what if you take a year to focus on you? Your grief from your dad's passing is going to be raw—and stay raw—for a while. I understand because when my mom passed away, it took longer to grieve than I expected. It just takes a while to feel like yourself again. I don't know how long, because it's different for everybody. So, why don't you just take some time for you?"

"For me?" Alex didn't even know what that meant. She thought she'd been living for herself for so long.

Why *did* Alex always need a man around? Most of them wanted to make her into something she wasn't. A housewife, a maid, a cook. Randy mostly wanted a piece of eye candy on his arm and his boat, when it was convenient for him. Which was flattering, sure, and way better than being his servant or his maid, but still a lot to live up to when she wanted to stay home on her nights off lounging and reading. Come to think of it, with everything else going on in her life, trying to be what he wanted her to be was exhausting.

Then there was whatever this was, with JT.

"Yeah. For you. A year of Alex, or whatever." She laughed again. "How's your book coming?"

Her book. She hadn't so much as opened her book, since the last thing she had done was send a draft to her dad and ask him to read it and comment on it. She didn't even know why she had, as it wasn't his style of book. He had liked mysteries and cop stories, and her book was . . . not that. Maybe she had wanted his approval. Or for him to say for once, "I'm proud of you." Her mom had given the book back to her after he passed, and Alex didn't know if he had really read it.

"My book," Alex said. Kara also didn't seem to think much of anything was private. "I haven't opened it since my dad died." Sometimes it felt like she was prying.

"Well," Kara said. "Okay. When you're ready to pick it up again, you will. But I want to read it when it's done. And you've got this cool new teaching job. You've got so much going for you, Alex. I'm so *proud* of you. You're doing great with sobriety. Maybe see if you can get out to a meeting today."

"I'm in Tennessee," Alex said and laughed. "I don't really even know where I am."

"There are meetings everywhere," Kara said. "Look it up and let me know what you find. Today or tomorrow, okay?"

"Okay."

"So, what are you gonna do?" Kara asked. She always asked this at the end of their conversations. Alex was supposed to give her a recap.

"I'm going to do a fourth step about my argument with JT. Then I'm going to find a meeting close by, if I can. Then I'm going to see if I can stay single for a year?" She said this last part like a question, because she wasn't sure if she could do it.

"Good. Okay. Oh, and Alex?"

"Yeah."

"Don't drink."

"Okay." This made her smile. She hadn't always made the best of decisions, but going to that first AA meeting and asking Kara to be her sponsor was one of the smartest things she'd ever done.

"I love you," Kara said. "Call me back if you need me."

"I love you," Alex said. "Thank you."

Before she put down her phone, she looked up *AA meetings near me*. Of course, there was one at the church next to the marina. Five o'clock. She had fifteen minutes to get there.

She grabbed her notebook and checked herself in the mirror. She did like this tennis dress. She put on some sunglasses to cover her puffy eyes, grabbed her notebook and pen, and slowly walked upstairs. She thought she'd just sneak out the door, but everybody was in the kitchen. Pauly, Bingo, Jessica, Vanessa, and JT.

"Hey!" Vanessa said. "Did you have a good nap?"

Alex glanced at JT, whose lips were flattened in a serious face. His eyes were sad like a rainstorm.

"I did." Alex clicked the ballpoint pen in her hand off and on.

"Girl, I know it," Vanessa said. "Todd and I tied one on pretty good last night. Both of us crashed out for two hours this afternoon." She winked. "Also, this guy." She pointed to Charlie, who was sprawled out on his side in the corner of the living room, snoring.

"Yeah." Alex smiled. "Vacation is nice like that. Taking a rest when you need one." She looked back at JT. She couldn't read his face. "I'm going to go for a walk," she said. "I'll be back in an hour or so."

JT followed her out. She kept walking, slowly, down the three wooden steps of the porch and onto the gravel. The flag swayed in the light breeze. A large, gray cumulous cloud had settled in front of the sun.

"Hey," he said. "Where are you going?"

"I'm going for a walk." She turned left onto the path and headed toward the marina. "I just need to clear my mind."

He grabbed her hand from behind her, locked his fingers in hers, and said, "Can I walk with you?" A part of her was relieved.

"Sure." She had no idea what she should say, but she knew she had to say something. She clutched the notebook in her other hand.

He quickened his pace, so he was next to her. "Look, I—" She cut him off.

"I'm sorry, JT!" she said, in more than a cry than a statement. "I shouldn't have said what I said. I'm supposed to do a fourth step about it and figure out what happened just a minute ago, but I'm going to a meeting to get my head right. I'm so confused."

She hadn't been able to bring herself to look at him, but she did now, and his eyes were still puffy.

"You're probably right about her," he said. Kindness and forgiveness glowed out of the gold.

"What?"

She slowed her pace now, their steps synching together on the gravel.

He squeezed her hand. "I knew she was too good for me when I met her. And I never liked the way she looked at Curtis. Something about it, ya know?"

She shook her head. "No! I think I was just saying that because I was hurt. I'm so confused right now. My feelings don't make any sense. I didn't mean to direct all my confusion at you, and at her. JT!" Alex pleaded. "She was *not* too good for you. You are the *best human* in the world, and you deserve to have . . . *everything*."

He cocked his head, his eyes barely peering out from under his baseball cap. Alex's flip flop caught on a pink rock and kicked it. She bent down, studied the sparkly pattern on it. She picked it up and put it in her pocket.

"Every girl looked at your dad like that. Why wouldn't Emily, too?" JT shrugged. "He just had this magnetism about him. People wanted to be around him. Guys *and* girls."

It was true. Alex always hated the way girls drooled over her father. Older ones, younger ones. What was it they saw in him? To her, he was her geeky, flawed dad, who left a lot to be desired in the parenting department. In a way, she hated how women pined over him, because she'd never, not once in her life, felt like she had his full attention. But guys were drawn to him, too.

"Even for dudes," he continued. "Man, I really looked up to him."

Why did everyone think her dad was such a god-like figure?

"Curtis looked at the establishment, and said, 'Not me. I'm not playing your game anymore.' For those of us already stuck doing jobs we didn't dream about, it was really something to watch him follow his dreams. Your dad was so inspiring." JT started swinging his arm, and hers, too, playfully. "He put his life into songs and was wide open on stage. Man, it was so fun to watch him play." JT must have seen her face. "But as your new boyfriend, for a week, I can see how that might have seemed stressful."

Always pragmatic JT, considering what it's like to walk in someone else's shoes. And somehow kinder than she deserved, and even funny again.

"He just . . . never grew up," she said. "You know?" She clutched his hand, their arms intertwined now, and studied a mailbox shaped like a frog. The path wound around in front of them, up a hill, and then down again toward the marina and the chapel. "I needed a dad, not a rock star."

"Yeah," he said. "That makes sense." They walked in silence. Alex pointed out a large bush of orange flowers, and a tree with pink blooms hovering over the path.

"Hibiscus," he said. "You're going to a meeting?"

"My sponsor said it would help me get my head on straight. Figure out what to do with all these feelings I don't know how to feel."

"Ah," he said. "Okay."

"She told me that Randy was toxic, and that I should figure out how to stay single for a year."

He laughed, but the look on her face must have cancelled out his joy.

"What's funny about that?" she asked.

"I love how Brittany Spears lyrics have become professional psychological terms. And we're using them to describe your ex-boyfriend. She's right about him, though." He put his hand on the bill of his hat. "For a year?"

"Yeah." Alex said. She perched her sunglasses on top of her head.

She knew Randy was a jerk when she met him, but she went out with him anyway. Truly, he hadn't asked a lot of her, and that was enough at the time.

"I can't remember the last time I didn't have a boyfriend," she admitted.

"But what about your new boyfriend for a week?" He stopped, grabbed her waist, and looked into her eyes with his sweet, chiseled face.

How was he always so sure of himself? Her body felt broken in all places, her heart, her stomach. There were so many feelings; she couldn't name them all if she tried. Fear, anger, sadness, guilt. *Desire. Longing.*

The chapel sat in front of them. An arch over the door said, *Everybody's Welcome.* A single man in sunglasses stood outside, smoking a cigarette.

"I don't know, JT. I'm so confused right now?"

Her own voice sounded weak and unsure.

"Okay," he said, and pulled her into a bear hug. She loved the safety of his body around hers, the way it contained her completely even though she felt so out of sorts.

He nodded and pulled back.

"I'll wait for you."

Chapter Thirty

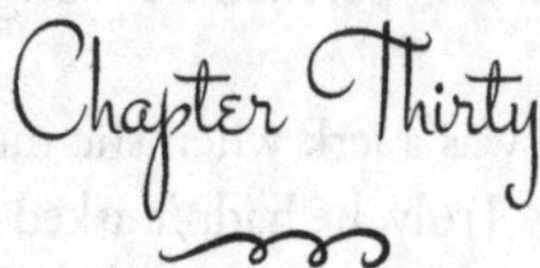

There was a certain structure to an AA meeting Alex liked. They always opened with the Serenity Prayer, and then there were readings of the Twelve Steps and the Twelve Traditions. Alex liked The Promises the most—what would happen if you could get sober and stay sober.

The smell of cheap, freshly brewed coffee surrounded the group. A small air conditioning window unit struggled in the corner window.

The attendees went around the room and introduced themselves, an eclectic group of young and old, different backgrounds, all with this same thing in common. Somebody brought up a topic. *Honesty.*

There it was again, as if it were haunting her. Or, as if this higher power was trying to tell her something.

Had she been so dishonest?

She didn't want to do a fourth step, but she would. She hated to see her insecurities and her mistakes all out on paper. But it was necessary, Kara said, to heal. Someone talked about how the fifth step had released them from the guilt and shame of their past, and Alex wiped a couple of tears. "When you can name your feelings," somebody said, "then you can feel them, and then let them go."

She loved the wisdom of these rooms. *"It's simple, but it's not easy,"* they said.

Afterward, the women hugged her. Strangers. She hugged them back. She had absolutely no energy after the day's events, and in the pit of her stomach ached a tired despair, like a draining. She found JT on a cement table outside in the courtyard, sweating and staring at his phone.

He stood up quickly when she exited. She noticed something in his eyes she hadn't seen in a while.

Fear? His confidence was gone.

"What's up?" she asked.

"I have to tell you something." He wiped the screen of his phone on his shorts and held it out to her.

"What? I don't want to stare at your phone."

"Right." He lifted his ball cap and settled it back around his head. "Emily texted me a photo of us . . . at the marina."

It took a long moment for understanding to sink in. "Was she there? Is she here?" A new feeling gripped Alex's stomach. "This is so weird. Did she follow us?" Then fear overtook her, too.

"No, no," he said. She heard a slight hint of his accent again. "My mom must have told her that we went out of town, and she must have put together that we came here."

"So how did she get our picture?"

"There must be a web cam at the marina, facing the water where the boats ride in, where we parked the Jet Ski. And then, when I . . . kissed you."

What little emotional energy she had left, faded away.

"She must have taken a screen shot of it," JT said. "Look."

There it was, in the message from Emily: a photo of them at the marina. Both of their faces curled in smiles under the kiss. His hands gently placed at her waist. Their bodies slightly pressed together.

This could be bad. Could it?

She left *him*, though. So, why was it so bad?

"She said she sent it to Randy, so, he knows."

Randy? How the hell would she even know about Randy? He lived a thousand miles away from them, and she hardly ever talked about her relationships anymore, to anybody. Her circle had almost shrunk completely when her dad passed.

"She must have found him on Facebook," he said.

"Facebook?" Oh, God. Alex hated the internet. It had gotten too weird. She thought she had her privacy settings all the way up. The pieces of information were starting to connect.

"Well, this explains why Randy said that weird thing about *I know what you're doing.*" Alex didn't have any feelings left for any of it. Maybe the universe was breaking up with Randy for her.

"Emily said she got a lawyer. Said she was going to take Jared, and then take me for everything I had, because this," he said and lowered his head, "is clear infidelity."

Alex put her hands on his waist and wrapped her thumbs around his belt loops. "I'm sorry." Then she thought twice about it. What if there was a webcam on the chapel?

She glanced behind her to the marina and took her hands away, instead clutching her notebook and pen. A different band was playing now, and a country song about red solo cups drifted through the air.

He shook his head and tucked the phone into his right pocket. "I don't know what to do," he said.

Alex didn't either.

Chapter Thirty-One

They walked back to the lake house *not* holding hands, JT's hands tucked into his pockets and Alex with her notebook, clicking her pen. They didn't speak; the only sound was their flip flops against the gravel path. The sun was starting to hide behind some trees, and a barely-breeze whispered through branches as they walked.

A new SUV was parked in front of the A-Frame.

"Coach," JT said.

They opened the door and Charlie came running. He wagged his stub of a tail and bounced around, clearly having a good vacation. Coach stood in the middle of the living room with sunglasses on his head, two black strands of string connecting them to a rope around his neck. He held a black guitar case.

"JT!" he said.

"Missed you, sir!"

Coach set the guitar down and took two long strides toward them, wrapping JT in a firm hug. He pulled back, hands on both shoulders while he looked him in the eyes and hugged him again.

"How you holding up?"

"Emily finally left, but she took Jared," JT said. "Other than that, I'm great." He didn't say it sarcastically, but with a sense of defeat.

"I'm sorry to hear that for you," Coach said. He scratched behind his ear and put his hands on his hips.

"This is Alex," JT said.

Coach studied Alex, then wrapped her in a hug, too.

"Juan Canosa," he said. "Around here it's just Coach. An honor to have you." The bathroom door opened and a woman emerged. She was petite and soft, motherly. "My wife, Rhonda."

Rhonda approached Alex, lowered her elbows, and embraced her in a warm hug.

"Oh, hi! It's nice to finally meet JT's girl . . . well, his best girl friend," she said. Rhonda's eyes were big, brown, and friendly. Rhonda hugged JT. The hug lasted for a while, as if JT didn't want to let go.

"Sorry we're late. We got stuck behind a semi around the first bend off the mountain."

"That last leg is a rough ride," JT said. "Thanks for letting us crash in your house."

"Always," Coach said.

"This is your house?" Alex asked. "It's so beautiful."

"We do this every year. You're always welcome."

Alex was exhausted.

Rhonda turned to her. "Are you hungry? I'm making Chicken Salan for dinner." Alex didn't know what that was, but she didn't want to seem rude by asking. "Pakistani Chicken Curry," Rhonda said and smiled.

"Oh, that sounds good, thank you," Alex said.

"We could always eat," JT said. "I'm gonna go downstairs for a minute. Where are the guys?"

"Pauly got the boat running. Glad somebody on the team is mechanical," Coach said. "They went out tooling around. Should be back in an hour or so."

Coach pulled a beer out of a red and white plastic cooler. "Want one?" he asked JT.

"No, I'm good right now."

Rhonda was opening cupboards, peering in, and closing them. She opened the fridge, then closed it.

"I think I have what I need," she said. "You kids look tired." Alex wondered if she could tell they'd both been crying today.

"I think I need to crash for a minute," JT said, rubbing Charlie behind the ear. "I could use a little rest."

"I'll go with you," Alex said.

Charlie followed them downstairs to the ocean room.

Chapter Thirty-Two

JT all but crashed onto the bed. Alex wondered if she should sit on the balcony and write for a while. That fourth step. But she felt like she needed to tend to JT now.

He would recover from his marriage ending, maybe, but she didn't know how he would recover from not getting to see his son. JT loved being a dad. He'd given up music and baseball for him. He'd given up everything he loved and wanted for his future, and he never, ever complained about it.

She laid down next to him, but didn't want to pry. The earlier confusion of her emotions had transformed into a knot in her stomach.

Alex rubbed his back through his tee shirt. "It's gonna be okay in the end. One of my recovery friends says, *If it's not okay, it's not the end.*"

She meant it to sound brave and empowered, but it came out like a mumble.

He rolled over and stared at the ceiling. Charlie huffed and curled into a ball in the corner, propping his head on his front legs.

"I don't see the end of this. Emily is ruthless."

Alex felt foolish about the things she'd said about her earlier.

She had resolved in the meeting not to say anything else negative about her.

"I mean, we haven't been happy for a long time. Just going through the motions, you know?" He took his ball cap off and set it on the bed stand. It left a ring around his shiny black hair. "I thought it was just a phase; I thought we would grow back together after we had grown apart." He sighed. "When she gets mad, though, it's bad news."

Alex couldn't see that about her, but Alex had most recently not done a good job of thwarting her own anger.

It was fear. That's what would come out in her fourth step. This feeling in her stomach.

"She's going to take me to court and trash my reputation completely. And try and take Jared. All for revenge."

Alex stopped her hand on his back. "You asked her to marry you, you quit playing baseball even though you could have played in the minors, and you went back to Greenview instead of moving to Nashville like you wanted."

He sighed. "It's complicated, Alex. She wanted to move back to Virginia Beach. When her mom got sick, there was nobody else to take care of her, so she took Jared, and she went. I think she met someone there, but she'd never tell me. She talked a lot about this guy she'd met, one of her old neighbors."

"When was that?" Alex asked.

"I think Jared was two," he said. "But by that time, I'd bought the house, and we'd settled in Greenview. I'd started coaching and had gotten used to being with my parents again. I'm all they have, you know? We're all they have."

"Yeah." Alex understood. She propped her elbows on the bed and rested her face in her hands.

"After her mom passed, she came home, and she wasn't really the same. One day she found and . . . went through . . . my shop box."

"Your shop box?" Alex asked, "What's a shop box?"

"You know. Those memory boxes we made in junior-high shop class."

"Oh yeah," Alex said. Mr. Short had them measure out the pine wood, cut it, stain it, and add nails and hinges. "Mine was all janky so I threw it away."

One side of his face smiled. "I kept mine and stashed all my important stuff in it. Concert tickets, senior pictures, that kind of thing. But she found these . . . letters I had written you in college."

"Oh, pro-tip," Alex said. "Don't let the new partner go through your old things without supervision."

One of Alex's first boyfriends, if you could call him that, had found one of her old shoe boxes of memories and she'd had to explain herself for weeks afterward. She'd stashed that box in the back of Diane's closet the next time she was home, and vowed to not let anyone else ever go through it.

"Thanks, Alex," he said. "*Really* helpful."

"Sorry. But you stopped writing after your freshman year?" Alex had dropped out of school and was couch-surfing, anyway, so they probably wouldn't even have gotten to her.

"I never stopped writing," he said. "Even after I met her, and even after she got pregnant, and even after we decided to get married. Even though I didn't know where you were, or where to send them."

"I didn't know that."

"Yeah," he said. "I guess, I don't know. It was so much a part of me, you were so much a part of me, that I still like, needed and wanted a best friend . . . needed and wanted you, as my best friend. I thought I would send them eventually, but instead I just put them in the box, put the box in a storage suitcase and forgot about them."

Alex felt jealousy welling up in her. She didn't have a right to feel jealous. "She read my letters before I did?"

"And she proceeded to go out with the girls that night, and to not come home." He cried now, his eyes an amber tint and overflowing. Young and vulnerable JT, not the cocky, confident man that had shown up to her house yesterday. "I accused her of cheating, and she denied it, but I found a note in her purse the next day that said, *'Thanks for the night'* with a guitar pick wrapped inside of it. Some dude's handwriting."

She brushed a tear from his chin. "That's a lot, JT," Alex said. "I'm sorry."

"It *was* a lot. I told her it wasn't like that. That you and I were just friends. And then she and I got into an argument, and we didn't talk to each other for a week. Even though they weren't love letters, they were still maybe—she might have seen them as—intimate."

"Intimate?" Alex couldn't remember what they used to write back and forth about, only that they did. And it was always good and grounding for her at college to get a letter from home. Maybe she was being too selfish. She dialed back her questions.

"Writing to you was like writing in a journal," JT said. "I read the letters again and saw myself young and in love and full of hope for the future." There was a hint of regret.

In love?

"After we got married, I shut down except with my kid. And then after that night she didn't come home, I shut her out completely." He ran his hands over his hair. "The thing was, though, she'd go out a *lot* without me . . . and stay out really late. I thought there might be someone else, but I could never prove it. It was almost like she was looking for some kind of out . . . some kind of excuse to blame *me*. I'm not mad at her; we got married so young. I worked a lot. I knew she wasn't happy. We both thought staying together would be best for Jared. That pissed-off playlist came in pretty handy." His lips smiled, but his eyes did not. "Thank God for Limp Biskit."

Alex had no idea. They seemed so perfect from the outside looking in. "How long ago was that?" She smiled a warm smile.

"Ten years," he said. "I think it was ten years ago. Jared was still small."

She tried to think back to ten years ago. She was finally

finishing her bachelor's degree after dropping out of school and being lost and traveling. She was always behind her peers in everything, after those years of *going with the flow.*

Maybe the letters would have given her some kind of direction. Probably not. She was so strong-willed back then. She'd finished her writing degree and moved immediately back with her graduation money to the beach.

"We never slept together after that. We slept in the same bed sometimes, but I pretty much moved to the couch," he said. "And here we are."

"Wait." Alex said, "You haven't slept together for ten years? With your wife?"

"Marriage is *so fun,* they said." He scoffed. "I don't know, we tried counseling. It didn't help. I knew she was seeing somebody else. Sometimes she wouldn't come home until two in the morning, and sometimes she wouldn't come home at all. There was nothing I could do about it. And she would never admit it, anyway."

"I didn't know you'd been so unhappy for so long."

Alex couldn't judge her, though. Alex had never even had the same boyfriend for more than a year. Who knew what it would be like to be married?

She also knew that she was a different person now than before her dad died. Or, she was never going to be the same as she was before then. She didn't even remember who she was before then.

"Nobody knew. How would anybody know? I didn't even tell my parents." The tears had stopped running down his face, and Alex's eyes focused on his lips for a second. "I mean," he said. "I told your dad."

"You did?" she asked. "I knew you were friends, but I guess I didn't know you two were *that* close." So close that he would tell him something this important but wouldn't tell Alex.

JT finally smiled. "Curtis called me up one day and said, *Sounds like you're going through a rough patch. Wanna talk about it?* We talked for two hours. Every once in a while, he would call me up and ask me how I was doing with everything."

Alex couldn't remember the last time her dad had called her up and asked how she was doing. Or if he ever had. She'd spent her early twenties just rolling with everything.

Maybe she should just roll with this, too.

This was a lot to just roll with.

She rubbed the inside of his forearm, which was something her mom used to do to calm her when she was scared. Alex's guilt from earlier, from their time on the Jet Ski, had dissolved.

Maybe she had betrayed Randy, but he was a jerk. She didn't feel like she had betrayed Emily now. She adjusted her tennis dress and laid down next to him with her neck in the anchor of his shoulder, and her foot just slightly touching his.

They laid there like friends.

Chapter Thirty-Three

Alex woke up and the room was dark. JT was next to her, snoring, his face sweet and handsome. His perfect lips. He looked so innocent and so grown-up. He looked peaceful. The moon was full and beckoned her out onto the balcony. Charlie slept in his same spot in the corner.

A figure outside sat at the table. She rubbed her eyes. Maybe it was Pauly or Jessica, taking a little time alone. She stood up, half-asleep, and the face came into view. She opened the sliding glass and stepped out, feeling the warm wood against her feet.

"Daddy?"

He smiled his million-dollar dimples. There was this deep compassion in his turquoise eyes.

Was he really here?

"Hey, kid." A faint light wrapped around him, like the moon was shining only on him. A glittering. His deep voice reverberated in the night like a trombone.

"I missed you so much!" She rushed over and hugged him around his neck. He smelled like Old Spice aftershave. He wore one of his favorite shirts, a blue-gray stonewashed tee-shirt with a compass drawn on the chest, over his heart. He squeezed until she let go.

"Daddy, what happened to you?"

"I'm okay," he said. "I'm here. Took a wrong turn, or a right turn, depending on how you look at it."

She pressed on. "But what happened? Nobody will tell me what happened, and I miss you so much, and I'm sorry about the last week, I was so mad at you and then—"

"It's okay, kid. I miss you, too. It doesn't matter so much now about what happened, but more about what is happening."

"What do you mean?" She moved the chair with her foot and felt a piercing pain. "Ouch," she hissed. A splinter stuck out from her toe. She sat down and tried to pull the tiny piece of wood out of her skin, but she couldn't quite get a hold. He waved his hands, and there was light following his fingers, like a figure-eight of sparklers. The stars were so bright. The milky way stretched over them and reflected off the water below.

"Some things are destined, Alex. We agree to certain things in the spirit world, about who we'll meet and what we're supposed to work on. We have choices about what to do."

"Do you mean about what happened to you?" Alex crossed one leg over the other knee and continued trying to pull out the splinter, but she kept her eyes wide on his presence. "I mean, Mom won't tell me everything, you know, Mom, and then Drew and—"

He cut her off again. "It's okay, kiddo. You don't need to know right now. Your mom and your brother and me and you, we all decided before this life we would come here to learn together. But this next lesson is going to be only about you."

"Lesson?" She couldn't get the splinter out.

"You've always liked being alone," he said. "This next phase is going to be about what you do when you're alone, who you choose to be around, and which path to choose next." She felt suspended in time, like, maybe she was here, but maybe she wasn't really here. Otherworldly.

The pain in her foot was real, though. "What am I supposed to learn?"

"I can't tell you, exactly." He scratched his chin and put both elbows on the table. He flexed his biceps, un-flexed them, and sat back.

He smiled his joking smile then, the one Nana Kate always loved.

"It would take all of the fun out of it, anyway."

"I want to tell you I'm really proud of you." Tears gathered in her eyes. "People look up to you, Alex. You've forged your own path." His eyes looked like stars. "Like your Nana Kate. She was the same way. There aren't any wrong turns, so you can let go of the guilt and the worst part of it, the shame. It's unnecessary, anyway."

"But Dad," she said. The tears streamed down her face now. "I'm sorry I—"

He continued as if he couldn't hear her. "This next part is all about you, Alex. About everything you ever wanted. It might not look how you thought it would look." He stood up. "I've got to go . . . they're calling me back. Nana Kate says to tell you she loves you more than the moon and stars."

They? "Nana Kate?" She was bewildered; she didn't want him to go. She had so many questions and wanted so many answers.

She wanted to hang out here all night with her dad.

"Focus on what you truly want, Alex. And you're going to have to give up caring so much what other people think of you. Human opinions don't matter in the spirit world. You have to be true to *your* path, *your* journey, and *your* lessons. It's about passion and compassion, the balance between the two." His voice began to fade.

"Daddy, wait. I really don't care—"

"You *do*," he said, his silhouette blurring out of vision. "Let it go. Focus on what you want. Your intentions. It's 3 a.m."

He was gone.

She was outside.

Alone with the moon.

Chapter Thirty-Four

It was 10 p.m. She had just been with her father. Music came from upstairs, and she could hear laughs and talk around the song. JT was still in the same position on the bed, his head tilted toward her and their feet touching. Charlie must have gotten bored, or hungry, or both, and gone upstairs. She could feel the remnants of her dad's arms around her, his aftershave lingered in her nose.

Alex tuned into the sounds.

"We're going to wake them up," a female voice said. "We should keep the volume down."

Someone laughed. "Wake them up! We're on vacation!"

Some guitars began, and a drumbeat. Various voices in various intonations started singing Matchbox 20. Lyrics about cold and a raincoat. *3 A.M.* Alex thought. That song from the late 90's. The voices sounded jovial. JT stirred and opened his eyes.

"Guess we fell asleep," she said. She tinkered with the soft cotton sleeve of his black tee-shirt. He took a deep breath with a hissing noise.

"What time is it?"

"Ten. They started the concert without us." He took in another deep breath, and she removed her hand from his sleeve and propped her head on her elbow. Her knees tucked up against the side of his thighs. Ever since this morning, her body had been drawn to his.

She wanted to be close to him, without getting too close to him.

"I had a dream about my dad."

He propped himself up on both elbows, then one, and turned toward her so their legs were intertwined.

"What was Curtis doing?"

The moon still shone through the window, and the stars were sprinkled in the sky, but nobody was there.

"He was sitting on the balcony, right over there." She pointed. "I got to hug him."

JT wiped at one of his eyes. "Cool. My mom would say that was a visitation."

"A visitation?" She put one of her hands on his leg.

"When one of your ancestors visits you in your dreams." He grabbed her hand and rubbed her palm with his thumb. "Did he say anything?"

"I tried to ask him what happened, and he wouldn't tell me, and then he said this next part of my journey would be about focusing on what I want—my next lesson. Without the guilt and shame." She was hard on herself sometimes because somebody had to be, but was she too hard on herself?

"That's really cool," JT repeated. "And what do you want?"

She still couldn't answer that question.

She wanted to go back in time and make a million different choices in a million different scenarios. She wanted her life to be like one of those choose-your-own-adventure novels from the 1980s, and she wanted to go back a few chapters and choose differently. She wanted to feel like everything was okay. Not only now, but always.

Something opened up inside. "I want to write a best-selling book and pay off my student loans and open a used bookstore and to find somebody to share my life with who is attractive and fun, but who lets me be me. I want to not be such a failure in my career and my relationships, and I want to live by the water . . . and have a backyard and plant fruit trees and I want to live a free and peaceful life. Outside of everyone else's god-forsaken condemning opinions. I want to travel to all the Caribbean Islands and go out on sailboats, and go to Brazil to see Carnival, all five-hundred drummers playing at the same time." There. That sounded like something. "And I want to see the Redwoods before I die." She laughed. "That's what I want."

She felt naked, suddenly. She blushed. "That sounds like a lot. What do you want?"

He leaned into her, cupped her chin in his hand and said, "I want to unzip this tight black dress, take it off of you sleeve by sleeve, and see what's underneath it."

He kissed her.

She couldn't help but laugh. She pulled back, even though his tongue was teasing hers. "I am just having this seriously authentic moment, and you are just . . . being a guy?"

The kiss had aroused her.

"I'm sorry," he said. "I am a guy, and I just woke up." He pulled his tee-shirt over his head and tossed it onto the floor. His triceps flexed as he moved close to her and let his chest hover over hers, his hard body against her bare legs. "You want to plant fruit trees? Tell me more."

His sparkly gold eyes.

She breathed out a heavy breath.

"JT, I am supposed to be taking a year off men, remember? And our, relationships, everything . . . is kind of a mess right now."

He put his head in her chest, clamped his front teeth around the zipper of her dress, and tugged at it. He brushed his lips against each one of her breasts and then found her mouth again.

"Let's be a mess together," he breathed.

A ball of emotion welled up in her gut. She took his chin in her hand now.

"I'm sorry I can't be your mysterious vacation girlfriend for the week."

He kissed her once more, tenderly, and put his forehead against hers. "Then be my mysterious vacation girlfriend for one more night." He licked at her earlobe. "It's still July fifth," he whispered.

She heard laughter and cheering from downstairs. The song changed, a familiar electric guitar intro. Sad and longing. High and then falling. Prince's "Purple Rain."

JT continued, "You can start that single thing tomorrow, can't you?"

His breath on her neck and in her ear made her fingertips tingle.

She put her hands on the back of his head and let him pull the zipper all the way down with his teeth. She stroked his black hair. He turned her onto her back, and knelt over her, unzipping his shorts and removing his boxers. God, had he always been this smooth? She opened her knees so his body would fit in between. His rough hands rubbed her up and down, tenderly, as he pulled the dress around her shoulders, and then down behind her, running his fingertips down each leg as he took it off.

He nibbled at her bra, then at the blue lace between her thighs, held her with one hand behind her back and the other on her navel, moving his mouth around her until she was warm and ready.

"*God*, you're so beautiful," he said. "Could you want *me* for one more night?"

It was slower this time. Even more tender. He adjusted himself fully between her, his dark eyes on her face. She closed her eyes and sucked at the freckles on his shoulder, then his collarbone, allowing herself to be completely overtaken.

Until desire and climax met at the base of her spine and released in pulses.

Until both of them were trembling.

Chapter Thirty-Five

Her soft body curled up against his. She wanted to stay right here, in this moment, feeling this way.

"I don't know what's going to happen to us now," she said.

JT kissed her shoulder. "We'll figure it out."

Drums started, then what sounded like people banging on tables.

"JT!" a voice said, from upstairs. "You're missing your part!"

JT laughed. "Rusted Root," he said. "'Send Me on My Way.'" Alex heard a faint whistling in between laughs. "I usually lead the drum part."

"What do we do now? I don't even know how we move forward from here."

If there was a time to use the L-word, this was a time to use the L-word, but Alex did not, on principle, just use the L-word. Saying *I love you* had never worked out for her.

Not anymore. Not since before Sam.

"*We go back to being friends.* Wanna go to my friends' amateur concert upstairs?"

She rolled off the bed to find her intimates and her tennis dress. He slid on his shorts. From the open door of the bathroom, where she went to check her hair, she asked, "Did you just quote Dave Matthews Band to me?"

There was a time when she was nineteen, where she thought if she could figure out how to make money—how to sell jewelry or poetry or anything else—and follow Dave Matthews Band around the country on their tour, then she would have.

He came into the bathroom and kissed her neck, then took a swig of mouthwash. "Number 41," he said, and spit the green liquid into the sink. "I didn't do it on purpose. It just came out of my mouth."

"Is that on my playlist?" she asked.

He kissed her quickly and patted her on the butt. "Of course, it's on your playlist. Let's go be friends."

"This is going to be hard," she said, as she followed him up the stairs. "Not being able to touch you."

He smiled and cocked his head.

"I feel like I'm just starting to get what *I* want."

A wonderful smell of onions and garlic permeated the living room. The lights were turned down and Charlie stood up and greeted them when they entered. JT's college friends all cheered.

"It's about time," Todd said. He got up from a djembe drum and gestured for JT to sit down in front of the hour-glass shaped instrument. "Start it over, you guys."

Todd sat on a cajón—a square drum that looked like a box—next to JT. There were two new people in the room. Rhonda came over to Alex and handed her a plate.

"We saved you some. The guys almost ate it all, but I stopped them." She smiled.

They stopped playing as JT situated. When he started playing, the rest of the friends, who were placed on various couches and chairs, chimed in after. Pauly and Coach played the guitar, Jessica shook a tambourine, and Vanessa played a small keyboard. Of the two new people, one guy played a bass guitar, and the other guy had a shaker going.

"Thanks," Alex said to Rhonda, and sat down at the dining

room table adjacent to the living room. She didn't know they had brought all these instruments. The song sounded just like the *Rusted Root* CD. Coach sang the first verse, and then Pauly sang the second.

They were really good. The food was savory.

When the song ended, JT was smiling from ear to ear.

He looked at Alex. "You wanna play?"

It had been so long since she played. She didn't even know if she could.

Coach said, "Alex, this is Tito and Sarge," he pointed to the two new guys. "Guys, Alex."

"JT's Florida girl," Sarge said, and adjusted the strap of the bass. "Nice to finally put a face to the name—you're prettier than he said you were." He ran a hand through orange hair.

Alex smiled.

"Nice to meet you," Tito said. "Don't mind Sarge, he's been drinking all day." He was tall with creamy skin and dark curly hair. Crow's feet spread around his eyes when he laughed.

"Anyway, song," Jessica said.

"I'm pretty rusty," Alex said. "I haven't played in a while."

"What do you play?" Coach asked.

"The last thing I played was a cajón," she said.

"Here," Todd said. "Have a seat."

Jessica said, "Do you sing?"

"I don't usually sing and play at the same time," Alex said.

"What's next?" Vanessa flipped her braids over her shoulder, smiled, and turned a dial on the keyboard.

"Ring of Fire," Pauly said. Jessica rolled her eyes. "We gotta let Alex hear the Asian guy sing bass."

"Hey," Coach said. "It's Pacific Islander." All the guys laughed.

Rhonda said, "He's from the Philippines. It's a running joke." She took the empty plate from in front of Alex.

"Go play," she urged.

Alex sat on the drum next to JT. She forgot how comfortable

and powerful she felt on the cajón. Hers was in her Florida apartment tucked next to her bed; she hadn't even looked at it this year.

Coach started in on the guitar.

"You know this one?" he said to Alex.

She started playing. JT came in with her on the drums, and Vanessa started on the keys, then the rest of the band came in.

"She does," Coach said. He started singing the verse. He sounded just like Johnny Cash. Alex had forgotten how much fun it was to play. She glanced over at JT, and he was staring at her with a sultry gleam in his eye.

He closed his eyes then, but his hands kept moving to the beat.

When the song was finished, Sarge said, "Not bad for a white girl."

"Hey!" Jessica said. "Easy."

"What? You don't see white girls on the drums all the time."

"Someday," Tito said, "we'll get him cultured enough to live up to the multicultural dorm assignment. Cheers."

"That was good," Vanessa said. "What's next?"

Jessica turned to Vanessa. "Don't you play Alicia Keys?"

"Oooh," Vanessa said. "I don't know if I can sing that one tonight. I might need help." She started on the intro to "If I Ain't Got You," and everyone else chimed in.

Alex stared at JT and this time it was she who closed her eyes while she played.

Chapter Thirty-Six

Alex played and sang a couple of songs, and having JT next to her while they were playing brought back more memories of their youth. How she felt safe with him. How, when they were younger and when they were playing together, she felt free. How much fun they always had together.

They played some other songs and ended the night with Bob Marley's "No Woman, No Cry." Now Alex and her best guy friend-turned-boyfriend for the week cuddled on the bed in the beach-themed bedroom with a giant Rottweiler at their feet.

Alex propped her chin on her elbows and turned to him.

"How is it that all of your college friends who are baseball players, are also musical?"

JT laid on his back, folded his hands across his stomach, and stared at the ceiling. "SOU was a really good school. Better than University of Southwest Florida," he joked and squeezed her waist. "Nah, I mean, Coach kept us out of trouble."

"How so?" she rested her hand on his knee.

"He threw parties at his house on the weekends. Rhonda cooked, and we'd all get out his instruments or bring ours and hang out in the basement. We drank, I mean, we brought booze if we didn't have a game the next day. But there were absolutely no drugs allowed, and he only allowed women to come if we had been dating them for six months." JT kissed Alex softly on the shoulder. "We weren't allowed to drive if we'd been drinking—so we crashed in the guest rooms. He had this music room in his house with a bunch of guitars. We all started jamming together, kind of for fun and then it became like a tradition. Jessica and Vanessa came eventually, after their six months, of course. And they both just fit right in."

Alex wondered what it would have been like if she would have played sports in college. She might have walked a straighter path if she'd had a coach around to keep her in line.

"I forgot how much fun it is to play," Alex said.

"You sounded good," he said. "It was fun to play with you again."

"I miss those days," Alex said.

"High school?" he asked. "You couldn't wait to get out of there, and out of Greenview for good."

"I guess I didn't know how good I had it, you know? How easy it was." She put her head between his collar bone and his neck. He still smelled faintly of sunscreen and cologne.

"We did have it good," he said. "Remember that Saturday band contest when you threw up on the bus?"

"Oh my gosh," Alex said. "That's probably still one of my most embarrassing moments."

"Because you had a crush on Ryan, the trumpet player."

"And he made fun of me. I was mortified."

"Remember that band contest where you lost your glasses, and you kept bumping into me the whole show?"

"I do. I begged my mom for eye surgery after that."

Alex's mind wandered now. To how she and JT wrote back and forth all the time her freshman year of college, and then how they just lost touch.

"I'm sorry again," she said. "About leaving you high and dry like that."

"High and dry?"

"Sophomore year, I met this guy that I thought was the one. The first one I thought was the one."

"Aaron," JT said, turning to her now. "I remember."

She sat back up. "I told you about him?"

"Right before you stopped writing back."

Those few years after were all fuzzy. That guy had broken her heart into pieces, and she'd self-destructed, without even being aware of it. She started hanging out with anybody who would hang out with her, smoked weed for the first time, experimented with other things, and her life just got blurry. Maybe that's what she was trying to do then, numb the pain of the breakup.

She was young, but that's when she'd learned she might not be relationship material.

"What was so special about him, anyway? And what stupid thing did he do to let you go?"

"Aaron?"

"Yeah." He pulled a pillow under his chin and looked her in the eyes. He still had a faint hat ring around his hair.

"I don't know," she said. "I liked his smile. He had a great personality. He played sports, like us. He was smart, funny, nice. I thought he really liked me." In fact, she'd lost her virginity to him because she thought he was the one she could see herself with.

The one. The ideal she'd created in her brain of a husband. Back when she believed there was *a one.* "He had a girlfriend back home." Even now it hurt. "A high-school sweetheart. He didn't even tell me about her until she came to visit."

"You've had shit luck with men." He smiled and his eyes were gentle now, compassion in the golden sparks. "What do you see in Randy?"

She hadn't thought about Randy for hours. Funny, how they'd been on-again-off-again for more than a year, and he hadn't even crossed her mind, even with all the angry text messages. Maybe she *was* ready to move on from him.

"I don't know," she said. "He's fun, kind of. He plays music and has a boat." He kind of had an inflated ego.

"Fun . . . kind of?" JT's face lit up when he laughed. "Maybe you need to raise your standards." He used a mocking voice, "I play music." He puckered his lips and moved his chin from side to side like he was being sassy. "Maybe I'll buy a boat."

She laughed. She liked confident, sexy JT, teasing her.

"Honestly?" she said, "Randy asks very little of me, and I work two jobs and write on the weekends, and he wants me to come to his shows sometimes, but other times, I can just be alone."

He kissed her again. "You're dating a guy so you can be alone?"

"It's complicated," she said. She didn't really understand it. "And anyway, we're not dating anymore, not since Emily called him to tell him that you and I are here at the lake, kissing at the marina. Which we have to stop doing."

He leaned in close again to kiss her, let his lips and tongue feel around on hers this time, and then leaned back. Her body tingled.

"It's still July fifth," he said.

"It's not. It's July sixth now."

"It's July fifth until we go to bed. After we wake up, then it will be July sixth." She was trying hard to resist him, to not think of the future, and to not get lost in the past.

But she'd been wondering about this thing he said.

"Do you think I could read them?" she asked.

"Read what?"

Alex didn't want to bring up anything hurtful, but she was curious about the letters he talked about.

"The letters." She wanted to kiss him again, but they were not going to be able to keep doing this. She wondered why she had just stopped writing, why she had let their friendship fall away.

"I'm sorry, JT," she said again. This time her heart warmed up when she said it.

He smirked. "Didn't your father come to you in a dream last night to tell you to let go of your guilt and your shame?" She pinched her lips.

"Yeah." Alex rolled over and stared out the sliding glass door into the night. Charlie rustled at her feet.

"I burned the letters in the fire pit," he said. "Trying to let go of the past, or whatever."

She tucked her head back in the soft space between his neck and his shoulder, and tried not to think of what could have been. Her eyes were heavy. "We're going to have to go back to our lives soon. What are you going to do?"

"I'm going to ask Todd in the morning what he thinks my best options may be. I can't lose my son."

Chapter Thirty-Seven

In the morning, she woke up alone. She used the bathroom, grabbed her notebook, and started up the stairs to the coffee. Vanessa and Jessica were sitting outside on the balcony in front, and Todd, Pauly, and JT sat around the corner from them in the shade.

The sky was cloudy and overcast today, and the water below had a browner tone than green.

Alex poured herself a cup, still groggy, and walked out into the morning air.

"Hey," Jessica said.

"Good morning," said Vanessa.

"Morning," Alex said. A mug of coffee sat in front of Jessica and something that appeared to be a smoothie or a protein shake sat in front of Vanessa.

"You sounded really good last night," Vanessa said.

"We all did," Jessica said, and lifted her coffee cup.

"Where are Rhonda and Coach?" Alex asked.

Jessica said, "They went into town. She needed a stronger wi-fi for work."

"Too bad she has to work," Alex said. "What does she do?"

Vanessa cleared her throat. "Sorry," she said, "from singing. She owns a women's magazine."

"That's cool," Alex said. Through the glass she watched Sarge and Tito emerge from the bedroom, both in their boxers. "Wow. They're pretty comfortable."

"Oh," Jessica said. "You have no idea. V, how many times have we seen them naked?"

Sarge was built like an athlete, and Tito's sun-burned beer belly hung over his waistband. Vanessa laughed. "Oh, God. Like, a hundred-thousand times."

"They're a couple," Jessica said.

"What?" Alex asked. "Were they both on the team?"

"Yeah," Vanessa said. "The guys say they didn't know in college, but I think they did."

"That's cool," Alex said. "I would have never guessed."

"They joke around a lot," Jessica said. "But they're really sweet to each other."

Vanessa stirred the drink in front of her. "Coach and Rhonda didn't have children, so I think they see all the guys as theirs."

Alex wondered if both women had kids, but she didn't ask people that question anymore. When she was younger, she thought about children. It went along with the perfect romance, then marriage, then the white picket fence. None of which had materialized. Now, with her student loans and apartment living in her thirties, she knew she probably wouldn't have children. Aunt Skylar didn't have kids, though, and she was awesome.

Alex picked up her notebook and excused herself from the table. She descended all one-hundred and nine wooden stairs carefully and sat at the very end of the dock. She put her toes in the water.

The morning sun reflected on the calm green. A man with a fishing pole stood on the other side of the river with his line in the water. She thought of her grandfather.

They had stayed up so late, her eyelids burned. She wrote for a while, recording her random thoughts. She made a list of the things she was grateful for: JT, her mother, the dream she'd had, playing drums, being at the lake, her job, her sponsor, being sober.

She was daydreaming over the sparkly water when she felt JT behind her. He kissed her neck, took his sandals off, then sat down next to her and put his toes in the water. For a guy, he had nice feet.

"Hey," he said. "Good morning."

"Morning," she said. She really needed to paint her toenails. A tiny splinter was still stuck in her foot.

"Whatcha writing about?"

She closed her notebook and held the pen between her lips. "Just random stuff."

"The next Great American Novel?" he asked and smiled.

"Just writing my morning thoughts down. Getting the whirlwind out."

He kissed her shoulder. "I really wanted to take you out on the Jet Ski again, but I've got to head back home."

"Really?" They had only been there two days. According to Jessica and Vanessa, more of the team would arrive as the week went on.

"I talked to Todd this morning, and Coach." He scratched his chin. "Todd says I'm going to have a nasty custody battle in front of me. That some of the states aren't so nice to fathers, so I'm going to have to keep my nose clean and my wits about me."

"You always keep your nose clean." More freckles had formed on his face from the sun.

He splashed some water up with one of his feet. "I'm going to have to explain what I'm doing here to the court. And, maybe, what you're doing here."

"But—" She felt a pang of guilt in her stomach.

"This is not your fault, Alex," he said. "This is Emily being crazy and mean." Her mind had quieted after writing, and now it was full of questions again. "I asked *you* here. Not the other way around."

Alex put the notebook down and sat back so she was resting

on her palms. The sun felt good on her legs. She wasn't ready to go home yet.

"Todd said he had a friend from law school he could hook me up with. He said a female lawyer might be better able to negotiate my custody arrangements."

A female lawyer.

She couldn't be jealous of that, right? She and JT were just friends, anyway.

But what would they be now? After this?

They packed quietly and said their goodbyes. Alex thanked Rhonda and Jessica for cooking, and Vanessa for leading the songs at their "concert." The girls hugged her and said they hoped they'd get to see her again.

"We'll be here next year," Vanessa said. "The first week of July."

"Send me your book when you're finished," Jessica said. "Seriously, I want to read it."

Alex agreed but knew she probably wouldn't.

They had made Alex feel welcome, and she was sad to leave them. Coach, Pauly, Bingo and Tito all gave her bear hugs.

"Sarge is passed out again," Tito said. "But he would want me to tell you to come back, because we haven't seen our catcher here happy in a long time."

Alex blushed, petted Charlie on the head, and said, "It was nice to meet you all."

JT didn't seem to want to go, either. They loaded their bags into the Jeep, Charlie jumped in, and they started the journey back up north.

Chapter Thirty-Eight

The radio was mostly static while they wound through the mountains, so Alex flipped through JT's CD book and reminisced.

She found Outkast and Green Day and then Alanis Morissette, *Jagged Little Pill*. The CD insert had red, green, and blue swirls on it, like paint over images of grass, and two silhouettes of Alanis's profile, one looking up and one looking down.

Alex missed getting CDs in the mail, then listening to them for the first time while flipping through the artwork and lyrics. It was half of the fun of discovering a new artist. She used to cruise the country roads around Greenview and sing every word of this album at the top of her lungs. She popped it in the player.

"Alanis," he smirked.

"You love Alanis," she teased.

"You're right. I do." The guitar part started with its driving rhythm, and then the vocals to "All I Really Want." Alex turned it up. She tapped the drumbeats out on the dashboard and bobbed her head.

It was mid-day, and there were only a few scattered clouds like popcorn puffs dotting the sky. They drove slowly through the mountains and JT downshifted for sharp turns. Alex tilted her seat back and kept her sunglasses on.

She did kind of feel like she was on vacation, if only for a few more hours. It was a four-hour drive back north.

"What's your book about?" JT asked.

"What?" Alex heard him, but she never liked to talk about what her book was about. It was hard to distill into an explanation.

"What's your book about?" He turned down the radio.

She knew she would eventually have to talk about it if she wanted to publish it. "My book is about a girl in her early twenties trying to figure out life." She stopped drumming and fidgeted with the edge of her blue sundress. A part of it had started to fray.

"Is it autobiographical?" She heard that plain as day, too, and thought she might say something else to stall, but instead she just answered him.

"It's fiction. It's all made up—the characters, the places, I made them all up." She smiled to herself. It was hard to explain a book. Especially when it wasn't done. "It is but it isn't? It's kind of hard to explain."

"How do you even write a book?" He put his signal on and changed lanes. "I wouldn't even know where to start."

"Sixty-thousand dollars of graduate loans," she joked, "and I think I've almost got it." He scrunched his face. "I turned down a full ride for a master's degree," she said, "because I didn't want to take literary theory."

"No, you didn't."

"I did." She laughed nervously. "Literary theory was like taking a putty knife to an oil painting . . . like ripping up someone else's masterpiece bit by bit. I don't know, maybe I didn't get it."

She'd been thinking about this question of *how*.

"I mostly sit at my desk and daydream. Then I start typing." She left out the part about how when she was really in the zone, the characters take on lives of their own and start writing the story, without much input from her.

"Is the main character yourself?" he asked.

"She's not," Alex said. How to answer this honestly? "She's brave."

"*You're* brave," he laughed.

"I'm not brave," she said. "I'm afraid of everything."

They came out of the mountains and into a town.

"Can I read it when you're done?" he asked. "I mean, after Jessica?"

It was only a few more miles to the interstate.

"I don't know if I'm going to let anybody read this one."

She wasn't sure she wanted anyone to read this one, because the last thing she'd done with it was send a working draft to her dad and asked him to read it. When he'd called her and used the word *cute,* she'd gotten mad and told him that he wouldn't even know good writing if it slapped him in the face, and that if he wasn't so immature, he might have seen it was a meaningful story.

And then she'd hung up on him.

Three days later, he was gone.

Alex didn't let her mind wander here very often. To the last week her dad was alive. But something about here, this day, in JT's Jeep, heading back into her old life and her new reality, she let her mind wander there.

Alanis's angry "You Oughta Know" played softly.

Where are your feet?

At work she'd had a certain feeling, then she'd seen her mom's text, but she was too busy. How important in one moment it had been that she bring a roomful of customers drinks and food on time, and then how meaningless it all seemed in an instant.

How the shock lasted for days. How it was like living in a bad dream she hoped she'd wake up from—but everyone else had been there, too, in the same bad dream.

How they had to make decisions and there were so many people around asking questions and everybody wanted to know what happened and dammit, Alex wanted to know what happened, too.

But most of all, she wanted to go back to the beginning of that week. Tell her dad she loved him so much and thank him for the feedback. Thank him for reading her manuscript and caring enough to call and talk to her about it while he was out in California recording a new CD.

And even though he wasn't perfect, thank him for being her dad.

"How about you?" she asked JT. "Why didn't you study sports management or sports medicine? You could still be around baseball. Maybe work in the big leagues."

"Nah," he said. "You know the high you get from playing something? From playing sports or playing drums? I didn't want to ever be on the sidelines," he said. "I always wanted to be in the game. I always just wanted to play."

She wondered about his day to day.

"Do you ever get tired of driving?"

He pursed his lips. "I like the solitude of it. Being alone with my thoughts. I plug my phone in and listen to my playlists, or turn up the radio and listen to the beats. Then I stare out at the countryside and watch the world go by. Other drivers make me crazy sometimes. Too many people on their phones while they're operating heavy machinery."

They were on the on-ramp at I-75 before the music changed to the third song on the disc, "Perfect." A humble and sweet track where Alanis sings in a high voice. Alex rubbed her knees.

"If you don't let anybody read your book," JT said, "then what do you get out of it?"

She considered. "Writing makes me feel weirdly present."

"I get that," he said. He turned to Charlie in the back seat and gave him a pet. "So why not keep teaching? And write on the side?"

She cupped her hand around her chin to think.

She thought about books. And she got excited.

"Have you ever been feeling low, or something, or been lost and confused, and then you find a book laying around—or someone gifts you one just at the right time—and you read it and you're *blown away,* like it can change your *whole worldview?* Like, maybe you learn something you didn't know before or you just . . . feel less alone, because this story, this book, this author . . . hit your soul in a way that made you feel like everything was just . . . okay for a few hours?" She sipped in a breath. "I want to be part of that club, you know? Give people a little escape, and when they're finished, that feeling that, like, everything is going to be okay."

Maybe she was getting better at being honest. She added, "Writing is the only thing I've ever seen myself doing."

"So, what are you so afraid of?"

Kara always asked her this. *What's your fear?*

She hated it.

"Typos."

He laughed. "No, seriously. What's holding you back?"

"Seriously." She sat up straight in the seat. "I read this beautiful book a few years back. I mean, gorgeous. I looked up the author online to see what she was about. I wanted to know who she was and how she did it, you know? And there were all these mean reviews and people saying horrible things about her and about her book, and . . . man, some of the stuff was *so low.* They were attacking her *personally.* It was like all the mean girls in high school had shown up on the internet and ganged up on her." Alex shook her head. "It takes *years* to write a book. I mean, a good book. I think. I'm still learning. And it takes every bit of your *heart* and your *soul* and your *time* to do it."

"Those mean girls on the internet probably don't have hobbies?" JT said.

God, he was great. She smiled.

"Yeah. It just made me think, maybe I don't want to be in that club, you know? I left all the mean girls in high school. On purpose." She shook her head.

"I have an idea." He smiled his half-smile and put his tongue on his canine tooth. "Why don't you write a book about a sexy

Latino All-American baseball player who majored in percussion performance in college."

She laughed a loud laugh, but she humored him.

"Okay. So, what does this sexy Latino All-American baseball player who majored in percussion performance want?" she asked. "What's his motivation?" She studied his face. He was up to something.

JT reached over and held her hand. Clasped his fingers between her knuckles.

"He wants to get the girl in the end." The tone of his voice reminded her of Drew's. "Naturally."

She shook her head. "And, so, what is standing in his way?" she asked. "What is *he* afraid of?"

He took his hand from hers, pulled his baseball cap up, and settled it back down.

Matter-of-factly, he said, "Flying."

She breathed out another laugh. "You're still too scared to fly!?"

"We're *not* meant to be up there in the air that high," he said. "In a man-made machine of all things."

"I'll work on that," she said.

"I'm joking," he said. "But, since when does Alex Ward care what anybody *thinks?*"

How had she lived so many years without her friend?

He changed lanes.

A question tugged at her. A feeling of a question.

"JT?" Alex asked.

He had been around during the funeral, but peripherally. There with Emily and Jared at the funeral, and she had even brought a casserole over to Diane's house in those first confusing days. But they had never talked about it. Never had a conversation.

"Why didn't you ever ask me what happened to my dad?"

The rumors were astounding. They were everywhere in Greenview, because after Nana Kate passed, her dad had quit his nine-to-five at the bank to be a full-time musician again, announced he was going to record a new album, and had surprised and inspired a new wave of people.

And people like to talk about people doing unique and inspiring things.

Everyone wanted to know. Everyone had asked. He'd been in California recording, so nobody from Greenview had a first-hand, eye-witness story. Even Alex.

But why had JT never asked?

As the Jeep sped up on the on-ramp and into traffic, he did a double-take at her and didn't say anything. She tuned into the lyrics of the song, about parents telling kids they must be perfect, and the kids never feeling good enough.

He still hadn't answered, so she reached over the gear shift and tucked her pinky finger under the lip of his cargo shorts, resting her hand on his knee, and asked again.

"Why haven't you ever asked me what happened to my dad? Everyone in Greenview wanted to know all the details. I wasn't there, you know? I don't know what happened. But, you never asked."

JT took his hand from the gear shift, settled back in his seat with his left elbow on the door handle ledge, and took her hand with his right hand. He squeezed it. Then he pulled his sunglasses up so she could see his eyes. He had a tan line around his face, where the sun had brought out the copper of his skin around the line of white where his sunglasses had been. He said the words slowly.

"Because I know what happened."

He squeezed her hand again.

The Jeep had settled into a flow of traffic in the left lane between two semis. Charlie stood up in the back seat, readjusted his legs in a circle movement, and laid back down with a humph sound.

"I'm sorry?" Alex said.

It was not computing.

He knew *what happened?*

"How do *you* know what happened?"

She didn't mean for the tone of her voice to sound so condescending. She released his hand and rubbed her fingertips over her face, trying to clear out her eyes. Trying to see and think clearly. She didn't like this feeling.

Maybe he knew what happened the way her mom had told her Curtis had an undiagnosed heart condition, and because he wasn't home, it was normal for there to be police and detectives and interviews afterwards.

Something about his heart.

Maybe she shouldn't have asked; maybe she didn't want to talk about it.

She looked out of the passenger side window. She watched patches of trees go by, then turned back to focus on his face. His dimple was flexing off and on. He watched the road but glanced sideways at her. She propped her feet up on the dashboard and put her knees up to her chest, tucking her dress around her.

"Alex," he said. "I didn't tell you, because your mom asked me not to."

Her mom?

Her mom . . . asked him not to?

As if they were best friends or something?

She spoke slowly, choosing her words carefully.

"What did my mom ask you not to tell me?"

He signaled and slowed the Jeep, navigating them to the right lane.

"I know what happened because I was there," he said.

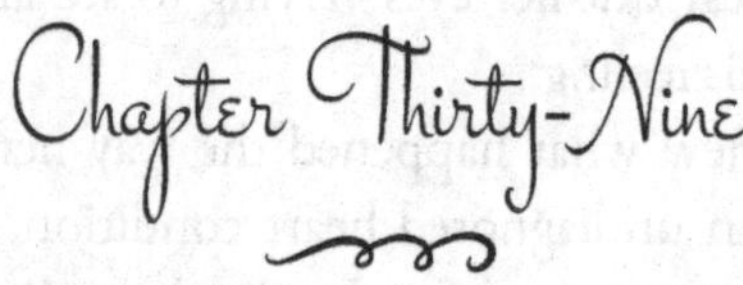

Chapter Thirty-Nine

If his words were a vehicle, then they were a semi-truck. Running right over her heart. Her whole body turned to solid lead. Anger, shock, exasperation, fear, grief, devastation. She couldn't name all these contradictory feelings if she tried.

Disbelief.

"You were where?" she asked. The meekness in her voice came out like a child's whisper.

He studied her for a moment, then focused back onto the road. The truck in front of them braked, and JT slowed down.

"I was in California with your dad. The night he passed."

No, no, no, this was too much. Too much. She couldn't even ask what happened, but what happened? What happened and JT was there? How was he there? Why was he there? What was he doing there, and what happened?

She wasn't sure he was telling the truth.

"If you were there then what the hell happened?"

"Your dad overdosed, Alex."

JT's voice cracked, like a string on a guitar breaking in the middle of a song. "An accidental overdose. His heart stopped."

If she would have believed these words, they would have pulverized her.

Thank God she didn't believe them.

"Pull over. *Please*, pull over."

She pressed her temples with her fingers. Why would he lie? He was her best friend. Why was he lying to her? They had talked for three days about being honest, and now, was he being honest? Right now? About this?

Her dad didn't drink or smoke. There was no way. Why would JT lie about this?

Undiagnosed heart condition.

"Alex, look, I—"

"No!" She cut him off. "There's no way. Why are you lying? About this!?"

"You asked. I'm being honest."

Accidental overdose.

"No, no, I can't. He didn't. Pull over, *please*. JT." Her voice shrieked out. She was on autopilot now. Reacting.

He eased the Jeep over to the shoulder, and before he even dropped it into first gear, she opened the door. JT slammed on the brakes. Charlie bumped into the back of the passenger seat.

Alex jumped out of the Jeep and fell onto the concrete shoulder. She banged her knees. Gravel pierced her palms. She didn't feel anything.

She stood up and started running.

His heart stopped.

Tall grass chafed her legs. A tree line. She was headed for a tree line. She tripped over one of her sandals, caught herself, and kept running.

Farther and faster and she ran until she reached the pine trees, and then she fell to her knees on a bed of pine needles and sticks.

She heaved and gasped.

Her hand found a rock. She clutched the rock and pounded it into the dirt. She was sobbing. Seeing stars and shapes. Her vision cloudy.

Her soul was breaking into tiny little parts, as if she weren't in her body anymore, but the pain of this knowing what she hadn't known was dissolving her.

Caught under a wave.

Accidental overdose.

She heard a noise. Charlie licked her face and then knocked her over. He stood over her, nudging her with his snout. JT's voice.

"Charlie, sit!"

She sturdied herself on her hands and knees. JT was behind her, holding her in a bear hug. She tried to twist out of his arms, but he was stronger.

The dog panted and licked at the air.

"Alex, it's okay," JT said. "I'm here. We're okay. *Breathe.*"

"I am not okay."

She sniffled a huge ball of mucus. It dripped down her face.

She was not okay. He sat on the ground and his knees wrapped around her.

She struggled one more time to get out of his grasp and then finally let herself surrender. She let the weight of her body fall back against his and used the strength she had to wipe her nose with her dress. She heaved and shook. Alex knew she was going to speak, but it was like the words were on their way, and she was not in charge of them. The words were not a part of her.

She gritted her teeth. "Honestly, JT."

She sat cradled in his knees. His breath whooshed in and out against her ear.

"Breathe, okay? I'm being honest with you, Alex."

She hugged herself by the elbows.

Undiagnosed heart condition.

Accidental overdose.

"What the hell really happened?"

His heart stopped.

Something about his heart.

The words were outside of her. Like her soul was outside of

her body because her body hurt too much. Like her brain wouldn't connect. But it sounded like her voice.

He entwined his hands with hers. "I've got you."

Alex tried to breathe.

She squeezed her eyes closed and tried so hard to listen.

She should pray, she tried to pray.

God grant me the serenity.

JT spoke slowly and calmly.

"Your dad called me up to see if I would play on one of his new tracks. His drummer had backed out at the last minute, so he needed someone who knew his style."

His voice was calming.

"I drove out to California for the weekend. We spent most of Saturday in the studio, and then we went back to his manager's place. He was throwing a party."

His words were not calming.

"A big Fourth of July thing." She wiped more snot from her nose. A breath kicked up in her chest.

"This dude was loaded," JT said. "He had this L-shaped swimming pool and four stories on the beach. There were a bunch of big names there. Guys in bands and girls everywhere."

Alex wanted to get up and run.

JT squeezed his arms around her and clasped his hands around her tighter. "A DJ was spinning down by the pool." She huffed. "We had a couple of beers and then your dad was getting ready to crash for the night. He was saying he had a headache."

Where are your feet?

Alex moved her gaze from JT's hands to the sky. Focusing on the color.

Blue. Focusing on anything. *Trees.*

She closed her eyes again. *Charlie the dog.*

"Lou came around with some high-end shots of tequila. Curtis got to feeling good, quick. Someone handed him a joint, and he looked at me and said, *It's legal here, right? We're almost finished with the track.* And he laughed. Like he was really having fun. He could be so serious in the studio."

Alex heard some more words come from her mouth. "My dad did not smoke pot. Or do drugs. Ever."

JT squeezed her closer. "I know. I only saw him drink one other time, at a New Year's Eve show."

"Once. He drank one time. At a special occasion. People drink and smoke pot all the time. And it doesn't make their heart stop."

JT sighed and nudged his chin into her neck.

"A girl came around. She was handing out pills. Before I even thought about it, your dad took one and popped it in his mouth. It was late, you know? And loud. I didn't hear what she said it was. I wouldn't even recognize her if I saw her. . .

"The party was raging. There were fireworks. We were just some, un-famous people at a famous people's party. A couple of minutes later, Curtis said he was tired, and he went to bed. We still had that track to finish. In the morning, I thought he was just sleeping off the hangover. Then it was one o'clock. Then it was two."

He paused. His knuckles tightened around her hands.

"I went in to check on him, finally, and—" JT's voice came out like a mix between a hiss and a whisper, "—and he was already gone."

His voice shook now, and he gripped her even tighter. His knuckles white.

They sat there in the grass together, him clutching her from behind.

His arms holding her close.

Charlie panting.

Traffic whizzing by in engine noises.

Something about his heart.

He sniffed in a deep breath.

"As long as I live, I will forever go back to that night, rip the tequila out of his hands, push that girl away, and make him go to bed."

But he couldn't.

She couldn't change this.

They couldn't do anything now.

"They found Fentanyl in his system. That prescription medicine they use in hospitals after surgery? They couldn't pin it down to the weed or the pill, and they couldn't find the girl." He inhaled a deep breath. "They don't know which it was." He gave her the tightest squeeze. "But that stuff slows your breathing," he said. "And too much can make your heart stop."

He was heaving now.

Undiagnosed heart condition.

"It's not your fault," she whispered. "You know it's not your fault."

They sat there for some time, under the pine trees adjacent to the Kentucky interstate. Cars and trucks sped by.

Zoom noises came and went.

JT held her from behind, and they both cried.

Alex picked a handful of grass and threw it in front of them.

Charlie whined but stayed sitting.

Finally, Alex said, "Why didn't my mom tell me? Why wouldn't anybody tell me?"

JT sighed into her ear. He released one of his arms from her and used his tee shirt to wipe his face. "Your mom asked me not to tell you, because, since your grandmother had just passed, she thought you might, self-destruct."

She swirled these thoughts around in her mind.

Self-destruct?

Alex stared at Charlie, who panted, stuck his ears up, and tilted his head.

JT's breath in her ear.

"She was afraid that if you knew the truth, you might start drinking again, or run away from everyone even farther, or worse."

"Or worse?"

"She's so proud of you, Alex, even though she never says it."

Alex did not think her mom was proud of her. She'd felt like a general screw up for most of her adult life. But this year was altogether different. She'd had to let go of everything and just try and survive. It was a miracle she hadn't started drinking again after her dad passed.

A miracle thanks to Kara and AA, and her . . . higher power.

"So that's why there were police and detectives and rumors?"

She inhaled.

"They interviewed us for hours. Me, Lou, and a handful of others at the party. It was all so devastating. Surreal. I was in shock for weeks. I wanted to call you, or to talk to you at the funeral, but your mom, she just wanted to protect you." She felt his body soften, relax around her. "The only thing I've been hanging on to, is how they said he went peacefully, in his sleep."

Peacefully, in his sleep.

She exhaled.

God, grant me the serenity, to accept the things I cannot change.

Chapter Forty

The Jeep was still running when they got back to it. Alanis Morissette's "You Learn" sang out of the speakers.

Alex's knees and legs were bleeding, and JT pulled a first aid kit out of the trunk, wiped away the blood, and applied some antibacterial gel and some bandages on the larger gashes.

She propped herself up by clutching his shoulder. Her wounds stung now.

JT climbed back into the driver's seat, and they headed north again. They drove in silence for a while, listened to "Head Over Feet," and the rest of the Alanis CD.

After the secret track, JT ejected the disc and handed it to Alex. She flipped through the CD book, but she couldn't make a choice.

The waves of grief had her under for now.

She flayed the book open on her lap and said, "Will you choose something? Something happy?"

He thumbed the pages while he kept his eyes on the road, glancing back and forth as if he knew where all of the CD's were situated. He paused on Counting Crows' *August and Everything After* but then turned to Eve Six.

He slid the CD in, played the "Open Road Song" track, and then ejected it and put in Blink 182.

"What's My Age Again" poured out over the speakers, but neither of them spoke or sang along. When that was over, he put in the Green Day *Dookie* CD, "When I Come Around." She loved this one; she used to practice it on her dad's drum set.

After Green Day he chose Dave Matthews Band, *Live at Red Rocks*. She stared out of the window and let Dave Matthews sing to her.

It was 5 p.m. when they passed the city limit sign that read Greenview Falls Exempted Village. What did that even mean?

Before they walked inside Diane's house, JT turned off the ignition and put his hand on her knee. Her legs were all battered up.

He turned to her, lifted his sunglasses and said, "For what it's worth, it was fun being your vacation boyfriend for a day."

His eyes were still red and puffy, and she imagined hers were, too. He kissed her swiftly, but she pulled his chin back into hers, and kissed him harder, trying to hold on to the one thing good that had happened this week.

He pulled back and put his forehead against hers. "You made it through the Fourth of July."

She hung onto his eyes. The yellow flecks. "Thanks to you."

As they unloaded Alex's bag, Charlie bounced up and down, excited to be out of the car. JT led him out back to tie him up against the deck, and Alex noticed Mrs. Stephens across the street in her flowerbed.

Had she seen JT kiss her? She thought about it briefly, but then she didn't have the energy to care.

When she opened the front door, Aunt Skylar was standing there to greet her.

"Oh, Dear Alex," she said and hugged her. She smelled like Nag Champa incense. "I was hoping to see you." She held Alex by the arms and studied her face, then her legs. "Are you okay? You're all cut up!"

"I was running earlier, and I fell."

"Oh my." Aunt Skylar was wearing a colorful flowing dress, and her purple-red hair was tied in two long braids. The edges of her eyes crinkled up, with some smiling lines on her nose to boot. Wrinkles that made her look as if she had spent most of her life smiling.

"How are *you*?" Alex asked.

"I'm okay," she said. "We made it through." She pulled Alex into another hug. "Your mom told me you went to the lake with JT and his friends."

"Yeah," Alex said, and set her bag down by the front door. "Serenity Lake."

"How was that?" Aunt Skylar's eyes were glowing now.

"It was fun, mostly. I had a dream about Dad."

Skylar was an elementary school art teacher and had this gift of making you feel like you were the most important person in the world, no matter what you were doing or saying.

"A visitation?"

JT had used the word visitation. "I guess?"

Drew and Diane emerged from the kitchen at the same time JT opened the sliding glass door and came in.

"Hey, Sis," Drew said. "Welcome home." He had a sandwich in his hand. Diane wiped her hands on her apron and pulled Alex into a hug.

She smelled her mom's familiar lotion.

"I'm making pot pie for dinner," Diane said. "JT, can you stay?"

"I wish I could. I, we, actually came home early because I have some stuff I need to take care of."

"Tell us about your *dream*," Drew said, and took a bite.

Alex sat down in her mom's favorite chair.

"I didn't know I was dreaming, but I walked out onto the balcony, and he was sitting there in his blue shirt." She made a circle close to her heart with one finger. "With the compass on his chest. I don't remember it all now, but he said he was okay, and that I should stop feeling so guilty for all my choices." She laughed at herself, uneasily, and continued. "He said I needed to stop being so afraid of what everybody thinks, and that I should start focusing on what I really want. My intentions . . ." her voice trailed off.

She had forgotten about the last part until right now. "And he said Nana Kate said, 'Hi.'" She remembered the splinter in her toe, but she didn't mention that part.

It had been a whirlwind of a week.

"I had a dream about him this week, too," Skylar said. "He was just hugging me really tightly, and I woke up feeling hopeful." Skylar wiped at her own eyes. "You know, he was a big pain in the ass, but I didn't know it was humanly possible to miss somebody so much."

Drew and JT were quiet. Diane said, "I'm glad he came to visit you two."

"I better get going," JT said to Alex. "I wish I could stay longer, but I can't."

"It's okay," she said. "I'll walk you out."

He said his goodbyes to Alex's family, and they walked out the sliding glass door to Charlie. Before they got back out to the front with Mrs. Stephens and everybody else's prying eyes, Alex wanted to kiss him one more time.

She put her hands on his waist and was looking for the words to thank him.

To say goodbye again.

She felt her eyes welling up. Maybe next year she'd be able to stop crying.

"What happens next?" Alex asked. "With us?"

He pulled her in tightly to him, and she let his solid body get as close to hers as it could. He just held her there, JT, solid and strong, stable and kind.

"I don't know. We'll figure it out." She kissed him then, a long, soft, and slow kiss that turned into something bigger and deeper. A kiss that seemed like the stuff of the movies.

Alex lost herself for a minute in a free fall of emotions. Then she finally pulled away and blushed. JT's one dimple showed.

"You're supposed to stay single for a year, right?"

She rolled her eyes. "I guess so."

"Well, I've got some stuff I need to take care of, I guess . . . so what if we meet back here in a year? And ride down to Serenity Lake together?" He smirked. She could tell a joke was coming. "Me and my friends from college meet there every year at Coach's lake house. I think you'll like them. They have Jet Skis."

Alex smiled. He hugged her one more time. She relished the comfort of his body against hers, the way she felt so safe and protected in his arms. She was going to miss this.

She was going to miss her best friend.

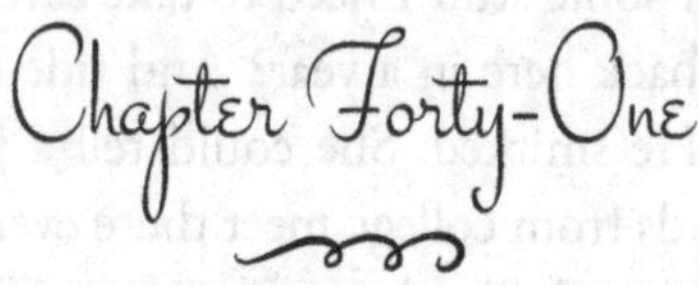

Chapter Forty-One

Alex didn't know how to get back to her regular life. Drew and Diane were in the kitchen laughing at one of Skylar's stories about school, and Alex felt like a zombie again. What was she going to do next? She had to start thinking about going back to Florida, about going back to work. She needed to call Kara.

She took her phone down to the basement. It was chilly down here; she hated being cold in the summer. She pulled a throw blanket from a chair and wrapped it around her shoulders. There were new text messages, but she ignored them. The L-shaped couch was worn-in and inviting, but instead Alex paced.

Kara answered on the second ring.

"How's it going?" she asked. Alex started to cry again. "You okay?"

Kara had been this strange person Alex didn't even know at first, but she'd trusted her because she'd wanted to quit drinking so bad that she would do anything to accomplish it, including telling this new stranger all her personal business. Alex had been desperate.

Kara wasn't a stranger now. She had become one of Alex's best friends.

When the words finally came, Alex managed to spit them out.

"JT told me what happened to my dad." Her voice creaked and croaked. Kara had heard Alex cry before, so it wasn't something new. What Alex loved about Kara was that she had never used those awful words, *"What happened?"*

"Umm-hmm," she said. "It sounds like it was tough news."

"JT was there. There was . . . tequila, weed . . . some kind of pill . . . laced . . . fentanyl . . . made his heart . . . " Another hiss escaped her. "JT was the one who found him."

"Awe, Alex, I'm so sorry," she said. "I didn't think your dad even drank."

Alex settled into a slow cry. Her body shook less, and the words came clearer.

"He didn't. He was at a party, and he had a headache."

This was the part where she thought Kara might throw some kind of 'program' at her, refer her to a chapter in the Big Book, or tell her to write something down and pray about it. But she didn't.

"He knew that you loved him. And he loved you. The best you can do is keep going, one day at a time." Kara held some space in silence over the phone for Alex to process her feelings. "Try and honor his memory with how you live."

Kara was good at uncomfortable silences.

"Did you make any amends this week?"

Amends.

"I um, didn't," Alex said. "Except for JT. I apologized to JT."

"Good. How did it go?"

"He didn't even flinch. It was like all this guilt I was hanging on to wasn't even on his radar as something that bothered him . . . like he didn't even care about it."

"See?" Kara laughed. "We think amends are for other people, but they're really for us. You still have your list?"

"Yeah." Alex had this long list of names on a piece of notebook paper with notes about how she had acted in the past, and then how she might be able to apologize for it all.

"You're going through a lot this week but see if you can cross any more of those off of the list." Her voice sounded sing-song-y. "You'll feel better."

Alex felt calmer after they hung up. She laid on the couch with her feet hanging over the arm and stared at the ceiling. A ray of sunlight beamed down through a high window, and she could see a small chunk of turquoise sky.

How should she honor his memory with how she lived? She remembered the dream again where he was telling her to forgive herself and to focus on what she truly wanted.

What did she want, though? She wanted a million things, but mostly to be able to live in peace.

Her phone rang. *Randy* showed up on the screen. She let the call go to voicemail and blocked his number.

She rubbed her eyes. Underneath, the skin was raw and tender.

She smelled an incense smell before she realized Aunt Skylar had come downstairs.

"Hey," she said. "Just wanted to check on you."

"Thanks. I just got off of the phone with my sponsor."

"Your sponsor?" They'd never talked about recovery before. Alex didn't talk about it much, but she knew her mom had probably at least told the family that she had quit drinking and was going to meetings.

"AA. Helped me quit drinking."

She sat down next to Alex's legs on the arm of the couch. "I'm so proud of you!" A large, purple stone dangled from a silver chain on her neck.

"Thanks. I miss my dad. And Nana Kate, too." She realized that Skylar must equally miss her mom and her brother.

If Alex felt like a piece of her heart was missing, then her aunt must feel like that, too.

"How are you?" Alex asked. "Last year was kind of a lot."

Skylar patted her on the knee. "It was. I'm glad your mom let me stay here for the week. It's weird being an orphan."

"An orphan?"

"I have this picture," Skylar reached into her dress pocket and pulled out a colorful pouch with a moon embroidered on the side. She pulled out a polaroid of two adults and two kids. "This is my nuclear family—Nana Kate, your grandpa, Stan, and your dad." Curtis wore a Star Trek tee shirt and that ornery grin from ear to ear. The family of four was staged in front of a big oak tree with a rope swing hanging from it. Nana Kate sat on the swing with a young Skylar on her lap. "This was when we lived out in Middle Falls." Alex studied the tree, their faces, and how they all looked happy and free. "I'm the only one left." She frowned.

Alex took this in. What would it be like if something happened to Drew and Diane? Many times, she had felt alone in the world, but she always had someone to call. She still had her mom and her brother.

"I'm glad I have my job," Skylar said. "And my students."

"I bet your students love you."

"Without them, this year I probably would have lost my marbles." Alex handed the photo back to her. Skylar tucked it into the pouch.

"I'm actually teaching, too."

"Your mom told me! How's it going?"

"It's hard, but it's fun. I'll be kind of glad when this semester is over, though. It's a lot of work."

"It is," Skylar said. "But you're making a difference. What's next after that? You ever think about moving back home?"

Alex didn't know what she was going to do next, really, except for go back to her life in Florida, and her job teaching, and her job waiting tables.

Break up with Randy for good, just in case he hadn't gotten the memo. She never thought of moving back to Greenview. She'd rather move to the other side of the country. Maybe to Washington State.

"Not really. I kind of ruined my reputation here in my twenties." And maybe again this week.

Skylar laughed then, and a sparkle rose up from deep in her

eyes. "You ruined your reputation in your twenties? In Green-view? That was fifteen years ago." She laughed again. "I mean, how do you think that? Why do you think that?"

"I dunno," Alex said. She sat up and adjusted her sundress around her knees. "This is a small town. People talk. I dropped out of college and had that one wild summer; I heard people talking. Dad sat me down one time and gave me a lecture and told me that people kept asking him if I was sober. They thought I turned into a big druggie or something."

"Oh. I remember that summer. Your mom *was* disappointed about you dropping out of college. But school changes people, Alex. I bet you learned so many things about the world you wouldn't have ever learned in Greenview."

"I did." She had wanted to take a year off after she graduated, to figure out what she wanted to do, but Diane made her go to college since she had some scholarships. She remembered her senior year as being so busy, she just wanted to rest. Or to party with her high school friends. She would have probably screwed up if she had stayed home, too.

Going to college was a gift. She wasn't mad at Diane. But it completely broke her naive worldview. Shattered it. The things she thought she knew about race, religion, politics, marriage, and love. So many things came to light and contradicted all the other things she'd learned up until then. Including that the world was good and kind. That there were happily ever afters.

"And now, maybe looking back on it, I was kind of devastated at the world, and so I hid from it. Just ducked into bars. And men . . . "

She'd gotten so adept at numbing her emotions, that she had flitted from relationship to relationship looking for some kind of self-love that she wouldn't have been able to get from the world. She thought when she found the right guy, the rest of her life would fall into place.

It had been a lot of trial and error, mostly error.

Her life had not fallen into place.

She had finally, after working through all the twelve steps with Kara, replaced her obsession with men with whatever kind of thread of a higher power she'd been able to understand. Which was something. Though she hadn't perfected it yet.

"Weren't you just driving around smoking with your friends? That's normal teenage stuff. People grow out of that, and people grow up."

She and her friends had spent that one summer driving to bookstores and record stores. The guys were always looking for elusive CDs from underground bands they liked. She was always looking for the next good book. Listening to music, going to concerts, and laughing. It wasn't like they were shooting heroin and living in a trap house. But if you asked anybody in Greenview back then, the rumors were that she'd become strung out.

The valedictorian voted most likely to succeed, turned into an addict and a failure.

That's what she imagined anyway. Kara always told her to watch out for her catastrophizing . . . making small things seem like huge disasters.

Her brain really could go wild with fear.

The truth was, she'd looked around to the adults in her world and what they were doing, and none of them seemed particularly happy. So, she had started living day to day, adventure to adventure. If going to the bookstore and the music stores were adventures.

It *had* been fun. She had wanted to make her own way for herself. She had wanted to do something different with her life. Coming of age for her, though, had been bumpy. And then Nine-Eleven had happened. Which changed everything, again, especially her view of the world.

Being in recovery rooms had taught her there was no shame in any of it. Alcohol, opioids, heroin . . . all of them could be gravely dangerous, and almost impossible to quit without support. She was so grateful for recovery rooms.

"Oh, honey," Skylar said. "You're so hard on yourself. Everybody goes through a coming-of-age learning process. Your brain wasn't even developed yet. Give yourself some slack. It takes a while to figure out adulthood. Heck, I'm almost fifty, and I'm still figuring it out." She smoothed one braid back behind her ears and then took Alex's hair and began to braid it. "Your Nana Kate was wild in her twenties. You get it honestly; it's in your blood."

"Nana Kate was wild in her twenties?"

"Oh, yeah." Skylar's eyes shined with fondness. "When she passed, your dad and I found these letters to this musician who lived in Florida . . . Marco Del Rio. Your grandmother fell in love with him at first sight and spent quite a bit of time trying to resist him. Grandma and Grandpa didn't approve, of course. But she had moved to the beach against her mother's wishes, and back then in the 1960s, it was uncommon for a woman to set out on her own. She could hardly rent an apartment, and you know, women couldn't get any credit, credit cards or car loans or anything. It was really brave of her."

"Wait," Alex said. "Nana Kate lived in Florida? How did I not know that?"

Skylar's eyes deepened into a kind of wild excitement. "She never talked about it. Your dad and I didn't even know until she passed. We found the letters in her keepsake trunk. Your dad," she smiled, "made me open them. I felt like it was too personal. But the letters were full of all this love and desire and happiness. She had a hot and heavy couple of years with this guy, Marco, and this really interesting group of friends who were like a cross between beat poets and hippies. I went to see him. I found him at this retirement home. He was old, but as lovely as the letters described. I gave the letters to him, since they were meant for him in the first place. But yes, Nana Kate lived not too far away from where you live now. Just for a couple of years, and then she moved home when the war started heating up."

She wondered why Nana Kate never told her, or any of them. She thought they were close. "Vietnam?"

Skylar nodded. "It was a turbulent time. The Civil Rights

Movement, political assassinations. Protests. There were lots of unknowns, and a lot of people were upset their friends and brothers were getting drafted, and some of them weren't coming home. The country was divided."

"Why didn't Nana Kate ever talk about it?"

"I'm not sure," Skylar said, "except she might have thought it was disrespectful to talk about it in front of Dad? This time in her life that was fun and free and wild? Her first love. The letters were memories, and they were kind of steamy."

"So, this is why Nana Kate always encouraged me, and never gave me a hard time even though I was screwing up?"

"Honey," Skylar said and grabbed her hand. "You were *not* screwing up. You were discovering who you are and looking for your place in the world. You're here. You're okay. You are a capable, lovable, *imperfect* child of God. Like all of us. A lot of people look up to you."

"Umm," Alex said. "Who looks up to me? People don't look up to me."

Skylar laughed. "You think there aren't a handful of your peers who wish they would have been able to go to school, to move to a new state, and to be single? I mean, some of your friends from high school might be happy, but some of them might be stuck in jobs they hate with husbands who are mean, and they might wonder what it would be like to go out on their own and try and do something different with their lives." She finished one of Alex's braids and started on the other. "I'm not speaking for anyone, but a ton of women would be afraid to do the very things that you have absolutely been compelled to do—or they wouldn't have been able to figure out how to pay for it." Alex noted that she had gone into plenty of debt in order to pay for it, although her mom and dad had always bailed her out when she got into a bind. "You've got to give yourself some credit for having the courage to really live *authentically*. You take chances, Alex. Not everybody is brave enough to live authentically."

Alex tried to see herself this way. As brave, as independent.

What made her so hard on herself? What made her always see her flaws and her failures instead of her positive attributes and her wins?

She *had* accomplished some things. She had made a kind of a way for herself, even though she'd made mistakes.

"Your dad was really hard on himself," Skylar said. "I didn't really see it until this year, after he passed. Even though he'd put the band back together and was recording a new album, some of those final songs were really sad, and now when I listen to the lyrics, I see him in a different light. He really struggled sometimes, as humans do. But he also beat himself up for things out of his control. Our dad, your grandfather, was not a happy man all the time. And I think maybe some of it is genetic. The sadness, I mean. I don't really know, though. It might be something to watch out for. Life gets low for all of us sometimes, shakes us up. But then it evens itself back again. We've just got to keep going and doing our best."

One day at a time.

Aunt Skylar's eyes misted over. "Your Nana Kate was really in love with that musician in the sixties. I think you're actually named after him."

"Named after him?"

Skylar laughed. "Your dad never told you that?"

"No. My dad did not tell me that."

"Your dad was really young for having children at that time. He and your mom decided not to get married, which caused a stir among the neighbors. But Nana Kate was there for every step of it. She hardly left your dad's side, and then when your mom couldn't decide on a name, Nana Kate suggested *Alexandra*. Your mom liked it right away sand your dad went along with it, because he wanted you to be a boy." She laughed. "He was glad he could call you *Alex*. Nana Kate never told us about her first love, but his full name was Marco Alejandro Riviera Del Rio. Which is a long way to say, I think your grandma chose your name."

How did she not know all of this?

"Here," Skylar said. She reached around her neck and unclasped the silver chain around her neck. "This is an amethyst." Skylar rolled the purple stone around in her hands, held it to her heart and then handed it to Alex. "It's an intuitive stone, protective." Alex cradled the stone in her hand, studying the violet and white patterns at the top. It was almost shaped like a pyramid, but it had been wrapped in bright silver wire. "It was Nana Kate's." Skylar helped Alex secure it around her neck. "It might make you have interesting dreams. Or maybe you'll have another visitation."

Diane came downstairs. "Hey girls, the pot pie is ready. Can I get you something to drink?" Diane touched Alex on the arm. "Are you okay, honey?"

"Mom," Alex said. "How did I get my name?"

"Your Nana Kate came up with it," Diane said and smiled. "I knew it was perfect as soon as I held you in my arms."

Diane's pot pie was made with gluten-free crust and tasted every bit like the real thing. The four of them sat around the table—Drew, Diane, Skylar, and Alex.

Diane started to make small talk by bringing up something from church, but Alex couldn't keep her emotions in.

"JT told me what happened to Dad," she blurted out. Drew's fork clinked on his plate, and he took a gulp of his lemonade. Alex started to cry again; she was getting so used to it, she just talked right through it. "I understand why you didn't tell me."

"Oh, Alex. I'm sorry," Diane said. "We didn't want to you to . . . I was afraid you'd start drinking again. Or run off somewhere. You've been doing so well with your recovery."

"I'm sorry," Alex sobbed. "For all that stuff I did when I was drinking and all of the awful things I said, and all of those times that I worried you and didn't come home and wasn't myself . . . I was young and dumb, and I didn't understand how dangerous it all was, or how I could have maybe ended up like Dad . . . " she trailed off. "I just didn't know," and again the tears came so hard she couldn't speak for a minute.

She looked at Drew's face, and he looked proud. Satisfied, almost. Aunt Skylar reached across the table and took her hand.

"It's okay, honey," she said. "It's all in the past now."

Diane got up from the table, walked around, and hugged Alex from behind.

"I don't know what I would do if something happened to one of you kids," she said. "The most important thing I have ever done was give birth to the both of you. I wasn't a perfect mom. I was so young when you were born. But I've done my best, and I am *so proud* of you." She turned Alex's head toward her and cradled it in her hands. "I forgive you, Alex. There is nothing in the world that you could do to make me stop loving you. You've handled this last year better than I could have imagined, and I don't know how you've done it. I am in awe of the woman you have become."

Alex and Diane both cried now. Drew picked up his fork and started eating again, nodding as if he were amused.

Skylar quietly said, "Amen," got up from the table, and returned with a box of tissues. Alex and Diane wiped their eyes and their noses, before the four of them settled back into a silence, sat back in their chairs, and went back to eating.

"It's really hard to believe sometimes," Aunt Skylar said. "But I think we are always, always, exactly where we are meant to be."

After they ate in comfortable silence for a while, Drew asked, "You going back to Florida?"

Chapter Forty-Two

She'd booked a red-eye flight to go home. As Alex and Drew were loading into the truck the next evening, a Pathfinder showed up and parked on the street next to their mailbox. Black with tinted windows. Mrs. Stephens sat across the street on her front porch and waved. The sun was slipping under the horizon, covered by some purple-tinted clouds.

"Who's this?" Drew waved back, clicking the button on his key ring to unlock the doors of his pickup.

"No idea," Alex said. "She hoped it were JT coming to see her off, but she'd never seen this car.

The engine stopped, and Gracie emerged.

Gracie was the last person Alex expected to see. She dropped her backpack into the passenger side of the minivan and closed the door.

"Hey." She approached, wearing a long green dress and looking classier, and less slutty-soccer mom.

Alex berated herself for her judgy thought. "Hey, Gracie."

The dress looked good against her red hair. Alex wore her black yoga pants for the airport, and her short black airport dress. Trying to look nice, and comfortable.

"*Grace*," she said. "I go by *Grace* now. Anyway, I'm sorry to just roll up on you like this." Gracie tucked her hands in the pockets of her dress and lowered her head.

Grace.

"No problem," Alex said. "I like your dress." What did she want? Alex hoped she didn't want to ask her any more questions about her dad. Greenview and its nosy neighbors. "We're on our way to the airport. I'm headed back to the beach tonight."

"Hey, Drew, good to see you." Grace sent a reluctant smile to him. "Could we have a minute alone?"

This was strange.

"Yeah, sure. I'll just be right inside." Drew shot a look over to Alex, as if he were telling her to play nice.

"I'm sorry I just ran away from you the other day," Alex said. "I guess I'm still not good at answering questions about my father. I don't really want to talk about it, actually."

Recovery was also teaching her to have better boundaries.

"No, no." Grace had stopped about three feet away from Alex, faced her openly, and moved her hands as she talked. "I'm sorry I asked that question. I know it's hard to talk about. Grief is such an asshole of a thing."

Alex lowered her defenses. "It *is* an asshole of a thing." She chuckled.

Grace smiled, then her face changed to concern. "I don't really know how to do this, but I'm in a program, and my sponsor is helping me to . . . umm . . . apologize to people?"

She was the last person Alex expected to see, and this was the last thing she expected to come out of her mouth.

Alex's eyes widened. "I'm in a program, too."

"You are!?" Grace's face brightened.

"Yeah, AA!" Alex said.

"Same!" Grace said. "God, it was so hard to quit drinking, right? So, umm, *thank God* you understand. I'm making amends. And you're at the top of my list."

"It was," Alex said. "It is. The top of your list?" Grace had been awful in high school, but it was mostly guys and family members at the top of Alex's list.

Grace blurted out the words. "I'm sorry I was mean to you in high school. I'm sorry for being a self-righteous, name-calling bitch. In the steps," she huffed a breath, "I realized I was jealous of you. And jealous of you and JT. It was *pride*."

Alex's heart softened.

She understood. But the last part?

"Jealous of me and JT?"

"Yeah." She kicked at a rock with the tip of her sandal. "I had a crush on him in high school."

"You had a crush on geeky JT?" She felt like chuckling again, but she didn't want to ruin the moment by being rude. "I didn't know you even knew who he was."

"He sat next to me in algebra," she said. "He's so funny! We used to get in trouble all the time for laughing. But when you were around, he would never even look at me."

Wow, Alex thought. But she didn't say it out loud. She didn't say anything.

"And those eyes." She stared off at the sunset. "And the way he used to practice drums by padding his hands on the desk?"

"Yeah," Alex said. "He's got great eyes."

But all this information was perplexing.

"Anyway." She looked Alex. "I hope you'll accept my apology. I was immature and didn't know how to handle jealousy, or my emotions, and I turned on you and tried to tear you down. I knew you were going places, and I resented you for all the things you had going for you."

A sorrowful feeling wrapped around Alex. Forgiveness and almost pity, but more like, humility.

Sadness that their friendship had ended.

"Then that time you made fun of my hair," Grace continued. "I never forgave you for that, but now, I do. I get it."

Alex didn't remember this at all. "I made fun of your hair?"

"Sixth grade. The year I cut my own bangs. I came to school, and you said, *'Nice haircut,'* in English class, and everybody, even Mr. Gardner, laughed."

"Oh, gosh. I'm so sorry. I don't even remember that."

"That was just a hard day for me," she said. "My mom had been on a tequila tear, and that morning she didn't wake up when it was time to take me to school. I had to walk, and it was snowing, and I ended up being late. She hadn't bought us any winter boots, so my feet were freezing when I got there. I probably took it more personally than I should have."

Alex stepped toward her hugged her. She smelled like lilies and musk. "I'm *so* sorry." Alex held her until it seemed like the right time to part. "I didn't know you were going through all that then. It was an awful thing for me to say."

"It's okay. I didn't talk about it much. My parents and stuff."

"Is there anything else I should apologize for?" This was a question Alex was supposed to ask during amends.

"I mean, there was that one time you asked me if I was trying to gain weight on purpose." Grace's face saddened again.

"Oh, *God.* I didn't say that did I?" Alex would remember that, wouldn't she? To Alex, making fun of someone's weight was the *lowest* of the low.

"Ninth grade biology," she said.

"I'm so sorry, Grace! I am such a horrible person!"

"You're not. We were kids. We were all such good friends when we were young, and then high school got so weird."

"It did get so weird. But you always had the nicest clothes," Alex said as an afterthought. "Gap and American Eagle . . . I was so jealous that your mom would buy you Abercrombie and Fitch. My mom would never—"

"Goodwill." Grace blushed. "My mom took us to thrift stores on the rich side of Middle Falls."

"I had no idea." They had been so close as young people. "That must have been so hard for you. We were good friends when we were kids. We laughed a lot together." Alex smiled gently, hoping her old friend would forgive her.

Grace's face lit up. "Remember New Kids on the Block?"

They both smiled and said, "Danny, Donnie, Joe, Jon, and *Jordan!*"

"Your sleeping bag! And Boyz II Men!" The joy of them singing along to the radio using their hairbrushes as microphones brought up the scent of Aussie hairspray and lots of giggles. Gracie had even choreographed her own dances for them.

"We did have a lot of fun together." She flipped her hair. "We don't have to be best friends again, or anything, but I'd like to keep in touch over social media or something."

Grace had sent her a request. Lots of people had sent Alex requests after her dad died, and she had ignored them all.

"I'm not really on social media much," Alex said. "But if you're ever in Florida, I could show you around."

"I've never been to Florida."

Alex reached out for her phone. "Here. Put your number in. I live closest to Tampa International Airport."

"Cool," she said. "Thanks."

"Yeah," Alex said. "The coolest part is driving over the Howard Franklin Bridge. It's like driving through an ocean-sky portal." Grace's face puzzled. "I'll show you," Alex said. "It's best to visit in January."

"Deal." Her shoulders had straightened, and her eyes were brighter. "We have a class reunion every year in June." Alex had gotten the invitations in the past. Reuniting with her high school class after all this time did *not* sound fun. "Everyone has grown up and changed," she said. "I mean, some things are the same. We'd love to see you there next year."

Alex gave it some thought. "Maybe I'll try and come home next year." Maybe Greenview wasn't as awful as she'd made it out to be in her head.

She made a mental note to tell Tiphanee Banks about this conversation the next time she saw her. After she went to college on her softball scholarship, of course.

"Plus, I could use a sober friend," Grace said.

They hugged one more time.

"I better go and catch my flight. Thank you for stopping by, Grace."

"Friends?" She held up her pinky finger for a pinky-swear, like they did in grade school.

Alex reached out her pinky and clutched onto Grace's.

"Friends."

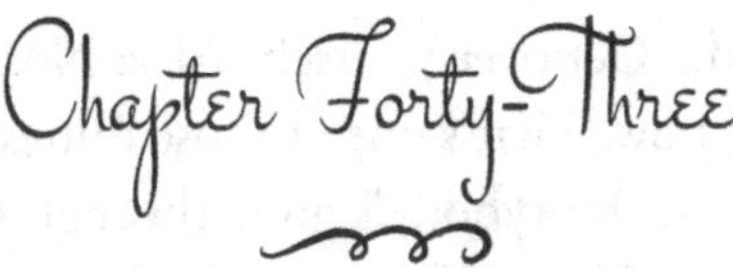

Chapter Forty-Three

"What was that about?" Drew asked, after they settled into the truck and started driving.

"She came to apologize to me for being such a bitch in high school," Alex said. "I guess I was kind of a bitch, too."

Tom Petty's "Mary Jane's Last Dance" played over the radio. Even in this big truck, Drew's presence seemed large.

"Everyone was kind-of-a-bitch in high school," he said. "It's part of growing up."

The air conditioning hissed out of the dashboard.

"It's weird how we all spent eighteen years together, and then just all lost touch so easily," Alex said.

"You're the one who ran away," Drew said.

Alex rolled her eyes, his same old lecture. "She invited me to one of those class reunions. You ever go to those things?"

"I go every year," he said.

"You go to your high school reunion every year?"

"It's good to catch up with the guys. Most everyone is married and settled down, but we get to be young and immature for a few hours. Tell funny stories at laugh at our old selves. You don't go to yours?"

"I've never been," Alex said.

"They have mailing lists," he said.

"I'm on the mailing lists. I just don't go. Why would I go? What would I even talk to people about? My life is so different than everybody else's now. I did so many stupid things since then. Well, and I'm so, different."

Drew laughed. "Get over yourself, Alex. Nobody was perfect in high school, or now. That's one of those things Dad was always writing songs about. Everybody's gone through something hard, done something stupid they thought was unforgivable, or treated someone like crap and didn't know how to apologize for it. Everybody we went to school with has grown and changed. But in a way, everybody's the same. Does that make sense?"

She considered this.

He continued, "But you sack up and face it. You gotta have the balls to look at your past and your friends and show up for them. Greenview was the best place to grow up in the world. Hometown people will always have your back."

She didn't feel like Greenview people always had her back. She felt disbanded, abandoned, forgotten sometimes. Under the microscope others. Like her mom's church friends looked at her some type of way—like they were disappointed in her.

"Remember Friday night football games?" He smiled. "The whole town would be there, and right before the game started, there was this energy. This excitement. We were all there together for the same reason."

She did remember. Drew uniformed up in his football gear, and Alex on the sidelines playing cadences with JT and the band. It made her smile to think about it. The crowd cheering as the fight song started and the team breaking through the cheerleaders' good luck sign and onto the field. There was an energy to it, an electrical excitement. There weren't adequate words to describe the feeling.

"That *was* fun," she said. "I don't know. I guess I feel kind of embarrassed, for how I acted when I first got out on my own. I made some really bad choices, and I know people around town were talking. Mom's church friends . . . "

"You're so self-centered," Drew said fondly. "You got that from dad." His voice deepened. "Nobody cares what you did in your twenties, and nobody cares what you're doing now. Unless you show up and share it with them. They're not thinking about you and all of your mistakes and adventures and shortcomings. They're thinking about themselves."

Sometimes he did sound wise. "Mom's church friends pray for us every Sunday. And probably through the week, too. If you don't think that's something that matters, then you're really on a high horse and somebody needs to knock you off of it."

This could be true. Could this be true? Kara always said this thing about *selfish, self-centered,* and *insecure.* There was something about it in the Big Book.

It did really matter, she knew.

Prayers really did matter.

"I just don't know what I have in common with anybody anymore," Alex said. "I mean, it's been so long."

Drew reached over and put his hand on her shoulder.

"Look," he said. "You remember how many people came to Dad's funeral?"

"Vaguely," she said. "It seemed like a lot."

"The whole town came out," he said. "And you know why they came?"

"Because they all thought that Dad was some kind of rock-star saint?"

Because they all wanted to be a part of the rock star drama?

Because they all wanted to know what happened?

He shook his head at her. "They came because they loved him. And they love us. And that's what Greenview does. They show up for people." He squeezed her shoulder and turned the air conditioning down. "How many people reached out to you this year? From home?"

"I don't know," Alex said. "All of them. There were so many girls, though." She meant to say the last part to herself.

Drew stared at her, then back at the road.

"There were so many girls, because Dad was a one-of-a-kind dude. Dad cut through all the bullshit. When he asked you *how you were doing,* he really wanted to know how you were doing. In your life. In your *journey* of life. People felt comfortable around him, Alex. That they could tell him the God damn truth about themselves—without being afraid he would judge them. He was like that with everybody. Guys *and* girls." He scratched his face. "How many people did you respond to? Who reached out?"

"I don't know," Alex said. "Some of them."

Not very many of them.

She hadn't known what to say.

Some of them she didn't even know.

"You think that was easy for people? To track you down and tell you that they gave a shit about us and our family? They reached out because Greenview is a village, in the truest sense of the word. I don't go to church anymore, but I know there's a God. When they said we were in their prayers, they meant it." He turned onto the airport access road. "I love you, Sis," he said. "I'm struggling, too. But sometimes you need a reality check."

She stayed quiet as they wound around the airport entrance, through parking lots, and to the terminal.

"What about you and JT?" he asked, as he put the truck in park. He turned down the radio.

"What *about* me and JT?" She lifted her backpack over one shoulder, opened the door and got out.

He came around to her side of the truck. "JT's our hometown hero. He's got a heart bigger than Ohio, and he's always had your six. From the outside looking in, it's like he was put on earth just for you . . . since we were kids. The only time I've seen you smile this year is when he was in the room. What's-her-name just did you a huge favor, you know. Might want to take a look at that."

"I am supposed to stay single for a year," she said. "My sponsor, or whatever, suggested it to me." She hugged him. His giant arms squeezed her tight.

"Good luck with that," he said and laughed.

This was the part where, in the past, she would have defended herself, made some kind of excuse for her bad behavior, justified that her actions, however bad, were not entirely her fault. But now she stood still. Felt all of these feelings. Sat with the truth of her actions. Digested them. Processed his words. Without running.

"You mad at Mom?" he asked. "For not telling you?"

"No," Alex said. "I get it." She adjusted her bag. It was heavier, somehow.

"You mad at me?"

"No, I'm not mad at you." She was mad at the world, that she could run wild and drink hard and try this and try that, but their dad—who never drank or smoked—had one night where he let go of all of his own rules for a little fun and . . . paid the ultimate price.

Tears brimmed beneath her eyes.

"It could have been *me*, you know? It should have been *me*."

"Alex!" He hugged her with his whole being. She heard his voice cracking. "Life just sucks sometimes. I wish there were some profound way to say it, but there isn't. It just sucks."

They cried there together, cars stopping, travelers getting out with their suitcases, cars moving on.

"Go catch your flight," he finally said, and tapped her on the arm. "Text me when you land."

She felt so small as she walked through the narrow hallways of the airport, this sense of humility spreading inside of her. When she got to the gate, she pulled out her phone and went through her messages.

She began to answer them one by one. Each person who had taken the time and gone out on a limb to reach out to her during the hardest year of her life.

"Hi," she wrote. "Thank you for thinking of me and my family. Your prayers have really mattered to all of us . . ."

Chapter Forty-Four

It had been easy to find friends at the beach, as if she'd already belonged there. There was something specific in the spirit of someone who moved to Florida from some other place, and that something specific recognized itself in others.

The desire to live at a different pace. The desire to leave the rat race somewhere else; the desire to live amidst the ocean and the sky, and the general overwhelming desire to be free.

Alex got off the plane after an uneventful flight. When she drove over the bridge, she felt like the indigo water was pulling all the negativity from her body and washing it all away. Like any form of bad energy would dissolve into the salty wind. Like she was back where she was meant to be.

Everything on the outside of her apartment was just as she'd left it. Two tiki statues on either side of the door, the placard that read, *Life's a Beach.* Her white mailbox shaped like a fish. When she opened the door, though, she was stunned.

Her couch.

It was torn up. Covered with spray paint? She had to settle herself before she could take in the scene. Scribbled words. The word *'slut'* rang out in her mind. She moved her eyes to the spare key on the coffee table. *Randy.*

The word hurt her more than she wanted. It cut into her soul, as if it had been painted on her forehead instead of her couch. *Slut.* She stared at it in disbelief.

She snapped a photo of it with her phone and sent it to Kara. A text came back almost immediately. "That's what he meant about *'sorry about the couch?'* Break up with him and then stay away from men." Another text, "For a year. Call me if you need anything."

A heart emoji.

This was clearly *not* a healthy relationship. He *was* clearly a toxic jerk. Why would she be with a guy like this in the first place? Her life was a mess.

What was the next right thing?

Like all the unexpected things that had happened this year, she couldn't believe this was happening. She shook off the pain, tried to clear her mind, and then said the familiar prayer.

Courage to change the things I can.

This was one of those things.

She finally stopped staring at it. She had to get ready for work.

In the kitchen, she checked on her Betta fish. He was dancing in the bowl when he saw her, and she smiled at him and told him she was sorry she'd been gone so long. She sprinkled some food into the bowl, and made a note that she would need to freshen up his tank water later. Her bamboo plant was still going strong, but the Christmas cactus was wilted on the ends. She gave it a drink of water.

Alex changed into her work clothes and then headed toward the Sailor's Inn. She had forgotten how she hated wearing tennis shoes in the summer, but they were the only safe shoes to wear to work. Back to real life—socks and shoes and bringing food and drinks to regulars and tourists. Back to breaking up with Randy, and time to be alone for a while.

The air was hot, thick, and wet, but the palm trees and the sun sparkling off the water gave her a sense of wellbeing she couldn't put into words. Being by the ocean cleansed her heart and her emotions. Somehow, despite the state of her apartment and her anger at Randy, she felt lighter and airier. As she drove to work listening to the radio, The Killers came on, "Mr. Brightside." She turned it all the way up and sang.

The large wooden building sat on stilts and looked over the bay. Customers came by car from the bridge that connected Tampa and St. Pete, from the water by boat, and sometimes customers rolled up on their Jet Skis. Not too far away was the Beach Sports Rental, where you could rent boats, Jet Skis, and paddle boards.

Her manager greeted her when she arrived, and Layla was making a frozen drink behind the bar. Layla's green eyes matched her Sailor's Inn tank top, and her hair was pulled back tight into a high ponytail of curls. Customers sat around the square bar on stools; a few of them smoked. It was good to be home. She felt like this was home.

"Hey," Layla said, and came around the bar to hug her. "Welcome home. We missed you."

"I missed you guys, too," Alex said.

"I like your necklace!" Layla said.

"Thanks." Alex clutched the amethyst around her neck. "It was my grandmother's."

She clocked in and her first table was a group of girls in bathing suit tops and sundresses. Alex tried to talk them out of piña coladas and strawberry daiquiris—it was a chore for Layla to keep cleaning the blender after every drink—but the July heat brought the need and want for ice and sugar, lots and lots of it.

As she took their order, Alex heard one of the girls say the name, "Randy." She tried not to flinch but also tried to listen. One of the girls was looking at her funny. Judgy. They all ordered grouper sandwiches and french fries. The judgy girl looked at her phone, then stared back at Alex and giggled.

"I think he starts at 6:30," she said. An older gentleman pulled up on a small speedboat, and the girls waved at him. He wore sunglasses tied around his neck with a strap, and a baseball cap. As he got closer, she realized it was Randy's friend, Ryan.

Alex punched in the girls' orders and then went to the server well to pour them waters.

"Layla," she said. "Randy doesn't play tonight, does he?" She tried to say it quietly so the bar regulars wouldn't hear. Layla poured rum and piña colada mix into the blender and pushed the button.

"I tried to call you. He's playing on Sundays now. He'll be here soon." One of the glasses of water spilled over. Alex barely caught it and propped it back up onto the mat to refill it with the soda gun.

She had prepared a speech for him, but she wasn't ready to deliver it. Not here at work, anyway. He'd been so mean.

Maybe it wouldn't be that hard to break up with him for good. She carried the glasses of water to the table of girls. One of them asked for a straw. She retrieved it, and then delivered their daiquiris, garnished with orange slices and cherries.

Layla twisted a towel around her wrist and stopped Alex on her way to the kitchen. "You haven't been on your socials, have you?"

"No," Alex said. "I had to take a break from my phone this week. The condolences from people about my dad . . . it was too much."

"Makes sense. You might want to look at it, though. Randy posted a picture this week of you . . . kissing some dude? I don't know if it's real. But there's some girl on there who chimed in and said it's her husband. It's kind of blowing up."

Alex didn't have words. What the actual f—. Randy had proved himself to be a total asshole, but this? Okay, this.

She *was* kissing JT at the marina; he *was* still technically married. Her professional network was also on her socials . . . her teaching friends. Some of her writing friends from college. Her reputation could be . . . completely ruined.

"You might want to untag yourself," Layla said. "And deactivate."

Shit.

She had taken Facebook off her phone. She couldn't remember the last time she logged in. She knew social media was precarious, but this was too much. "I'll be right back. Cover me?" She ran around behind the building and sat on the bench in the parking lot. Thank goodness she remembered her password. She logged in from the mobile site, and there it was on Randy's page.

"*My girlfriend,*" the caption read, "*kissing a random dude while she's supposed to be in Ohio mourning her father.*" The initial headline read, "*This is my HUSBAND,*" from Emily. "*With his SLUT-friend Alex.*"

It had been shared 234 times. Now 235.

Shit.

The photo brought back feelings of that day. Carefree. With JT, laughing and joking. The day on the Jet Ski, when she felt suspended in time, like she didn't have a care in the world. Just he and her, the water, in a place where nobody knew them. Her vacation boyfriend for a week.

The playlist, *B-sides for A.* Dismounting in the hidden cove, making love on the beach.

The rainbow.

Billie Myers's *Kiss the Rain.*

Maybe she should deactivate.

Maybe she should comment.

Maybe she should share the photo and explain herself, so that her professional network didn't see it.

Shit, what should she do?

There was nothing in the comments about how Emily had just taken his kid and left him. There was nothing in the comments about how *she'd* cheated on *him,* and he'd stayed with her, anyway. Maybe she should make a post about that.

Maybe she should deactivate.

She stared more closely at the photo. It was a screenshot. Time-stamped.

July 5th, Serenity Lake Marina Cam.

If you didn't know him, you wouldn't be able to tell it was JT. The shot was angled from high up, zoomed-out, and pointed toward his back. She studied his lean calves, his jawline, but the baseball cap shaded his eyes. The camera angle was, however, exactly pointed at Alex's face. Her eyes were closed, her lips were slightly open.

Alex studied it the longest, though, because she looked . . . *happy.*

She was smiling in the photo.

JT had just cracked a joke, and they both had started to laugh.

How long had it been since she'd been happy?

This was not good.

None of this was good. She panicked. She had to push one hundred buttons to figure out how to get to the privacy settings page. Then she found it. *Deactivate.* She pressed it. Her screen logged her out. Crap. She walked back around to the bar.

Layla was still slinging beers for the people crowding onto the deck. One of the regulars said, "Alex, your trip made you famous!"

Oh, gosh. Oh gosh, oh gosh, oh gosh. She could leave. She could tell her manager that she got sick, and she had to go home right away—that she had to—something.

Or she could *not* run, for a change. She could stay and face whatever this was, whatever was about to happen when Randy walked in to play his set.

She could have a drink.

The kitchen bell rang. "Alex, order-up!" She moved to the opening of the kitchen and gathered all four grouper sandwiches. She stuck a bottle of catsup and a bottle of hot sauce in her apron and approached her table.

Alex didn't look any of them in the eye, she simply put their baskets of food in front of them. Arranged the catsup and hot sauce bottle. The judgy girl asked for another daiquiri, then they all did. She moved to the computer, rang them in and stood staring off into space. *A drink.* A drink would take the edge off this. A shot of tequila. It would be warm down her throat. It would erase her mind for just a moment. Long enough that she could think straight.

She went back around behind the building and called Kara. The heat was stifling.

"I was wondering when you were going to see it," Kara said. "But you've had enough going on."

Was this some kind of theme? That everyone else seemed to know what was going on in her life but her?

"I just thought about taking a shot," Alex said. "These girls are here, these friends of Randy's, and he's coming in."

"Alex. Whatever you do . . . Do. Not. Drink over this. There is nothing so bad that a drink won't make worse."

Kara was right. Okay. Kara was always right. This was heavy, though. This was a lot. This was not how she thought getting back to her life in Florida would look. "If you have to leave work to not drink, then leave work to not drink." Alex couldn't leave work. "Avoid it like a hot flame, okay? Pray." And before she hung up, she said, "I love you."

Alex had promised herself she was not going to text JT for at least a week. God, it was supposed to be for a year.

She texted him, anyway.

"*OMG, Facebook. The picture from the marina.*"

"*I know,*" he wrote. "*I deactivated. My lawyer told me it was safest.*"

She didn't know what to type back.

"*It's going to be okay in the end,*" he wrote.

She wandered back around to her tables in a hot daze.

Layla handed her an ice-cold towel.

"Put this around your neck." The cool jolted her back into reality.

Where are your feet?

Randy arrived, carrying himself equally cocky and glum. Ryan, the guy from the boat had joined the table of girls, and they were all laughing loudly. Ryan got up to help Randy load in his equipment. Randy carried in an amplifier and set it down beside the railing of the deck.

Alex had six tables going and was clearing one away for the next people.

She didn't look at him. Tried to pretend he wasn't there. She escorted a family of six to the table she had just cleared off, set them up with menus, and went to the bar to pour them waters. She avoided looking at the liquor bottles.

"You okay?" Layla asked.

"I deactivated." The bar regulars were all staring at her. The ones who weren't staring at their phones, anyway. "You should see what he did to my couch."

"Have you talked to him?" Layla lifted a bottle of rum with one hand, and the soda gun with another, and refilled one of the regulars' drinks.

"Not since he blew up my phone on my dad's death date and called me a whore," Alex said.

"Screw *him*."

"Yeah." Alex set the waters down for the table of six while Ryan and Randy set up their instruments. She was afraid there was going to be a scene. What should she say? What should she do? The sun was still high over the water, and she was angry. Hot and angry.

"Look!" One of the kids at the new table said. "A dolphin!" Alex looked up just in time to see the dorsal fin poking over the water and then disappearing underneath the surface again. The tourists all smiled.

Alex smiled at the boy. "Usually, the dolphins don't come out to play until sunset." Alex said. The mother of the family ordered a salad, and the rest of them ordered fish or chicken.

She watched Randy out of the corner of her eye, but still, he hadn't looked in her direction. As she walked to the computer to ring in this new order, she felt him slowly approaching.

Alex glanced at Layla, whose eyes were wide. The regulars all stared at them now.

"Hey," he said.

"Hey," she replied. She did not want to hash this out here. Did not want to talk about it.

Was this her tendency to not deal with things? To run?

Before he had a chance to say anything else, Alex turned to him.

"Look, it's not working out for me. I've got some work to do on myself, and you've been kind of a huge jerk this week. So, let's break it off, okay?"

He reached out for her arm, and she pulled away.

"*Don't* touch me. What you posted was awful."

His face, scruffy but smiling, seemed surprised. His beer belly poked out from above his khaki shorts.

"I'm sorry. I was drinking when I shared that post. But that was you, right? I thought you were going home to mourn your father, not to hook up with some random guy—some girl's husband."

She felt the fight rising in her.

"That *random guy* is my best friend. And maybe I was happy for the first and only time this year, and maybe you don't know the details, and maybe you don't really even know me, and maybe you can delete it and never talk to me again. And fuck you about my couch," she added. "I'll send you a bill."

"Cool." He started to walk back up to the makeshift stage, but he turned back and said, "I'm sorry for what I said. It was out of line. I'm sorry again, about the couch. I was into a bottle of whiskey, and I overreacted." He put his hands in his pockets. "I think you're a great girl. Just not for me, I guess."

She turned back to Layla, who was nodding her head and smiling. "Nice," she said.

One of the regulars said, "You really told him."

Alex rolled her eyes.

While she delivered the rest of the drinks for the tourists, she saw Randy tinkering with his phone. Hopefully he was deleting that photo, but it was already out there.

Chapter Forty-Five

She didn't have much time to reflect on the incident, because she had to get back into her semester.

Class never seemed to go smoothly. There were always discrepancies with the syllabus, the paperwork, and the computers. She'd come to accept it, although it drove her nuts.

When the HR person had suggested the job for her, they'd said that adjuncting was so easy, because the English Department designed all the materials. Instructors just had to show up and teach.

There was a little more to it than that, a lot more to it. But the blessing of it had been that she had little time to think about anything else. When her mind went around in circles, it was at least about something constructive.

She had to connect the dots between the assignments, the syllabus, the papers, and the computers. Although the job was basically part-time pay, and she made about the same money that she made at the restaurant—sometimes less for her time—she liked being in the classroom with the students. She liked thinking she was contributing to the incarcerated students' second chances by helping them to get an education.

The prison classrooms were always hot, even in the winter.

July hot in Florida was different, though. Anywhere inland, away from the beach, you started sweating immediately. She had to walk through security, through a metal detector and two steel doors, past three security people, and through the prison yard to get to her students.

She was excited about a new semester, and a new group of hopeful students. Even though she hadn't been teaching long, she felt like she was making a difference. At least nobody in her professional network had mentioned the Facebook post, and Layla said that Emily had taken it down, too.

This semester her classes were smaller, and this made her happy. She could focus on each of their abilities, strengths, and weaknesses, and really work hard to teach each student individually what they needed to know to be successful in their next English classes, and then, hopefully, in their future careers.

Recidivism was lower for students who earned degrees while incarcerated, and she worked hard to make sure she treated them with kindness, dignity, and respect. Periodically, a student would get frustrated and have an outburst, but for the most part she experienced their personalities as kind, focused, and determined. As focused as you could be in prison.

She also thought a lot about boundaries in the classroom. She'd get to spending so much time with them in class and reading their journal assignments and getting to know them as humans, that she would start to really care about them. This semester, Corey Phoenix was making an impression on her.

She didn't know what he'd done to get in here—she never looked up their crimes, so she didn't carry any bias toward them —which was maybe smart, and maybe not, but she liked Phoenix. He had personality and potential. He was polite and easygoing. She'd heard him mentoring the other students. Once about navigating prison life, and once about hygiene, of all things.

Mid-semester he was asking questions about his research essay. He had the structure down, but struggled with assimilating his sources, which all students struggle with the first time.

At the beginning of the semester, she always began with a lesson about free-writing and quieting the 'inner critic,' and noticing imposter syndrome when it came up. It was one of her favorite lessons.

The inner critic is something all writers and students have, which she'd done a lot of work around in graduate school. We all have voices in our heads, the successful writers say, that tell us we aren't good enough or smart enough, or that lie and say we are incapable of trying a new thing successfully.

Alex reminded him of this today while she encouraged him to give it a shot.

"Don't be afraid to make a mistake," she said. "College is the place for that. Do your best and then see what happens." The rest of the students had finished their work for the day and left. "If you do your best, you can't be disappointed in yourself."

She wasn't technically supposed to be alone with any of the students. There was always a guard outside in the hallway, but anything could happen in prison, which they'd told her in her orientation. She should always expect the unexpected and be prepared for it.

She had never been afraid of any of her students; she was always more afraid of being too nice to them and catching some flak for being too kind. Prison was not the kind of place you wanted to get called into the principal's office. It was a weird balance between boundaries and humanity.

He shook out his hands and then put them back on the keyboard. "Do you still write?" he asked.

"Sometimes," she said.

"You ever publish anything?"

She worked hard to be authentic in the classroom, authentic and kind, without divulging any personal information, for safety reasons.

"Well," she said. She'd picked back up the novel she'd been working on, and she'd finished it again, and typed *The End*.

But she was still too afraid to show it to anyone. Even though

Jessica, JT's agent friend, had texted her and asked her how it was going, she'd put her off and said she wasn't done yet.

She could be honest. This wasn't too personal.

"So, I wrote a book, but I'm too afraid to show it to anyone." She laughed at herself.

Tiny braids sprinkled around his sandy-colored cheeks, and he smiled at her with a face full of kindness. "You're an em-peth?" he said, as if he didn't quite know how the word 'empath' was pronounced. She didn't correct him. Funny how he saw her that way. An empath was generally described as sensitive, kind, a conduit for soaking up other people's energy.

She did spend some time requesting the students remain kind with their feedback, telling them she was sensitive, and trying to model vulnerability in the writing classroom. She was working, especially in the last few months, on having better boundaries around her emotional and mental energy.

It was a process, though. Alex nodded.

"Ms. *Ward*," Phoenix said. He emphasized her last name like it was urgent. As if he were frustrated. "Can I say something to you, you won't take the wrong way?" His tone was a cross between a lecture and a question. Like he really needed to tell her this, but he needed permission in order to tell her.

Like he was mentoring her, but he couldn't switch roles without her go-ahead.

"Yeah." She was curious. "Sure, Mr. Phoenix."

"You spend all this time teaching us to be brave with our writing." He glanced up at her and then glanced back down at his keyboard. "Maybe you need to take your own *advice*." He popped the last word out with nonchalant sass. Like he was accustomed to being the wise teacher.

Phoenix lifted his eyebrows but kept his eyes on his computer screen and kept typing.

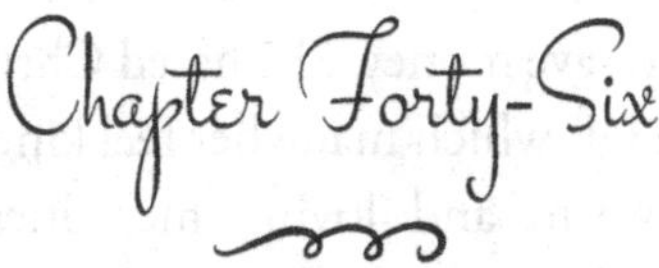

Chapter Forty-Six

Christmas came.

Alex had managed to stay single. She was lonely, but she didn't miss Randy. She missed JT.

She spent her extra time going to meetings and talking with other recovering women. She'd taken Diaz's comment to heart.

She'd sent a copy of her novel to Jessica on a night when she was feeling braver than usual, but she hadn't heard anything back.

Otherwise, Layla had turned her on to a shamanic healer from the Pacific Northwest who did guided meditations.

Alex spent mornings before writing picturing herself as a grounded tree, in a safe space where her confusing thoughts and emotions couldn't affect her, but instead, rolled off like water.

It seemed kind of woo-woo, even for Alex, but she was always calmer afterwards.

JT's mom had sent her a book called *The Magic* by Rhonda Byrne. She had written a note inside: *"For Alex, the daughter I never had."* It was a book about gratitude, with practices and lists to make about everything you were grateful for.

She already did a gratitude list in her morning writing, something Kara had told her to do. But this took the practice deeper. One of the first things it said to do was to find a magic rock, and to hold in your hands while you said what you were grateful for at night.

Alex had chosen her Nana Kate's amethyst, and she'd been wearing it every day since.

She'd decided not to go home this year. She was staying in Florida to work and save money. She hated Christmas, anyway.

Her mom loved it, which made her feel kind of guilty, but she didn't have any warm and loving memories of the holiday. Christmas past was her parents fighting, and being carted from house to house, from family-member to family-member's houses.

She didn't like the cold or the dark, and she always wanted to stay home and play with her toys when she was young. Or stay huddled under a blanket and watch movies as a teen.

One year when she was fourteen, she'd gone to her dad's, and they'd watched movies together while his second wife and their boys were traveling out of state. They must have been fighting since he didn't go along, but he didn't share that with Alex.

She was happy, for once, to have her dad around and to herself. They watched all the Christmas classics together, and then her dad had found his stack of old musicals on VHS. They watched *Fantasia*, *The Sound of Music*, *My Fair Lady*, and *The Music Man*.

The Music Man was her favorite. The songs were so fun, and the main characters were entertaining. She loved that song, "Til' There Was You." She and her dad sang all the parts together; it was one of the only things they'd ever bonded over.

Otherwise, he was always so busy with his job, his music, or his other family.

All this time, she hadn't texted JT, even though she wanted to. She thought of him almost every day. Wondered how it was going with Emily and the divorce, wondered what he would do with his house, and wondered how he was holding up.

She missed him, but she was doing her best to follow Kara's advice. She would stay single for a year, and to do what she needed to focus on herself and her career. She loved teaching, but she didn't know if she could do it forever. It was a lot of emotional and mental energy. She didn't know if she'd have the stamina for it her whole life. A few weeks off between semesters was nice, anyway. But it seemed to be getting harder instead of easier, with time.

On Christmas morning, she had volunteered to work at the restaurant so her coworkers with kids could celebrate around their trees and do the Santa thing.

She didn't usually work mornings, but she got up at 8 a.m. and clocked in at ten. Layla had volunteered to work, too. As she set up the salt and pepper shakers on the tables, the birds chirped, and she relished the quiet calm of the ocean in the mornings.

Down by the water, someone had decorated a palm tree with lights and shells from the beach. It *did* look festive. The sun flickered off the tips of the waves rolling in, and a light breeze brushed her shoulders. It wasn't warm, but it wasn't too chilly, either. She hoped they would have some business today. Whatever. At least she wasn't spending the day alone.

She and Layla didn't talk much at first, they just drank their coffee and set up their stations. A couple of boats puttered in and around the bay, sailboats and some trollers. That must be nice, she thought. Spending Christmas day out on the water. She put this on her bucket list of something she might like to do in the future. Maybe after she sold a novel. Was that ever going to happen? Her mind wandered to her mom. Diane had flown to Chicago to be with Drew and Elaine and their kids for the week. Maybe Alex should call her later and wish them a Merry Christmas.

The owners hired a Jimmy Buffett cover band to play for the day, two guys and a set of congas. At least they harmonized. It didn't take long for them to set up. She was, though, going to have to listen to "Margaritaville" most of the day. At least it wasn't that Mariah Carey Christmas song that Alex liked at first, but which they overplayed and overplayed to the point Alex couldn't stand it.

Layla unlocked the door and put the sign out: *Merry Christmas! We Are Open!*

One of the daytime regulars showed up, and then another. One of the women brought in little gift bags with their names on them. There was candy, socks, and a gift card for fifty dollars inside. Layla and Alex thanked her; Alex wished she had brought something to exchange with her, but she was grateful, anyway.

No tables yet; the band started to play "Cheeseburger in Paradise." She was daydreaming about the future, when she heard a familiar voice. Like a bass guitar.

"My long, lost vacation girlfriend."

Alex turned around.

JT stood there with a bouquet of daisies. JT?

At the Sailors Inn in Florida?

"I've been looking all over for you. I thought I'd never see you again." He smiled, appearing both cocky and vulnerable. "You're that girl I met at Serenity Lake this summer, aren't you?"

Alex looked at Layla, whose eyebrows were raised in surprise.

"I met this mystery girl over the summer, and she agreed to be my girlfriend for the week, but I haven't been able to stop thinking about her, so I came to see if she was here. I heard she worked here," he said.

"JT!" Alex ran to him and practically jumped into his arms.

"Hi." He felt so warm and strong. She fought back tears. Then she pulled back and gathered herself. "How are you?" She wanted to tell him she'd been thinking about him. Should she tell him she'd been thinking about him? "I was just thinking about you this morning."

Honesty.

"I'm glad I found you." He handed her the daisies.

"They're lovely. Thank you." JT was always so predictable in her mind, but this was a huge surprise.

"I wanted to come and wish you a Merry Christmas," he said.

She felt out his eyes, the golden sparkles under his baseball cap. He was confident, and he was also searching her eyes for something.

"Merry Christmas."

"Where's Jared?"

He put his hands in his pockets.

"We worked out a custody arrangement; he was with me last night. Mom and Dad came over and we exchanged gifts. Emily picked him up today and drove back to Virginia Beach."

Alex gestured for them to sit down. Layla and the regulars were all staring.

"You guys, this is my best friend from high school, Jason Torrez, or, JT."

"Saw a picture of you on Facebook," one of them said.

Oh, gosh. Alex shook her head.

JT didn't miss a beat. "You know, that wasn't my best angle. I'm going to go back there and do another photo shoot next year. See if the photographer can get it right."

Layla laughed out loud.

The regulars smiled and went back to their drinks.

"Sorry," Alex said. "Can I get you something to drink?"

"Yeah, what are you having, coffee? I'll have a cup of coffee."

Alex went into the kitchen, poured him a cup, freshened up her own, and then sat back down across from him. He wiped his hands on his cargo shorts. She was glad she didn't have any tables, so she had time to catch up with him.

Layla came over and handed Alex an empty Corona bottle filled with water.

"For your flowers," she said. As she walked away, she turned so only Alex could see her face and mouthed the words, *"He's hot,"* then turned back around.

Alex smiled and unwrapped the daisies from the plastic and put them one by one in the water.

"I have so many questions. When did you get here? How long are you staying? Where are you staying?"

He smiled his perfect smile. "Early-bird flight. I took another mini vacation from work. I was hoping I could crash on your couch. Unless that's too weird, I can get a hotel."

"Wait," she said. "Jason Torrez got on an airplane?"

He touched his tongue to his canine tooth and smiled.

"It wasn't that bad. There was a nice, old woman sitting next to me. She could tell how scared I was, so she held my hand the whole time."

Alex laughed. "You're so brave!" She wanted to kiss him. "I'd be glad to have the company. I'm glad you're here."

She thought about the state of her small apartment. She'd been working on her book so much since the semester ended that she had neglected cleaning duties. "It's kind of a mess, but it won't take long to put together. If I would have known you were coming."

"Yeah. Sorry. I kind of decided at the last minute. Last night was fun and all, but something was missing." That thing in his eyes became clear now. "*You* were missing. I was wishing you were there with me." Alex didn't know how to respond to this.

Vulnerability and honesty.

It was so pure, it scared her.

"You actually booked a flight on Christmas morning?"

He took a sip of his coffee, and his cockiness returned. "No. I booked a flight here as soon as I found out the arrangement last month. I didn't know if I would come or not, and I didn't want to tell you about it, in case you tried to talk me out of it. Or, in case I chickened out."

The band finished "Cheeseburger in Paradise" and switched into "Pirate Looks at Forty."

Alex loved this song. It was slow and reflective, and funny in the middle.

She loved how it referred to the ocean as *'mother.'*

"I'm glad you came. Why would I talk you out of it?"

"Because of your, whatever, staying single for a year?"

"Oh. Right." Something she was going to have to think about. Calling Kara and telling her he was here.

But it was Christmas.

She certainly didn't have to call her right now.

Anyway, she was at work.

"Anyway," he wiped his hands on his pants again, and this time pulled something out from the side cargo pocket. It was a small square wrapped in white paper with a blue, sparkly ribbon tied around it. "I brought you something. Merry Christmas."

Oh, gosh. She didn't have anything for him, either! This was one of the reasons she didn't like Christmas. Unexpected gifts brought unexpected guilt.

"I don't have anything for you."

"It's not from me. Well, it sort of is, but it sort of isn't."

It wasn't from him. Who was it from, then? "You know I don't like Christmas, right?"

"I *do* know. You haven't ever liked Christmas. Except that one you spent watching musicals with your dad."

"How do you remember that?"

Really, he had a memory like no other.

"Are you going to open it?"

She made one more joke before she resigned.

"Did you wrap this yourself?"

He smiled and licked his top lip. "It took me some time to get those curly cue things right with the ribbons."

"It's great. You did a good job. But who is it from?"

He still had tennis shoes on, but his foot found hers and nudged, then anchored against it.

"Open it."

She moved her foot farther in, so their bare calves touched.

The ribbons were too tight to untie, so she pulled at one until she unsnapped it. She tore off the paper and unveiled a midnight blue and silver CD cover with her dad's name on the bottom. *Curtis Ward.*

The cover art was glittered with stars; the constellation Orion, a shape of the infinity symbol, a small compass in the corner, and the title in cursive letters read, *Til' There Was You.*

Alex opened the CD case and pulled out the accompanying book and artwork.

She unfolded it slowly, and carefully, like a treasure.

JT lowered his voice now, the tone like a baritone.

"It's your dad's last CD. The one we were working on in California."

Her eyes fell to the dedication.

She read the words over and over. He watched her face.

"Lou was trying to get him to only release it digitally," JT continued. "But your dad wouldn't relent. He said, *'My daughter loves CD's, and we are making her a CD with artwork.'*"

She carefully turned it over and found the list of songs.

For Alex: The Brightest Star in my Constellation.
   1) Stars, Music, and Books
   2) A New Light
   3) Infinity in her Eyes
   4) My Only Girl
   5) Life as a Journey
   6) The Darkest Hour
   7) Christmas Musicals
   8) The Guy I Couldn't Be
   9) Free Spirit Heart
   10) Brilliant Mind
   11) 'Til There Was You.

JT held space and silence for her to let tears fall.

"From my dad?" She asked in disbelief.

"Your dad didn't know how to express his feelings," JT said. "He just, didn't know how to talk about how he felt. But, so, I think that's where his obsession for music came in. Like, he didn't know how to call you up to tell you how important you were to him, so he wrote a whole album for you, just to try and get it right."

Later at Alex's apartment, she gave JT the small studio tour and settled him in as best as she could. Randy had surprised her by buying her a new couch and arranging for the old one to be removed and trashed. Other than seeing him at Sailor's Inn, they hadn't really spoken.

She'd felt empowered by it.

Alex took a quick shower and put on her yoga pants, a hooded sweatshirt, and some fuzzy socks. She held the CD like a precious gemstone, then put her dad's CD in the player. JT sat on her couch in his cargo shorts and took off his hat.

She sat next to him and held his hand.

"This might be hard," she said. "I might cry a little bit. Or a lot."

"It's okay. I might, too," he said. She put her head on his shoulder and listened.

The intro of the CD was her dad's voice talking over a piano, saying that he loved her more than the moon and the stars. "Stars, Music, and Books" began, which was a whimsical guitar and piano number that talked about how magical his daughter was, and how she loved astrology, percussion music, and words—how there was nobody else in the world like her.

Alex cried through the whole thing.

JT stayed quiet, and sometimes when she looked over, his eyes were misty, too. One of the central songs, "The Guy I Couldn't Be," was full of apologetic lyrics, about how sorry he was that he wasn't a better father, and didn't make more time to spend with her while she was young.

The last song, "'Til' There Was You," made her cry the hardest. Curtis had reimagined it, so it was upbeat, alternative rock. It had a fast tempo and an arpeggiated guitar solo in the middle, but the lyrics were the same. The ones they'd sung together that Christmas.

She didn't have the energy to call her mom when the CD was over, but she curled up next to JT and fell asleep on the couch.

When she woke, she was lying on the couch under a blanket, and JT was in the kitchen fiddling with the coffee maker.

"Good morning," he said.

She sat up.

"I think I'm figuring it out," he said. He pressed the brew button, and the water started heating up with a hiss.

"What's your fish's name?" He peered into the bowl.

"Panther," she said.

He laughed. "Your Betta fish's name is Panther?"

"I wanted to get a cat, but I didn't want to get a vet bill or a litter box."

He laughed again. "Hi, Panther." The fish danced around in the bowl. "He's pretty lively."

"He has a lot of personality."

She was still waking up. She thought about telling JT about how Panther liked to meditate with her to Deepak Chopra, and how one time he spun around and around when Deepak came on PBS, but it was too much to get out of her mouth before coffee.

"What do you have to do today?" JT asked.

"Nothing," she said. "Well, I don't know. I'm off work, and I'm sure I have some things to do, but I'm not sure what they are." The semester had ended with her grading 40 researched essays and 40 final exams, so she was glad to be getting her energy and her mind back together.

"You made it through Christmas," JT said.

"It wasn't as hard as the Fourth of July." She rubbed her face with both hands. "Thank you for bringing me my dad's CD."

"You're welcome." He leaned against the counter and looked out her window. "You have a pool?"

She nodded. "It's too cold to swim in right now, but it's fun in the summer. We have apartment cookouts, sometimes." She thought about their first swim at the falls in Greenview, and how she'd been attracted to him for the first time.

How she'd felt awakened and adored at being close to him, despite being so emotionally broken.

"I can see why you love it here," he said.

The coffee finished brewing with a gurgle, and he poured her a cup. "Still coconut milk?" He retrieved the carton from the fridge and added a dash into her cup before he brought it to her.

"Thanks." She hadn't thought about drinking at all since she'd faced Randy at the Sailor's Inn. Other than going to meetings at least once a week, and sharing with her group, she had started to feel stable in her sobriety, like, maybe it was a thing she could do for her whole life.

One day at a time.

"What do you want to do today?" she asked him, as he poured himself a cup. She felt a bit emotionally raw from yesterday, but she was learning to accept feeling that way. "You're on vacation."

"I'm on vacation," he repeated. "You want to be my vacation girlfriend for the week?"

"JT, I—"

"I'm just kidding. I've never been to Florida. Let's go to the beach. You want to go to the beach?"

"You've never been to Florida!?"

"It kind of reminds me of Acapulco, where we used to go see my cousins when we were younger."

She'd never invited him here; never invited him in college.

"Yes. Let's take you to the beach. I'll show you my favorite parts of Florida."

It didn't take her very long to get ready. She packed her bag with the necessities and checked her phone. There was one new message from Aunt Skylar.

"*Merry Christmas, Dear Alex,*" it said. "*I love you to the moon!*"

She typed in a heart emoji and put her phone in her bag.

There wasn't much in her fridge, but she grabbed some club

sodas, and some sandwich wraps and crackers, and put them in the cooler for later.

He had rented a blue Jeep. They took the windows out and put the top down.

"You want to listen to your dad's CD again?" He rested his hand on the gearshift.

"Not now. I'm tired of crying. What else do we have?"

"I didn't bring my CD book, but you can be the DJ or pick a playlist from my phone."

Alex tinkered with the nobs, looking for a station. She scrolled through "Stairway to Heaven," a country station, then stopped on "Knee Deep" by Zak Brown and Kenny Chesney.

"I don't know where I'm going, so you've got to be my navigator." The fresh air caressed them as they ambled down her street. One of her neighbors waved, and they waved back.

"The beach is probably going to be busy since it's the holidays. People come from inland to celebrate. I know about a quieter place, though, where we can go. Turn left, up at this light."

For the first time since yesterday, her mind started to twist.

Was she taking JT to Sunrise Beach?

Where there weren't many people at all?

Was that smart?

She was supposed to still be single.

Where are your feet?

Chapter Forty-Seven

She navigated them toward Sunrise Beach. It had been an old military fort years ago, and there was a museum there, but there wasn't too much touristy traffic. Tourists tended to stay close to the hotels on the other side of the bay.

As they crossed the bridge and turned off onto a narrow road, JT said, "Are you taking me out to the middle of nowhere to seduce me?"

Alex laughed. She scanned the radio again and settled on the hip hop station. Nelly and Kelly Rowland sang "Crazy Over You."

She changed the subject.

"What happened with Jared, with your custody agreement?"

JT adjusted his hat and leaned his right arm onto the console. "Todd hooked me up." The line between his bicep and triceps flexed. "That lady lawyer he knew from law school did some digging."

He took a deep breath as Alex pointed to a sandy path.

"Turn here," she said.

The path curved between two large sand dunes on either side and opened to a hidden parking lot. There was a white truck with a trailer parked perpendicular to the lot lines, but otherwise, they were the only ones here. Nobody else on the beach.

He parked so they stared at the water. It was a pretty blue today, layers of indigo and turquoise. A fishing pier stretched out toward the sky, and a container ship inched against the horizon in the distance.

He lifted his sunglasses, and Alex noticed sorrow in his eyes.

"My lawyer discovered that she has not only been sleeping with your dad's guitar player for the last ten years, but she is now pregnant with his child."

"Oh, JT." She reached over and took his hand, wrapping her fingers over his and clutching. "I'm so sorry. My dad's guitar player? Mike? From The Yamahas?"

"So," he reluctantly nodded, "the judge forced her to share custody with me."

Alex had always liked Mike, though she didn't know him very well. "I always liked Mike," she said aloud. She'd never even seen Emily talking to him.

"Same," JT said. "The good news is, they are engaged. So, I'll have to pay child support for the next few years, but I won't have to pay her anything else. Which works out, because she could have taken me for a lot more money."

Alex wasn't sure what the right thing was to say.

"Guess you never really know about someone." She gave him some time for his feelings.

"It's a relief that it's all over."

Alex squeezed his hand tighter. She popped open the passenger door and pulled her cooler around her shoulder.

"Let's go stare at the ocean," she said.

Alex arranged the blanket, so it was half under the pier and half in the sun. Pelicans sat on the pylons of the pier. Seagulls squealed and moved in circles, and there was just enough breeze to make it almost chilly.

"It's supposed to be seventy-one today," she said. "But the sea breeze makes it cooler."

JT took off his shirt, anyway. His perfect copper chest. She saw the scar above his hip again.

"What's that scar from?" She pointed. "I saw it before at the falls, but I didn't ask you about it." Alex kept her sundress on and wrapped her sarong over her shoulders.

"From a long time ago," he said. He didn't act like he wanted to talk about it, but she was so curious.

"Did you have surgery or something?"

"Nah." He'd taken off his shoes, and he reached his foot over toward hers and played with her anklet, a light blue string with a cowry shell tied into it.

"Did you get into a bar fight you didn't tell me about?"

"I'm the guy who breaks up bar fights, if you didn't know that about me."

She did know that about him.

"Are we still being honest?"

He laid down on his back, his face to the sky. "Emily and I got into an argument years ago, and she came at me with a knife."

"*What?* Why?" He reached his arms back and cradled his head between his hands.

"I'm really lucky because my parents love each other, and they've stayed together all these years." Alex laid down next to him. She put her own hands behind her head and stared up at the turquoise sky.

One tiny white airplane flew above them.

"She didn't have that," he continued. "Her parents argued and fought and split up. They took swings at her when she was little. She'd go to sleep crying at night, afraid her father was going to come in drunk and violent." A piece of Alex's heart opened for her again. "Sometimes, that stuff would come up for her and find its way into our house."

"That's awful for her. But it's awful for you, too. Did you call the police?" Alex asked.

He moved his foot from her anklet and rubbed at the scar with his fingers.

"It was just a flesh wound. I drove to Pauly's for the weekend, and his sister patched it up for me. She's a nurse."

"Oh, man."

"Pauly and Jess never liked her," JT said. "I guess I just thought we'd grow out of all this stuff."

Alex reflected on her own childhood.

"I wish I would have studied more psychology in college," she said. "Maybe we'd all have it more together by now."

JT rolled over and kissed her quickly.

She was surprised but kissed him back. Her lips felt him smile.

"We probably wouldn't. We'd just have more definitions and terms for the messes we've gotten ourselves into."

He lifted his ball cap and put his hand on her waist, and she was about to suspend all rationale and her staying-single-for-a-year rule, when she heard a familiar voice.

"Hey lovebirds! Get a room!"

JT rolled back over, and Alex sat up. Coming toward them was a small white troller, Layla's modest boat for puttering around the bay. She eased it up onto the sand and said, "Ahoy!"

"Hey!" Alex yelled to Layla. "What are you doing?" Another girl hopped off the side into the knee-deep waves and pulled on a line to guide the boat onto the sand.

She was petite, with short black hair and perfect eyebrows; she wore a black tee shirt and cargo shorts.

Layla was in her usual day-off attire, a green sundress that brought out her eyes.

The two beached the boat and then Layla jumped off the back and onto the sand.

"What's up, guys?" she asked.

Alex stood up and hugged her. She smelled like sunscreen and saltwater.

"This is my friend Gabriela," Layla said. "Well," she said shyly, "my *girlfriend*. We just made it official this morning."

"Gabby," the girl said, and reached out her hand. She had a strong handshake and pulled Alex in for a hug. "Layla's told me a lot about you. It's nice to finally meet you." Alex had seen Gabby at the bar at the Sailor's Inn, but she didn't know they were dating.

Gabby had warm and glittery eyes.

"So, great." Alex said. "Nice to meet you! This is my friend JT."

He stood up and rubbed his hands together to shake the sand off.

"Vacation boyfriend," he said, and reached out a handshake.

Gabby grinned. "You're kind of Facebook-famous around here." Her vowels sounded like a song.

"Working on being an influencer. Glad my posts are getting some reach." He smiled the cocky smile, cool and calm.

Alex could see herself dating JT, maybe. For more than vacation, and more than a week.

"¿A dónde eres?" Gabby said.

"De Ohio," JT replied. "Pero mis padres son de Acapulco. ¿Y tú?"

"Puerto Rico."

Alex thought they were talking about where they were from.

"¿Qué haces aquí?" he asked.

"Vine por la escuela."

Layla said, "You *guys*, I can't understand what you're saying."

"Sorry." Gabby smiled at her. She had deep-cut dimples. "I told him I came to Florida for school."

"What school?" Alex asked.

"Tampa Aerospace," she said. "I studied flight mechanics for a few years, and then I got a job offer, so I decided to stay."

"Wow," Alex said. "That's pretty cool."

Gabby put her hands in her pockets. "Yeah, thanks. I always wanted to work on airplanes, and now I do." She kicked some sand around with her foot. "Layla tells me you're a teacher."

"For now," Alex said. "It's a lot of work."

"What do you do, Vacation Boyfriend?" she said to JT.

"I drive a truck," he said, "and help out at my parents' restaurant."

"Cool," she said.

Layla smiled. "You guys trying to avoid the tourists out here? It's such a pretty day."

"It is," Alex said. "You want to join us? There's plenty of room on the blanket."

"We wondered if you wanted to come out on the boat with us?"

"I love boats," JT said. "And we like Jet Skis, too."

Layla tilted her head. Alex hadn't told her about their rendezvous on the Jet Ski at Serenity Lake; when she'd told Layla about her trip, she'd left that part out.

JT and Gabby sat up front, and Alex and Layla sat in the captain's chair and the first mate's spot. Gabby pushed on the bow of the boat as Layla put it in reverse. The motor made a low hum sound and then bubbled. The sky was clear, and the breeze smelled fresh and clean. There were a few more boats out than usual.

As Layla pulled back the throttle, they bounced over a couple of larger waves, then pointed forward and gained speed. Alex told Layla about her dad's CD; about how special it had been to listen to it. Then she quietly asked about she and Gabby.

"I thought you two were just friends."

"We are. I mean, we were." The boat started to plane out and Layla eased the throttle back. "We went out dancing last night and we had so much fun. She crashed at my house." Layla blushed. "And then we were talking at brunch this morning, and she asked me if I would be her girlfriend."

"That's great," Alex said. "I'm happy for you!"

"What about you and your vacation boyfriend," Layla smiled. "He really *is* cute." She lifted the sunglasses from her face. A few freckles had popped out on her nose. "You said he was chubby in high school? He grew right out of that." Then she lowered her glasses.

"Yeah. I don't know. I'm staying single, I guess? It's not complicated right now, and it's nice that it's not complicated."

"A hot guy staying at your apartment?" Layla said. "That sounds like it could get complicated. How long's he staying?"

"I think a week."

"There's a sand dance on New Year's Eve," Layla said. "We should all go."

Layla and Gabby stopped at the seafood market on the way home from the boat ride and picked up some crab claws. Alex and JT stopped at the grocery for steaks, asparagus, and potatoes.

When they got back to Alex's apartment, JT went out by the pool and fired up the grill. Alex seasoned the potatoes and made a simple salad with a vinaigrette. They gathered in the kitchen while the grill warmed.

"What should we listen to?" Alex turned the nob on her radio.

"Gabby is a huge Metallica fan," Layla smiled.

Alex found the rock station. Puddle of Mud was singing, "Blurry," and Alex remembered liking this song when it came out.

"And Layla likes country," Gabby said. "I'm getting used to songs with banjos about trucks."

"I get it," Alex laughed.

"You still have that mini blender?"

"I do," Alex said, and retrieved it from the tiny cabinet above the fridge.

"I brought some lime juice. I'll make us virgin margaritas." Layla plugged the blender in. "Be right back."

While Layla and JT were both outside, Gabby talked excitedly about Metallica.

"I saw them four times this year. I'm in their fan club, so I get backstage passes. Lars put a picture of me and him on his Instagram! I can't wait until they announce their upcoming tour." Her eyes lit up while she talked. She reached in her pocket, pulled out her phone, and showed Alex a picture of her and Metallica's lead singer. Gabby had a spiked mohawk in the photo, her fingers flared in the rock and roll symbol, and her tongue stuck out against the bottom of her chin. "It was a blast. He signed my tee shirt."

Layla returned with some lime juice and a small can of pineapple. "Found this in the bottom of the cooler. Can I use those bananas?"

The salad was ready. JT went outside put the steaks and asparagus on the grill. Alex had slathered the asparagus in olive oil and garlic and wrapped them in a foil pouch. The potatoes were in the oven, and when the virgin daiquiris were finished Alex said, "I appreciate you all not drinking around me, but you can if you want. I think I'm over the worst of it, you know, and I don't mind being around other people when they're drinking."

Layla held up her glass. "I'm so proud of you. It can't be easy in the bar business."

"Oh, yeah. Layla told me you joined AA. My mom's in AA," Gabby said. "It's made a huge difference for her. She said after she worked the steps, she was able to work all the way through some of her biggest roadblocks to happiness. She said she even worked out her daddy issues," Gabby laughed.

Alex laughed uncomfortably. "Her daddy issues?"

She didn't think much about her relationship with her father and her alcoholism, or how they might be combined or related. She'd done some step work around her anger issues, but she hadn't really thought too much about her dad.

She had mostly written about guilt and about shame when it came to her relationships. How many people she'd hurt by being emotionally unavailable, immature, or both.

"Honey," Gabby said, setting her drink down. "We all have daddy issues; we all have dads!"

"Steaks are ready." JT opened the sliding glass door. "You have an aluminum pan?"

They laughed over dinner and had another round of virgin daiquiris for dessert.

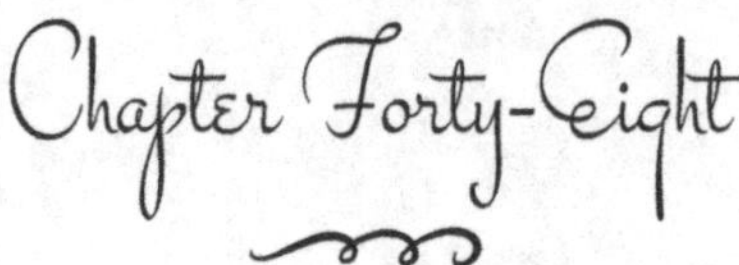

Chapter Forty-Eight

Alex had changed into her comfy clothes and JT sat on the couch.

"Sorry, I don't have cable," she said. "We could watch a movie, but the DVD player is in my room."

Alex plopped down on the couch, so she faced JT, and tucked one knee underneath of her.

"What movies do you have?" he asked.

"Oh, you know," she laughed. "The same ones."

"From the nineties?" he asked.

"Yeah, I sort of stopped buying movies when I stopped buying CD's. Started spending money on bar tabs." She had something on her mind, though, she wanted to talk about. "While you were grilling the steaks, Gabby said this interesting thing about daddy issues." She hooked her finger underneath the edge of his cargos. "Do you think you have daddy issues? Or is it just a girl thing?"

He cocked his head and squinted his eyes. "Are we going Psychology 101 again?"

She punched him in the shoulder. "Yeah. Or maybe Psyche 201."

He hooked her finger with his and gently rubbed her fingertip. "I'm sure of it."

"How so?" She'd always thought his family was perfect. They seemed happy, healthy, and they stuck together. His parents loved each other, they worked together, and they went to church together. Compared to his family, hers seemed sort of wild and broken. She rubbed his finger between her forefinger and her thumb and then pulled the rest of his hand into hers, so their palms touched.

"You know my parents. They're dutiful and work hard, and they always do the 'right' thing. There was a lot of pressure to be like my dad, even though I didn't want to be in the family business, even though I wanted to study music. But when we found out about Jared, there wasn't a question. The right thing was to get married and to get a stable job. That was it. That was my choice. Now I think, if we wouldn't have rushed everything, maybe she would have hooked up with Mike sooner, or I don't know." He sighed. "There's not really a reason to do the what ifs and could-have-beens."

JT stared at Panther for a second, then turned his attention to her.

"What about you? Do you think you have daddy issues, Professor Ward?"

He unlocked his fingers from hers, reached out to clutch her beneath her arms, and pulled her onto his lap.

She hugged her arms around his neck.

"I spent all these years feeling like something was wrong with me, like I wasn't good enough for my dad, or that he didn't love me enough to be around? But after last night, after listening to his CD, it turns out, he was just a flawed human trying to do the best he could—and like you said—he didn't know how to put his feelings into words, or maybe really show me that he loved me."

"Curtis told me he read your book," JT said. "I mean the whole recording thing was supposed to be surprise."

She squeezed him tighter. "I wasn't sure if he did."

"He said it was really good."

They sat there for some time and held each other. He put his chin in the cusp between her neck and her shoulder and kept his arms wrapped all the way around her in a bear hug. She wrapped her arms around his.

"You know, honestly," Alex said, getting sleepy, and close to dreaming. "I never thought she was too good for you." She'd been wanting to tell him this for years. "I always thought that you were too good for me."

After a while of sitting in silence like that he said, "Which movie do you want to watch?"

She thought of the night on the hammock after graduation, how their lives might have been different if she'd decided to stay in Ohio, or, if she would have been brave enough to act on the feelings she had for her best friend in high school, instead of running from them.

Maybe if she would have changed one, tiny action in the past, then this present would be completely different.

Maybe her dad would still be alive.

The what ifs never really left her.

Where are your feet?

She wiped a tear from her face.

A wave of grief was coming.

JT picked her up then, effortlessly. His strong arms carried her through her living room, past the bathroom, and into her bedroom. He laid her down on her white comforter and said, "*Good Will Hunting* it is."

She watched him scan her DVD collection, find what he was looking for, turn on the TV and put the disc in. Then he tucked her under the blankets and laid down next to her, so she was underneath the blankets, and he was on top.

They watched the familiar movie with the familiar characters. Brilliant Matt Damon, rough around the edges, meets brilliant Minnie Driver, who goes to Harvard. Robin Williams plays the psychologist. She fell asleep before her favorite scene; the emotional one in which Robin Williams tells Matt Damon that his abusive childhood wasn't his fault.

Alex fell into a dream. She was huddled under an umbrella with her mom, JT, and Drew. They were somewhere in California waiting on a valet driver to bring around their car. Then, around the corner of a tall building, came her father.

"Dad!" she said and ran to him. She hugged him tightly. It felt so good to hug him. The Old Spice smell.

"Hey, kid," he said. "I'm glad you got my message."

Behind him was a giant tour bus, complete with truck and trailer. It was large and long as the entire city block. The whole thing was aquamarine, the color of the water in the Caribbean.

"That's yours? You have a place to live?"

"I'm going to do a little traveling," he said. "But I want you to know that *I'm sorry*. And I want to tell you that you're doing a good job letting go of the guilt and focusing on what you want. The magic will happen for you. Give it some time. JT's a great dude, Alex. Some things are written in the stars. You can stop running, now."

There were so many things she wanted to ask him, and so many things she wanted to say, but just like in the other dream, before she could find the words to ask, he faded away and then she woke up.

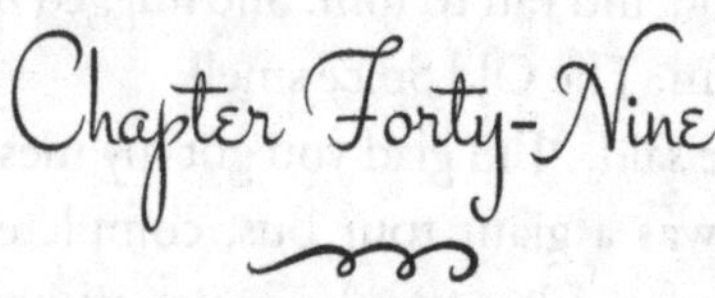

The Sand Dance was something only locals knew about, and they kept it a secret as best they could from the tourists. Mostly hospitality people and music people attended. They roped off a portion of the beach, checked IDs at the ropes, and built a stage behind one of the motels. The organizers and attendees went so far as to book up all the rooms in the motel, so they kept their locals-only party as Florida as they could.

Of course, some people from out of town were invited or stumbled in, but the Sand Dance was as Florida as taking the day off work for an impromptu fishing trip. Layla had taken Alex to her first sand dance when she'd moved here.

They had laughed and danced all night on the beach.

Alex splurged and booked her and JT a room next to Layla and Gabby, and they spent the day at the beach watching the setup crews get ready. There were at least five bands playing tonight, and for this special New Year's Eve Sand Dance, there were rumors of a boat parade and a drum circle. They ate shrimp and locally made fish spread at the Beach Shack.

"This is delicious," JT said. "What is this?"

"Fish spread, Vacation Boyfriend. It's a Florida thing." Gabby had taken to calling him *Vacation Boyfriend* every time she addressed him. Layla's eyes were full of light and love, and she laughed a lot at Gabby's jokes.

It occurred to Alex that she had never seen Layla this happy before.

Alex had worn her favorite blue sundress and had put on Nana Kate's amethyst. JT dressed as he always did, in a tee shirt and cargo shorts. He'd settled into flip-flops since he'd arrived, and she was getting used to having an attractive guy hanging around her. An attractive guy who knew her as well as she knew herself.

She'd forgiven him for not telling her what happened to her father. He'd always been solid as a rock in her life, and though he was due to fly back to Greenview tomorrow, she was trying not to think about it.

They all decided to take a nap and get cleaned up before sunset. The drum circle would start an hour before sundown, so they had two hours or so before they would miss anything fun. Alex had bought club sodas for herself and a sports drink for JT, and she'd told him that he could drink if he wanted to.

He didn't seem to have the urge.

She wondered what it might have been like to get that gene, the one that could take an alcoholic drink, or leave it. She was so grateful to Kara and to AA that she had finally been able to leave it.

The hotel room was a simple one, with one bed, a white tile floor, and a kitchenette. The windows were framed with old wood, but decorated with grays and blues, and the room's balcony overlooked the ocean and the beach below.

She loved Florida. She hoped she'd always get to live here.

Down below, the beach was busy with locals setting out chairs and tables and building a makeshift stage for the night.

JT removed his tee shirt in that one-arm thing that guys do, and Alex caught herself staring at his abs. His black boxers just barely peeked out from the waistband of his shorts.

Had he done a bunch of sit ups in the last five days? He'd gone for a run this morning while Alex was still asleep.

"What if I don't want you to go?" Alex plopped down on the bed.

She had told him about the dream with her dad in it, but she hadn't told him what he'd said about JT.

JT acted like he didn't hear her. Or he was joking, and he wanted her to say it again.

She smiled. "What if I don't want you to go back to Ohio tomorrow?"

Her eyes kept falling to the scar above his waist, the small and only blemish against his skin.

He sat down on the bed, picked up her left hand, and kissed it.

Sweetly.

"I see why you love it here. *I* love it here. But I have to go back to my son—back to work."

She studied his one dimple, the golden lights in his eyes.

His callouses had softened, so as he rolled her hand around, she felt the design of his fingerprints, the tiny ridges in his skin.

Just barely friction between them.

She wasn't sure what to say next, or what to do.

He squatted down onto one knee, reached into his cargo pocket, and pulled out a small, white box.

And opened it.

She froze.

"Alexandra Kathryn Ward, I have loved you since the first time I saw you at the park. Since the night after your graduation on the hammock. Since you flew off to Florida for college and went wild and free without me, and since you came to meet my friends at Serenity Lake." His bass voice shook. "Spend the rest of your life with me, Alex. Spend the rest of *my life* with me. I will hold you close, but I will never interfere with your dreams."

It was a shell ring.

Like the ones from her childhood, from Serenity Lake, with a pink heart carved in the middle. An aquamarine stone was embedded in the shell, surrounded by silver, wrapped in a wave shape. It was her favorite color.

Her mind told her to *run.*

She stared at the door, and watched a version of herself run through it, slam it behind her, descend the stairs and bolt toward the water. She felt the sand on her toes, soft and deep, then harder and more compact, littered with shells, sharp and painful.

She wanted to run far, and fast, and away. She ran and ran, oblivious to anyone and everyone else, toward the sunset sky, until she was up to her waist in water, and the next wave covered her completely.

She ran until she couldn't run any farther.

Until the water was so deep, she could drown.

She waited for some answer from the sky, or the clouds, for some kind of divine direction from anywhere, but there was none.

Just water and sky, and the sound of the waves.

The dream; her dad and his words.

You can stop running, now, Alex.

She watched that scene play out in her mind.

When it was settled, she stood in the ocean—her favorite place—but she was all alone.

So there, in their hotel room, she chose something different.

Alex didn't run.

She gazed at JT, familiar, calm and steady. He held her eyes in his as fear and uncertainty and the old impulses all swirled around her body.

But she found a small place in her soul, like a tree trunk with a door, and she opened the door and stepped through it, where the feelings couldn't control her.

She let the fear roll off her like clear water. She moved her mind into gratitude. For where her feet were. For her higher power. For *surrendering.*

She stood there, steady and motionless.

And the wisdom to know the difference.

Finally, when she was certain she was grounded, she said, "You remembered I don't like diamonds."

He was still lowered on one knee with her hand in his. His cocky smile emerged.

"Since you watched that documentary about the mines in Africa."

He cleared his throat. "I specifically asked that this stone be ethically sourced."

His tongue on his canine tooth.

He knew she was procrastinating.

"Marry me, *Alex*. You're my best friend. I'll be the best vacation boyfriend you've ever had."

She tugged on his hand, and he stood up. She pulled his body toward her and wrapped her legs around his waist.

The fear.

"You know I'm not marriage material, and I don't know what a healthy relationship is like, and I don't want to have kids, or cook and clean all day, and I am not the ideal wife in anyone's mind. I probably shouldn't be married to anyone, ever."

He put a finger under her chin, lifted her face, and kissed her.

His lips were soft, and she could feel him smiling.

"I don't want to make you into anything you aren't. I'm not going to trap you into some housewife role that you're not cut out for. You can write, you can travel, you can do all those things you want to do. We can open a bookstore; we can go see the Redwoods. I just want to hang out with you, indefinitely, forever."

The kiss was pure and warm, and there was some fire inside of it.

"You can do whatever you want," he said. "Except maybe you could just do it *with me*."

Indefinitely, forever sounded like song lyrics.

The small part inside of her which was still as clear water, held on to his hands and laid back on the bed.

She lifted her sundress over her head, pulled him close, and guided his body on top of hers.

She unbuckled his belt.

He kissed her neck and placed himself on top of her gently and slowly. She kissed his stomach, then his waistband, and then postured herself against the pillows. He pulled the comforter off the bed and then laid her back down in the crisp white sheets.

She didn't have thoughts; she only had feelings. Desire and trust and this feeling that maybe she was finally getting what she wanted, too.

Only maybe she hadn't known, this was what she wanted.

He took off his hat and placed it on the bed stand. He smelled like sand and ocean. And dreams.

Alex was completely open.

She helped him pull out of his boxers and enter her gently and the pleasure came almost immediately, so she had to wrench her neck back to take him all in. The energy trapped under her skin, flushed and fluttered until the hair stood up on her arms and her toes curled.

He held his tongue against his canine tooth and watched her face for every expression that went with every movement, then he licked at the points of lace of her bra and unclasped it with his left hand. He slid it from each shoulder and traced the shape of her arms with his fingers.

He put one leg under her, then one arm and then rolled them over, so she was on top of him, and he was on his back.

He kept his arms around her and studied her face and nipped at her lips, and she watched the sweat form over his brow, and drip down around his face. His heavy breathing.

She tasted the salt on her tongue.

She relished the moment when his eyes closed and he shook in small vibrations and clutched her back, then gasped a breath and let out a sound like a cat purring.

The fireworks in his eyes shooting across the sky.

He flipped her over again, and smiled while he kissed her and she felt like sand crushed into pieces, warm and safe and aware he was going to say something.

"*Marry me, Alex,*" he whispered.

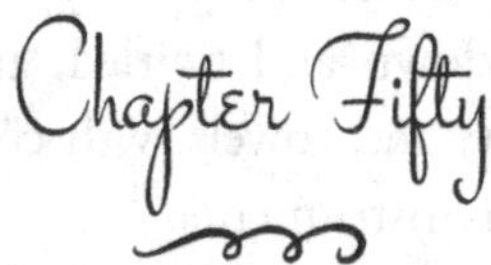

Chapter Fifty

She still hadn't answered him; she'd simply gotten up and led him into the shower.

JT washed her hair, massaged coconut shampoo from behind, rinsed it, and added conditioner. He rubbed soap into her skin and kissed her neck. As the water fell over them, she sat on his lap on the bench.

New sensations. Sensuality, coupled with trust.

Vulnerability, with confidence and passion.

All mixed into one experience.

The drums began.

Gabby and Layla knocked on their door before they were completely ready, but Alex opened it anyway.

She had one hand on her braids, finishing her two-braid pattern. They were both smiling.

"Hey," Layla said. "We're going down. You guys ready?" Alex gestured for them to come in. JT was putting on his shirt.

"Are we," Layla stopped, "interrupting something?"

"Whoa," Gabby said, and pushed past her. "What's that!?" She pointed to Alex's finger. The shell ring on her finger with the aquamarine. "Nice work, Vacation Boyfriend!"

Alex continued braiding her hair and felt her cheeks flush.

"Our girl here hasn't answered me yet," JT said with his cocky smile. "But I have a good feeling about it."

Down at the beach the sun was setting in oranges and reds.

A circle had formed, one inner circle of drummers, and then a layer of dancers—belly dancers, hippie types, and guys with long hair jumped up and down and twirled, and folks sat gathered farther out on blankets and towels with coolers and glow sticks and random percussion instruments.

"Welcome to the drum circle," Alex said to JT.

"This is rad." He clutched her hand. They found Gabby and Layla in one of the outer circles and Layla waved and motioned for them to sit down.

"Glad you found us." She reached into the cooler and pulled out a coconut club soda and handed it to Alex.

"Thanks," Alex said. Layla knew it was her favorite.

"JT, you want a beer? Or a club soda?" Layla held up a can of Corona with ice dripping down the side. "We brought some champagne for later. And we brought some sparkling apple juice for you." She winked at Alex.

"I'm good with water." JT held up a bottle from the room.

Gabby said, "Vacation Boyfriend, did you get down on one knee?"

"I did. I was going to wait until midnight, but it just seemed like the right time."

"So, Alex, what's the hold up?"

"Gabby," Layla scolded. It wasn't like Layla to edit Gabby so far, but Alex appreciated her standing up for her.

Honesty.

She just said it all out loud now. "You guys, I am not marriage material. I am not the kind of girl who wants to cook and clean and have kids." She took a sip of the club soda and held the bubbles in her mouth. The rhythms grew in intensity. It was strange that Alex felt comfortable enough to say all of this in front of JT. Usually she would consider this girl talk. It wasn't weird at all.

Gabby raised her voice over the drummers. "I know I just met you and you don't know me from a dude at a bar, but marriage doesn't have to look like what our parents told us it was supposed to look like. The 1950's are long gone." Gabby had apparently never been to Greenview. "Women's rights are *in*. You can make marriage look however you want, as long as you both agree on how it looks."

JT said, "Yeah, so, I'm going to go put my toes in the water. Let you girls figure out the details."

He walked toward the setting sun and Layla chimed in.

"I can tell he really cares about you. He seems like a great dude."

That last part chimed in to Alex's mind somewhere.

"And he's hot," Gabby said. "If I were straight, I would chase him."

Alex laughed. "I think my dad said that to me in a dream," she said, and poked at the sand with her toes.

"That he's hot?" Gabby joked.

"No," Alex laughed. "That he's a great dude."

"It's true," Layla said. "I can tell. And you're happy. I haven't seen you truly happy since before your dad passed."

The rhythms built the loudest just as the sun slipped under the horizon. Everyone on the beach cheered. Gabby and Layla got up to dance and Alex stayed on the blanket, taking in her Florida paradise.

She watched JT stare at the sunset sky. Her happy place. Maybe she did want to be with JT. But she didn't want to leave this. Florida was her home now.

The dancers jumped higher as everybody clapped and hollered, then they calmed down to subtle background music just as the boats started rolling by.

JT returned and sat behind Alex on the blanket, settling his knees under her elbows and tucking his chin on her shoulder. "The boat parade?"

"Cool, right?" Alex said.

It was Alex's favorite time of night. Twilight, when the sky and the sea and the air all had a gray-blue tint to them and the stars became visible. "JT, I want to be with you, but I don't want to leave this. I don't know if I can go back to Greenview."

He squeezed her tightly and said, "Maybe you don't have to. Maybe we can find a way to live in both places."

"Like snowbirds?" she asked.

"What's a snowbird?"

"It's a word we use for people who live up north half of the year and then migrate down here for the winter."

"Okay, yeah. Like snowbirds."

The boats glided by, lit up in Christmas colors and red, white, and blue—all of them different shapes and sizes: some sailboats, some tugs, and even some small trollers.

There was something magical and festive about it all.

A dinging noise. "What's that?" Alex asked.

JT pulled his phone out of his pocket and looked at it.

"It's Pauly." He put the phone up to his ear.

"Hey," he said. "Happy New Year! Yeah, we're at the beach. Watching a boat parade. I did." He looked at Alex from the side of his eyes. "She didn't answer me yet, but she's wearing the ring. Thanks for the encouragement. Yeah. Oh, really? Okay, I will. Thanks. Love ya, man. I'll tell her." He hung up.

"What was that about?" Alex kept his arms wrapped around her as the final boat passed by them. The caboose of the boat parade read, *Happy New Year!* on the back in lights.

"Pep talk. He wanted to know if you said *yes.* And Jessica is trying to get a hold of you. He said to check your texts."

She pulled her phone out of her bag. She had two missed calls from Jessica and one text. "Sorry to bother you on New Year's," it read. "But I think I've got you a deal. Call me when you can."

A deal? She'd forgotten she'd sent a copy of her novel to Jessica. Alex figured she would read it and maybe give her some feedback on what needed fixed. She hadn't really expected to hear from her.

JT read the texts from over her shoulder. "Call her." He nudged her.

"Right now?"

"They're at a party with a bunch of writers and editor people. Pauly hates those things, but he said Jessica really works them."

Alex clicked on the name *Jessica, editor,* and held the phone up to her ear.

"Hey!" Jessica answered quickly. "Look, sorry to bother you, but I loved your book. It was compelling and interesting and heartfelt, all the things that readers like. As soon as I finished it, I sent it to my editor friend. She's been looking for a book like this for two years. Anyway, I'm here with her, and she wants to meet you. She was just asking me if I thought you could write two more . . . make it a series . . . do you think you can write two more?"

Alex was already working on the next one, but she hadn't told anybody. "Yeah, I mean, I think so."

"Okay," Jessica said. "She's drawing up a deal this week. It's not one hundred percent yet, but I might be able to get you six figures. You'll just have to deliver, if you decide to accept," she added.

Six figures?

"Six figures?"

It sounded like buy-a-house money. It sounded like pay-off-your-student-loan money *and* buy-a-house money. It could be, for Alex, financial-freedom money. She clasped the amethyst around her neck. "Okay," was all she could think of to say. "Thank you."

"I'll call you on Tuesday with more details," Jessica said. "You might need to tone down the beginning stuff about the dreams. Oh, and Alex?"

"Yeah." She held the phone to her ear in disbelief.

"Happy New Year. Thank you for making our friend JT so happy. He's lucky to have a girl-*friend* like you."

"Holy shit." Alex turned to face JT. "Did you hear that?" *Holy shit holy shit holy shit.*

He put his hands around her stomach. "You've been reading that book my mom sent you? *The Magic?*"

"And making gratitude lists," Alex said.

He kissed her neck. "Maybe we can be snowbirds."

When Layla and Gabby returned to the blanket, Alex didn't want to say anything, but she couldn't help it.

"An editor liked my novel!" she squealed to Layla. "And I might be getting a deal!"

"Congratulations!" Layla said. "New Year's Eve is really panning out for you." She pointed to the ring.

Alex didn't want to make a huge thing out of it, but she felt like it was a huge thing.

She looked at JT. "She said something about I might need to tone down the stuff at the beginning about dreams?"

"That's weird," he said. "Everything starts with a dream."

"The bands are starting," Gabby said. "Vacation Boyfriend, you wanna go sand dancing?"

Alex laughed at her. "Gabby, if you weren't my best girl-friend's girlfriend, then I might be a little jealous."

They gathered up their blankets and towels and wandered to the stage. A crowd had gathered already. Two tiki bars were set up on either side of the sand dance "floor" and throngs of people laughed and danced. The band was covering The Black-Eyed Peas, "I've Got a Feeling." A couple of spotlights were set around the dance area, but otherwise, the sun had gone down completely, and they danced under the light of the moon.

The four friends stood in back on the boardwalk and watched. JT resumed his position behind Alex, holding her from behind. Gabby positioned herself behind Layla in a similar hug.

When they finished the song, the lead singer began talking. Some of the sand dancers stopped to listen, and some of them scattered to get more drinks.

"So, we lost a dear friend last year," the lead singer said. "A musician who made an impact on all of us in our early days." He pointed to his band. This was a common thing, Alex noted, to pay tribute from the stage to an inspirational mentor.

Her dad had done it at his shows when somebody passed.

"Curtis Ward," the guy said, "lived for and loved music. And he passed away in a tragic accident without releasing his last and final CD."

Alex's dad's name hit her like a windstorm.

Oh no, oh no, oh no.

God, grant me the serenity.

She squinted to see if she recognized the guy on stage. She didn't. She felt her body tighten. JT whispered in her ear, "It's okay. I've got you." She tried to picture herself as a tree, the water rolling off. She shot a look at Layla, whose eyes were wide. She didn't feel like a tree. "Breathe."

"His last CD was dedicated to his daughter," the guy said. "Musicians spend a lot of time on the road sometimes, and we spend a lot of time chasing our dreams. Sometimes our families get the short end of that stick. Curtis's last CD was dedicated to his only daughter, and we're going to play the title track, a remix of a song you might recognize from *The Music Man*. We know he's out there somewhere, in the big rock band in the sky, making sure every track is perfectly imperfect."

The guy put one hand in the air and pointed to the sky before he placed it back onto his guitar strings. "Curtis, this one's for you. One-two-three-four," he said. And the band started to play.

Every feeling swirled around Alex as she stood there in JT's arms with her friends at the beach, listening to her dad's version of the classic love song, which he had recorded for her.

Somehow, safe there with her best friend, she didn't break, she didn't shatter, and this time, she didn't run away.

When the song ended the guy said, "We're going to keep Curtis Ward's legacy alive as long as we live. Hug your loved ones tight tonight, and Happy New Year, sand dancers."

The drummer played a solo while the guitar players strummed a finale. People cheered. Alex stared out over the ocean. It looked like one of Aunt Skylar's paintings. Black and blue, the water and sky sparkling. Stars glowing in the dark.

The beach after sunset.

The lead singer lifted the neck of his guitar in the air, signaling the band to the song's end.

"Thank you and Goodnight," he said.

Chapter Fifty-One

EPILOGUE

"Ask me where I want to get married," Alex said.

The morning sun poured into their motel room on January first. She kissed JT and stirred him awake.

"What?" He kissed her back and wiped at his eyes.

"Ask me where I want to get married, before I change my mind."

She had the sheets pulled up over her bare body, in the room where they'd been since the clock had turned 12:01 a.m., and they'd excused themselves from the party.

"Did I take a time warp and land in some dream life?"

They had introduced themselves to the band, she'd thanked them for saying nice things about her dad, and the musicians had been gracious—with nothing but good things to say about Curtis. Then, they had danced.

The band had invited JT up on stage to play drums, and they'd sang that Prince song, "1999."

"If you run away," JT said, "I will chase you this time." He gathered her up in his arms and kissed her between the breasts, wrestling her for more kisses. "And I'm a fast runner."

"Ask me." She resisted his advances with giggles.

"Where do you want to get married, Alex?"

"Serenity Lake Marina. At that little chapel. Maybe all our friends can stay at Coach's for the week."

He sat straight up.

"Does this mean it's a *yes?*" He fished out her hand from the blankets and looked at the ring. "I thought I had a dream I asked my best friend to marry me, but she didn't answer."

"Yes," she said. "It's a *yes.*"

He reached for his phone and began pressing at the screen.

"What are you doing?" she asked.

"I'm rescheduling my flight. I want to spend New Year's Day celebrating with my fiancé at the beach."

Acknowledgments

Dear Lovely Readers,

I owe everything I am and everything I have to the Higher Power, God, *Spirit of the Universe* energy that protects, connects, and guides us all. Like Sonya in the story, I do believe our souls are eternal, forever interrelated, and I believe our lives are a precious gift. Thank you to anyone and everyone who has ever said a prayer for my journey and my family's.

Thank you to *Alcoholics Anonymous* for existing.

I owe this first edition to my mom, J. Lynn, who made it come alive after her initial reading (which she turned around in one week!). Her wise editorial comments helped me see the story from the outside, and ultimately deepened the characters and the plot. *Mom, I love you* with everlasting gratitude.

Onita, I wouldn't be able to write or publish anything without you. You. Are. The. Best. Writing. Partner. In. The. World. And I am lucky to know you. Monday Night Writing and your determination, passion, and knowledge carry me and inspire me.

Jimmy, my most favorite professor, my writing coach, and my friend. Without your mentorship, encouragement, and authenticity, I'm not sure where I would be.

Patrick, nobody has ever supported my writing in the way you do. Thank you for dinners, for listening, for putting up with my daydreaming, and my late nights trying to meet deadlines. Thank you for talking it all out with me, and for letting me pick your brain with endless random questions. Thank you for the road trip to the lake, the setting of which inspired this story.

Natalie, the trip was just what I needed that week.

Ericka, thank you for always answering the phone, for being so down-to-earth, and for keeping my spirit afloat and laughing. You continue to be the smartest person I know, with the biggest, and funniest vocabulary.

Melissa and Melaney, you two. Us three. Destined in the stars, I think. I love you.

Romaana, Nikki, Nicole, and Erin, boy did I get lucky when we crossed paths out on our own in the world for the first time. Your support carries me through some days, even with so little words, and from so far away. Nannette, Katherine, Karma, Gizella, Lisa, Tenisa, Holly, Melanie . . . thank you for being in my college world, for accepting me, and for teaching me.

Kristy, Dear, Kristy. I'm not sure there are words for this? Thank you for reaching back your hand to help me. None of my life would be possible right now: writing, teaching, living, or otherwise, without you, the Noon Group, and the recovery community. I love you to the moon and beyond for your serenity, acceptance, courage, and wisdom.

Autumn, I know we haven't known each other for very long but thank you for *listening*.

Sheri and Cindy, thank you for taking me under your wings and showing me around the beach. You made a girl feel welcome and loved. Vicki, Beth, Debbie, Jami, Beccy, Kimberly, Kimmy, Jane, Cathy, Michelle, Heather, Debra, Maddy, Angie, Koko, Chief, Joe and Maddy . . . all my beloved beach friends, say hey to the ocean for me. The next time I see y'all, we should go sand dancing.

Bridgit, your message meant the world to me.

I couldn't name all of my childhood friends if I tried, but you all were the best. I'm sorry for all the times I was a jerk in high school, and I'm sorry for being so far away for so long . . . let's go roller skating or something?

Thank you to WSU and AU Creative Writing Program: Rebecca, Denny, Katrina, Andrea, Adrian, C.K. Read, Dr. Gale, Jimmy C., Dr. Martin, Dr. P., Jen V., Dr. Pringle, Dr. Hunter, Dr. Jones; Antioch Writers' Workshop, and MV Writers Network. April, Tim, Jennifer, Judy: Y'all continue to teach and inspire me.

Thank you to my family, my hometown, my coaches and teachers, my first beloved community; my restaurant friends, my music people, my students, and my mentors—the folks who have kept me in their hearts and prayers, and always had my back no matter what.

Endless gratitude for my readers, and for those who have a hand in Green Sea Publishing.

This book is published in memory of Socrates, the best rescue protector-mutt there ever was. I know he's up there guarding the gate, and even I will have to know the magic word in order to pass through, (or I will have to remember really salty treats).

Wishing you all safe travels, happy endings, and sweet dreams,
Sincerely,
Sara

Sarasota Green is a writer, editor, and poet. She loves beach towns, live music, indie bookstores, boat trips, reading, and painting. She currently lives in the Midwest.

If you liked Serenity Lake Marina, it would mean a lot to me if you would give it some review stars somewhere like Amazon, Goodreads, or Barnes and Noble. Write me a message, sign up for my postcard list and newsletter, and stay tuned for updates and new releases at sarasotagreenauthor.com.

Coming soon!

THE LAST POSTCARD OVER THE GULF OF MEXICO

A vacation love story

Book Three in the Cocktails, Sunsets, and Music Series

Join Alex's Aunt Skylar as she's about to turn fifty, reflects on one wild vacation in Cancun, and gets a second chance at her own unrequited happy ending.

Learn more at sarasotagreenauthor.com